SINGING THE REDBIRD'S SONG

S.S. Wright

Illustrations and Cover Art by Nissa Henslee
Interior Design by Cameon Jackman
Printing by Gorham Printing
Published by Sandra S. Wright ©2025
Bonner's Ferry, Idaho, USA

ISBN 979-8-9932450-2-7

Cataloging Data
Wright, Sandra S., 1947—
Singing the Redbird's Song : Speculative Fiction / by Sandra S. Wright — 1st ed.

Dedication

I dedicate this work to Family (physical, extended, and spiritual)
who have seen me through many trials as well as triumphs. Your strength
and love have allowed me to grow into my essential self, that is and will
always be forever. I look forward to partying with all of you
someday on the Other Side.

Acknowledgments

Thank you, Michael, husband extraordinaire, for your love, support and patience. You've worked so very hard for me and our children that you have more than earned this retirement and what comfort you can find in this world. I love you and the life we are privileged to share.

Thank you, my children. Nissa, your beautiful, loving elfin spirit is a joy to us all. Jim, your strength of character and kindness shine from your golden soul. Melina, you are loved even though you are no longer with us physically. I thank you for showing me your journey through this lovely story. You have each brought me much joy and love.

Thank you, so many souls here and on the Other Side. Your loving patience, encouragement and inspiration have spurred me on in this task of love. Special thanks to my wonderfully clairvoyant cousin, Deborah Johnson, whose input blew open many blocks along the way.

Thank you, Bridget Cook-Burch. Your life-changing Inspired Writer's Retreat was the catalyst that is responsible for kick-starting me into finishing this work.

Thank you, Paul Hanson of Village Books in Bellingham, Washington, for your writing insights and encouragement in years past. Also, your Chuckanut Writers Conference was an important part of my journey by presenting me with contacts and tools to bring it home.

Thank you, Eve Costello, an amazing editor who understood my vision from the beginning, Erica Larson, insightful marketing manager, and Cameon Jackman, talented designer. You are the professional team who held my hand, patted me on the head and showed great patience. You have taught me so much that I may just have to do a sequel, hopefully more efficiently a second time.

Thank you, Ann Coughlin, an awesome spiritual teacher who started me on the last leg of this journey.

Thank you, Nissa Henslee. When I approached you with my vision for the cover and interior art designs, you understood immediately and created it perfectly. You know me so well and you lifted a heavy weight from my heart, mind and soul. I'm sure that Melina is grateful to you as well.

Thank you, Jordyn, at Gorham Printing, for guiding me through the printing process and for this beautiful book.

Finally, thank you all who have picked up this tale of Homecoming, Promise, and Remembering. "Serendipity" was my daughter's favorite word, and it has played an essential role in the events that made this story and the publishing of it happen. My wish is that you will find your own serendipity in these pages and that you'll discover any healing that you need along the way. Happy Reading!

In Love and Light,

S.S. Wright

Part One

HOMECOMING

One

"I'm tired of dying, Gramma," whispered the young woman. She fixed her gaze on her own delicate hands, which were resting on a silver flute in her lap. "I don't want to do it again."

Grandma Lilly bit her tongue. It was not in the protocol to reveal too much at once. There was a process, with options and choices to explore, to traverse the layers of physical and mental conditioning. This was going to be one of the rougher transitions she had helped with for some time. Her granddaughter was going to be a challenge even as she had been in life.

The two women were seated on the sunny front steps of a modest home in the Cascade Mountains of the Pacific Northwest. The June morning was redolent with fir, cedar, and the cool freshness that flowed from the Snoqualmie river near the back yard. Flower beds were alive with rhododendrons and azaleas, the pinks and purples of early summer.

Mari was a twenty-five-year-old strawberry-blonde woman wearing peach silk pajamas. Her sad, cerulean blue eyes revealed her current anxieties.

Lilly was a quintessential sweet little grandmother with sparkling hazel eyes. Her gaze emitted hints of sage wisdom and, most of all, her understanding. She looked up at Mt. Si where, according to Snoqualmie Tribe legend, Chief Si was fabled to be resting. Lilly wished for the wisdom of those ancient sages for guidance with this precious one.

"It's not for us to know just yet, Sweety," she offered Mari while she dusted a little flour off her apron. For this occasion, she chose to present her persona in the way that Mari would relate to. "There is a process. The resolutions to all those questions you have stirring inside you will require some patience."

"I know, Gramma," she replied. "Thank you for the reminder and, by the way, thank you for the flute. I've missed playing but I just couldn't do it. Hopefully I can now. I did the whole white light and tunnel thing, and I am grateful for that experience and to be here with you, but right now I'm not feeling the peace and contentment that I expected."

Lilly took hold of Mari's hand. As their fingers met, the translucent essence of Lilly's hands melded into the still more densely physical ones of her granddaughter. An effervescent flow of energy caressed Mari's hand, traveled up her arm into her body, then softly swirled around her heart. The healing could begin.

"Shall we move into the day?" asked Lilly. Mari pursed her lips and nodded then replied, "I think I'm ready."

A breeze stirred and they faded from the porch just as cars pulled up to the house and visitors began to emerge.

Two

Suzi closed her eyes and bent to inhale the perfume of a bouquet of white roses that graced the cabinet in the entryway of her home. They had been her daughter's favorite flower. Stepping back, she admired their purity and grace and thought of Mari as she breathed deeply to hold back the sometimes-overwhelming grief. She needed to get through this day.

Her attention was distracted by the painting on the wall that complemented the flowers. The rich neutral tones of the print revealed a man of firm and strong features wearing a hooded cloak that flowed around him in the breeze. A falcon with extended talons was preparing to land on the falconer's heavy glove. It was a powerful picture that Suzi had purchased on a trip with her three children to Cannon Beach, Oregon. She found it in a small quaint gallery built of old weathered boards that beaconed creativity. She resisted buying it but went back for it after she couldn't get it out of her mind. It spoke to her for some reason. It wasn't until months later that she stopped suddenly in her entry, realizing that the falconer warmed her heart because he looked just like her deceased father, Claus. Today she hoped that Mari was with her grandparents.

The ringing telephone pulled Suzi back to her need to stay focused today. She entered the dining room and crossed to the bureau where she picked up her cell phone.

"Hello," she said cautiously.

"Hey, Cuz," responded the voice on the line. It was her cousin Deirdre. "How are you doing?"

"Oh good. It's just you." Suzi breathed a sigh of relief.

"Considering your state," Dee continued, "I won't take offence at that."

"Thank you. I'm sorry," said Suzi. "It's just that calls lately have been difficult. Mitch tries to spare me, but he's getting things ready outside right now. He's always the diligent task master. Bless his heart. But it's good to hear from you."

"I wish I could be there. You know I'm there in spirit."

"I do. Thanks for that."

"I won't keep you, but I had to tell you that I was with Mari in a dream last night." Feeling the pervading sadness of the day, Suzi pulled a chair from the dining room table and sat to steady herself. Silence hovered in the space between Washington State and Missouri. Hugs could only be imagined.

Finally, Suzi broke the silence. "I'm happy to hear that. You know I respect what you get in dreams. Tell me about it."

"It's pretty fuzzy, but I want you to know that she is with your mom, Aunt Lilly." Dee, the family's clairvoyant, often shared with Suzi the images that she experienced in her dreams. "It was brief but there was something to do with a flute. I didn't get that part. What would a flute mean?"

Again silence. Suzi covered her eyes to hold back approaching tears. "Mari used to play the flute. I guess you wouldn't know that. It was when she was in school. She loved it. I enjoyed hearing her practice, but she hadn't played it for years since her illness. I'd forgotten all about that."

"Well, I guess she'll be doing it over there now," Dee offered. "I'll keep you posted if I get anything more. When are you expecting everyone?"

"People should be arriving at any time now," Suzi answered. "Thank you for the input. It's good to know that my mom and Mari are together. You and I will have a good long talk soon when things settle down."

"I don't envy you today but stay strong and know that I love you and I'm sending lots of good healing vibes."

"Thank you and I love you too."

Suzi smiled at the thought that Mari and her grandmother were together again. They had always shared a special bond. She liked the idea that closeness can live on.

Three

Mari and Grandma Lilly glided through the front door into the entryway just as Suzi returned. Suzi was unable to see her visitors, but she paused when she felt the warmth that was the energy of their presence entering the space.

Mari watched her mom fussing with the roses, then gazing at the painting of the falconer. She was with Suzi when she realized that it could be a painting of her grandfather. Mari looked down at the flute still in her hand.

"There are so many ways that I feel like a disappointment," she said more to herself than to anyone else.

Lilly smiled gently at her granddaughter, knowing that every soul had its own unique experience entering the afterlife according to the need to heal.

"My life should have meant more," Mari continued. "I used to want to be useful somehow. To contribute something positive. I totally blew that."

"Remember the process," Lilly replied. "Let's not get ahead of ourselves."

Mari held out her arms for balance as she suddenly found herself in her old bedroom.

"Whoa! Still getting used to the teleport thing," she told an amused Lilly.

"It takes a little time. You'll get it and be exploring all over the place soon."

Having regained her balance, Mari gazed around the bedroom that she and her illness had so recently occupied. She expected to find a dresser and night table full of pill bottles, syringes, insulin bottles, gauze, bandages, fluid-filled IV bags, and so many of the other medical supplies and paraphernalia that go along with serious illness. Instead, Mari found the room of someone with no visible illness whatsoever. Even the IV pole was nowhere to be seen.

The bedroom had been transformed into the room of a young woman who could let herself enjoy hopes, dreams, and fonder memories. Her mother had arranged the dresser with the Raggedly Ann doll that she had made for Mari, sitting on the hand embroidered table runner that Grandma Lilly had given her so many years ago. Mari smiled at the photo of her parents and her younger siblings grinning in their innocence. She tried to pick up the photo, but her hand only passed through it.

Beside the doll were favorite perfume bottles and the playbill from the performance of *The Phantom of the Opera* that was Mari's last birthday surprise. She had been quite ill, but pushed herself to be able to go, even though she had to go in a wheelchair. She confided to her mom that she could identify with the tragic figure of The Phantom.

The bed was prettily made up with Mari's Victorian Rose bedspread. It tempted her to lie down for a good rest with the copy of her favorite book, Gone with the Wind, that graced the nightstand along with a crystal lamp and a bud vase that held a single white rose.

Lilly looked out the window as more cars arrived.

"Well, Dear," she interjected into the nostalgic silence. "It's time we moved on. Would you care to change your look for the festivities?"

Mari stepped in front of the cheval mirror that stood in her room.

"How do I do that?" she asked, seeing that she was still in her pajamas.

"The mirror will help," answered Lilly. "Just imagine what you want to change into."

As a puzzled Mari gazed into the mirror, the glass took on a wavy texture that undulated with energy until an image like Monet's lily pond appeared.

She raised her hand to the image and her fingers melded into the waves. She was startled at first, but it felt so good that soon her whole arm was engulfed.

She looked at Lilly, who was smiling and telepathically encouraging her.

"That's it. You've got it. Just keep going."

Without hesitation, Mari lifted her leg into the mirror and entered it fully. The waves began to subside, and she stepped back out of the mirror wearing a beautiful Victorian gown printed with pastel watercolor lilies flowing around her. She was a vision to behold.

"Well done!" exclaimed Lilly. "Now you're ready for a party."

Mari watched as Lilly's attire changed from her housedress and apron to a lovely pink Channel type skirt and jacket.

"Really!" Mari exclaimed.

"Well, yes," Lilly sheepishly replied. "It can be that easy. But I thought you might enjoy a magical transformation." Mari just grinned and shook her head.

With that, they faded from the bedroom and appeared in the backyard, which was now filled with family and friends who had congregated to honor Mari and celebrate her life.

Four

A party atmosphere filled the backyard just as Mari had hoped for. She had shared with her mom that she wanted a party with champagne flowing. She was not disappointed. Flowers were everywhere and a table was set on the patio with refreshments.

Grandma Lilly and young Mari were a warm and loving presence, moving unseen through the assemblage of family, friends, and familiar hospital personnel. The two caught snippets of conversations.

"I just love what you have done for Mari today," the husband of a cousin was telling Suzi. "My family has morose funerals. This is lovely and classy. A great way to remember Mari."

"Thank you, Paul," Suzi answered. "Mari told me what she wanted. I'm sure she would be pleased that you are enjoying her plan."

Beside the table was an easel that held a poster board filled with photos of Mari with family, friends, and pets that filled her with so much joy. Among her favorites was a photo of herself when she was just two years old with her Uncle Joseph and his beautiful white Arabian horse, Ezmeralda.

She loved Uncle Joseph and that sweet old mare.

One of Mari's favorite nurses from Virginia Mason Hospital approached Suzi and gave her a hug.

"Thank you for sharing your home and showing us Mari's world," she expressed. "We love seeing that there is more to a patient's life than what we see daily. And Mari was a pretty special one."

"Well," Suzi replied, "I know that she would be happy that so many of the staff were able to come today. We all appreciate it. You were a big part of her life and ours as well."

Lilly and Mari continued watching as Suzi made her way through the well-wishers, until she came to a family that her children had grown up with. Their daughter was visibly shaken. Suzi hugged her and Amy told her how sad she was that Mari died so young.

"I've never imagined it with someone my own age," said Amy.

Mari wished she could comfort her young friend, but just then Mari's dad raised a glass and tapped it to get everyone's attention. The small crowd quieted, and a short but lovely service took place with Mari's favorite music and memories shared by many.

As it concluded, Lilly took Mari's hand and led her to the wooden gate in the back fence. She encouraged Mari through the gate, into the park, where the Snoqualmie River flowed.

Suzi felt a light movement of air behind her and turned toward the fence where it seemed to be coming from. She blinked in surprise. She could have sworn she saw a flutter of exquisite pastel fabric pass through the boards of the gate, and she hadn't even been to the champagne table yet!

Five

Lilly led the way into the park, but let Mari take her time to feel her new freedom on the grounds of her old home.

The green grass of the park and the deep forest green of the surrounding fir and cedar trees were taking on brilliant hues never imagined by Mari in her physical life. As she moved through the park, all the colors around her grew more vibrant and sparkling with light, and within those colors she heard soft music. It started faintly and grew in intensity with a rhythm that lightened her step. Mari remembered the time she tried to explain to her mother that, to her, music was color.

The colors and music intensified, from dancing geometric shapes and ribbons of light as she slipped into the memory of the time she tried to explain this experience to her mom.

Suzi asked, "Do you mean that you see each note as a different color?"

"No," Mari explained. "Music just is color. I experience it that way, but I really can't explain how it works. I guess I shouldn't have given up on the flute. I'd like to take it up again someday. Then maybe I'll get good enough to show you what I mean."

"I'm not seeing it myself right now," said Suzi, "but it sounds incredibly beautiful and a special experience."

Mari appreciated her mother's open imagination and acceptance of the possibility that individuals can experience physical life in unique ways. Suzi felt very blessed that Mari had shared this special insight that did much to broaden her own concepts of spiritual awareness. As Suzi wondered about it over the years, it made increasingly more sense. Scientists know that everything is made of energy, and music and color are related in that they are both vibrations created by exertion of energy. What a beautiful way for God to reveal the wonders of the etheric world through the physical senses of her daughter. Somehow Mari must have been getting a little glimpse of heaven.

With all the green surrounding her, the music that Mari heard and saw in her own colorful way began to sound like the lilting music of a Celtic harp. This astral body that she was becoming comfortable with began to take on a vitality that was new to her. She bent down, picked up the hem of her skirt and danced and twirled across the park lawn with the lightness of a feather across a rainbow. As the music mellowed she glided and bounced toward the river. She slowed to a walk toward it with a light kick to her step that made the hem of her skirt bounce in joyful waves.

She was so caught up in the thrall of the peace, joy, and freedom of this new existence, so free of physical pain, that when she arrived at the ultra-thin veil that separates and, at the same time, joins worlds, she had no awareness of the difference between then and now. Her initial passing, with the white light and tunnel, had been full of love from both sides. Her visit to the party to observe her life and death, through the memories of others, involved new processes that had proved difficult to Mari, but it confirmed that she had done the right thing by engaging in the physical realm of her recent past.

The river and the bench were, and yet weren't, the same as she knew in the physical world. Now it seemed more vibrantly alive. Having gone ahead of Mari, Lilly sat patiently waiting for her.

Smoothing the hem of her skirt, Mari reached down and gave the sides a bit of a Scarlet O'Hara flip as she lowered herself onto the bench next to her grandmother.

Mari turned and sighed, "Oh Gramma, I'm so relieved that you encouraged me to go to the party. It was lovely and I learned a lot. Maybe I did make a small but positive contribution to that life. Everyone was so kind."

"Well, Dear," Lilly started to say, but Mari continued in excitement.

"It was great. I didn't expect so many people to show up. Mom did a good job. The flowers were beautiful, and I'd forgotten about all those pictures of me with family, friends, and pets. Those were good memories to revisit. I was happy to hear our favorite song, Gramma, Willie Nelson's *Angel Flying Too Close to The Ground*. I have always identified with that song. Isn't it great that the sun was shining?"

Grandma Lilly closed her eyes and took a deep, deep breath, raising her palms up to her heart as she inhaled, then letting her hands down to her sides as she exhaled. She did this twice more, and Mari began to breathe with her. Then Grandma Lilly sent Mari a warm thought, telling her she heard and understood everything Mari was experiencing. She was not alone. Additionally, any question could be asked and answered with a thought in an instant, if she could focus on the exchange.

Then Lilly put her arm around Mari and said, "If you can take a break for a minute, there are a few surprises on this side before you settle in and begin your orientation." Lilly cupped a hand behind her ear and said theatrically, "I think I hear one coming now."

Mari turned toward an enthusiastic yipping that was swiftly approaching. The liveliest Pomeranian-poodle mix this side of whatever they were this side of, came bounding at a run around the corner. Ears flopped, tail flew, and short little legs seemed to never hit the ground as this brown fluff ball ran straight into Mari's arms and gave her face the moist, affectionate doggy kisses she remembered so well.

"Dolly! Dolly! Dolly!" exclaimed Mari through laughter and tears. "You're wonderful. You never looked so good! What a surprise! I've missed you so much."

Breathing excitedly with her tongue flapping, Dolly gazed lovingly up at Mari. Mari turned to her grandmother and through tears of delight, sent a mental, "Thank you so much. I never expected to see her again. But how can this be?"

"It wasn't me," Lilly said and shrugged her shoulders. "Dolly herself insisted on being here for you. We're all here to help you remember this part of yourself. When we return to this side, all the pets that we loved and lost in the physical world are here for us. They make us comfortable so we can adjust to this new world. Dolly was here for me, too, when I crossed over, and she's been anxious to see you. No one can tell us that our pets' love isn't eternal. This surprise and more are just part of what makes us know that we are truly at home on this side."

Dolly curled up on Mari's lap. The gentle petting strokes that she was giving were relaxing her and her furry spirit friend at the same time.

Mari became quiet. It was almost overwhelming. She thought deeply about all that she had to learn about this new life. In those thoughts came the idea of an education in the world of spirit. She loved learning and was a very good student. A's were normal for her and she hoped she could make up for the missed opportunity. She felt like a dry sponge waiting for someone to turn on the faucet.

She continued caressing Dolly and she reveled in the adoring pet's healing energy. The palms of her hands could feel that power being drawn into them, and it was a soothing ointment to her soul.

"I like the idea of learning," Mari shared with her grandmother. "I feel like my entire life was preparation for some important work somewhere and sometime. I loved school and I'm sorry that I had to put it on hold. Illness really messed me up. It was agony to watch other people around me going to school and moving on to productive careers. I know that I'm ready to jump right into whatever learning is available to me here."

"First thing's first," said Lilly. She was pleased to see the familiar enthusiastic energy of the old Mari. "I mentioned orientation. It's an important part of any new school experience. I know that you feel better than you ever thought possible, from where you've just been, and I'm happy to say that it's just the beginning. Right now you're still in a place where the memory of your physical experience is pulling heavily on your spirit. The restrictions you experienced on Earth are just one chapter in a larger soul journey, but I understand that chapter can feel like everything for a while until we remember who we are in a larger sense. Perceptions here intensify to a degree that requires us to slow down a bit, but I promise you won't miss out on anything.

"To get you on the right track," she continued, "you can start shedding the idea of 'time' as you are familiar with it. Release it and you might be able to free yourself from the anxiety that you may have missed out on something. It's not possible to miss anything that you choose for yourself because you'll be creating every experience according to the specific needs of your spirit."

Mari sat quietly watching the peace wash over Dolly's energetic aura as she seemed to melt into her lap with each petting stroke. She was deep in thought and didn't notice a change in their surroundings. A light mist rose from the river until the water, the park, and the trees vanished within it. The caressing fog was like a huge fluffy fleece blanket wrapped gently around them. It gave a welcoming feeling that Mari was just becoming used to.

"So where are we now?" she asked Lilly when she finally noticed the fog. The hesitation in her voice was evidence of her need for an answer, whether she wanted it or not. "Are we in Heaven?"

"I was wondering when you'd ask that," her grandmother answered. "You've been pretty patient with all the changes you've been through. The best way to respond is to bring up a time when you and your mother, sitting on this very bench, were having one of your philosophical discussions. She posed the idea that everyone stuck on earth is trying to come up with answers to these age-old questions. But the trouble seems to be that we are all using different words as well as different languages while we are all talking about the same things. Heaven, Nirvana, the Great Beyond, the Other Side. They're all words trying to describe where you and I are now. It's a world of love, light, energy and vibration.

"I guess I don't really need to tell you that there is a lot of confusion in the physical world about the subject. There are people who want to think, and have others think with them, that they have exclusive access to the Divine. But Heaven is not some tasty morsel that is dangled before humanity by some conditional higher being. So many think they need to fight, scratch and bite each other, competing for just a taste of it like a pack of starving dogs. They may have forgotten that our all-loving Heavenly Father/Mother/Higher Being taught love and sharing.

"Okay, I digressed to my soap box there. If I must give this place a name," said Grandma Lilly, "I just call it Home, my heart's place of peace in this universe. On that note, how would you like to see the house that I've created for myself? I've been looking forward to your arrival."

"House? Really? I would never turn down a chance to visit your home and I'm not about to start now. Yes please. Let's go," was Mari's exuberant answer. "I haven't thought about houses here. I guess I haven't thought about any details here at all. Like, how do we get there?"

A sound came through the heavy mist. At first Mari couldn't distinguish what it was. As it drew closer, she realized it was horses' hooves approaching. She glanced down and saw that the gravel at their feet had become multicolored paving stones that glistened with the moisture of the fog. They had hues that, for her, were giving off a light musical romp that heightened her expectations of what mystery might be headed their way.

Lilly rose and announced, "Here's our ride now." She added with a twinkle, "There may be more surprises in store for you."

Six

Like a fairy tale apparition, a pure white Arabian mare began to appear through the evaporating fog. To Mari's delight, it was pulling an open Victorian carriage. The mare held her majestic tail high in the air and lifted her head, nodding a happy greeting to the young woman in the flowing chiffon gown.

"How beautiful!" was all Mari could think, as the sight gave her heart a flutter.

"Yes. It is," Lilly agreed. "And look again."

Mari immediately recognized the horse from the picture with her Uncle Joseph. "It's Ez! It's Ezmeralda!" She jumped up from the park bench and ran to where the horse had brought the carriage to a halt. "Oh Ez, you wonderful old horse!" cried Mari, reaching up to hug and stroke the long snout of her old friend. Ez looked just as good, if not better than, she had in the picture. Her coat was glowing, and her eyes were sharp and alert. Mari's equine friend appeared pleased, and bent her head to nuzzle Mari.

Mari stood back to take in the stunning sight of the carriage and its gleaming harnesses, studded with multi-colored gems that sparkled in the mist. She turned to her grandmother. "I can't thank you enough, Gram," she said with a hug. "It's so great to see Ez again and the carriage is beautiful. No, it's stunning. Oh," she continued with a shrug, "I just don't have a word to do it justice."

"I'm glad that you like our little surprise," Lilly replied, "but I can't take any credit. It was totally the creation of Ez and your carriage driver. Even the animals assist in creating our realities here."

At that, Mari looked up to see that a somewhat mysterious but grand gentleman had appeared, and he was grinning down at her from where he sat in the tall driver's seat. She admired his ruggedly handsome and exotic appearance. His head was framed by the tall stiff collar of a cream-colored cape that was tied around his neck. His smile shone brightly on his friendly face with its long, Romanesque nose, twinkling dark eyes and prominent, rather pointed chin. His dashing, Robin Hood style hat was the same color, and on his right hand he wore a thick brown glove with a wide cuff that extended almost to his elbow. Mari didn't understand the glove until she caught sight of a red-tailed hawk on a perch next to him.

She smiled back, knowing that she knew this person, but she was perplexed about exactly who he was. Finally, she remembered being in the entry of her family home and seeing the painting that was titled *The Falconer*.

"Of course!" she exclaimed. "*The Falconer*. Mom said that the painting reminded her of you. And you are my grandfather, Claus. I didn't know you in life, but I know you for certain now."

Securing the reins, Claus stepped down from the carriage. He reached under his cape and pulled out a beautiful white rose and handed it to Mari with a slight bow. He took her small hand and raised it to his lips, then pulled her into a huge grandpa hug.

"Welcome, Sweetie," he said with a capricious grin. "I don't always look like this. I wanted you to have a reference that would help you remember me. And besides, I do share your flare for drama. I may just keep this look. It suits me."

"I understand your confusion about knowing me," he continued. "You see we have met, but not in the world you just came from. You were twelve years old, and in the hospital diagnosed with a diabetic coma. While your body was in trauma, your spirit was in a place of comfort, and I was thrilled to volunteer to help you bide the time there. We had a good time. When you start remembering more, you and I have a Monopoly game to finish."

"I remember now," she said quietly. "And I didn't want to go back. It was so great. I didn't want to leave you, but you said I wasn't finished on that side, and that we would meet again. I also remember coming out of the coma. Everything was all white and everyone was dressed in white. I thought it was heaven, but it was just the hospital. I was really ticked off when I realized I was back in my ailing body."

"Yes," said Claus. "You resisted some, but you knew what you had to do."

"I can't believe that I am remembering all of that. You helped me until I was ready to go back. But most of all you gave me the grandpa love that I needed, and I still need it. Thank you for being there then and here now. And thank you for Ez and this wonderful carriage. I love you. And," she added with a sly grin and a playful wink, "I do remember owning Park Place and Boardwalk."

"So, you did," said Claus smiling. "Well maybe we'll just forget about that game and start a new one. Anyway, Ezmeralda wouldn't allow herself to be tethered to just any old wagon when she heard that you were coming. She insisted that this one be special for this occasion. We both knew that you needed to see things that you could relate to. Our animals here are even more magical, loving and dedicated to our spirits than we can imagine on the other side. You're the first of your generation in this family to return here and you have a lot of love waiting for you from many sources."

"Speaking of waiting," interrupted Lilly from the sidelines, "are we ready to move along? We'll have lots of good visits and relaxation when we get to my house."

"Ez and I are at your service, Ladies," Claus said as he adjusted his hat and bowed deeply, gesturing toward the carriage. Mari curtsied, holding her skirt. Lilly had gone back to her more comfortable attire and apron. She used it to wipe the moisture from her eyes as she watched the touching reunion between Claus and their granddaughter.

Claus rose as the ladies glided past him. He gallantly opened the carriage door, and a step appeared for them. The elegant door revealed an inviting luxurious interior. He sweetly lifted each lady's hand as they took turns stepping into the carriage.

Seven

This was almost too much splendor for Mari. She loved to read books that described the opulence of different eras; however, she didn't feel deserving of it herself. Even now she had doubts. She had handled so many things poorly and her life had seemed such a mess. Now she had her grandmother and grandfather, and she looked forward to getting to Gramma's house and taking the chance to let it all sink in.

The carriage was even more beautiful inside. The seats were upholstered with such fine pewter colored velvet that Mari had to rub her hand across it to know it was real. The gleaming silver panels of the interior walls were trimmed with inset white satin braid with gold and silver threads.

Claus straightened his hat and rose to his seat. Picking up the reins, he looked back to be sure his companions were settled in place. He took in the beauty of the ladies with an ermine throw over their laps, surrounded by white pillows. Instead of interrupting their intense girl talk about their special carriage, Claus simply turned and gave Ez a mental okay to proceed. He was concerned for his granddaughter, but he knew that he had to trust this system, where love always prevails one way or another. She had a challenging road ahead and he wished he could make it swift and easy for her.

Ezmeralda raised her head. Her regal Arabian tail did a grand swish over her back, then she held it high in the lofty arch that is the trademark of that breed. Her hoof beats began a gentle pace as she pulled the carriage smoothly down the road that had appeared before them out of the mist.

Mari and Lilly sat facing forward so they could enjoy the panorama that was coming into view. As the fog lifted into the ethers, a world of light and sparkling colors began to reveal itself.

There was no glaring sun here. Instead, everything was emitting a light of its own. The brightness that radiated all around them revealed a pastoral scene. Mari's mother, Suzi, had raised her to appreciate the beauty of Earth, but this was beyond incredible. The colors seemed to be vibrating with fluid energy, yet they were still comfortable for her new eyes to distinguish. They had a life and warmth with an occasional eye-catching sparkle.

She knew at once that her physical eyes could never have tolerated the intensity. A memory returned to her of having her eyes dilated in an eye exam. She remembered the doctor had given her some dark glasses when she left the office, but her curiosity got the best of her. She took them off on that sunny day and was stunned by the brightness of the world without the protective mechanism of the eye's iris. Now, this experience with her astral body's eyes was even more intense, yet comfortable to her heightened senses.

As the carriage rolled on, the texture of the grassy fields looked like emerald velvet cloth that undulated over the rolling hills, with patches of wildflowers offering waves of color. Some of the colors seemed curiously different than those Mari had known on Earth, but they were part of the spectrum that was now being shown to her. In the distance, she could see clusters of trees that appeared to be moving with a breeze, but with a closer look, they were dancing to the symphony of color around them.

The fields showed occasional wildlife. Mari saw deer, moose, fox, raccoons, bear, and others that she recognized from around the world. Birds were dipping through the air, heralding the journey with their cheerful songs. Hawks, eagles, robins, hummingbirds, gold finches and multi-colored parrots shared the sky.

A bright musical whistle coming from above caused Mari to look up. A brilliant red cardinal and its cinnamon-hued mate dipped in their flight and flew directly in front of the travelers. They took Mari into a warm flash of memory.

She was a young child, sitting on the floor, gazing into an antique cabinet in her grandmother's home. It was filled with glass, ceramic and carved wooden figurines arranged carefully with plates and glassware that were vividly painted with images of vibrant red cardinals. She had spent many moments wondering about that fascinating bird that she had never met in person.

As she grew older, she finally asked, "Gramma, what is this pretty bird?"

"Oh, that's my Redbird," Lilly answered simply. "I grew up in Missouri where we would see them a lot. They were so pretty, and they had such a sweet song. My mother, Lenora, and every other woman in my family always loved them. That's the one thing that I miss since I moved to the Northwest."

Mari became very familiar with Lilly's love and longing for this beautiful bird that she referred to simply as the "Redbird."

Emerging from her memory, Mari was especially in awe of the scenes that surrounded her. It was as if her fantasies had come to life. Lilly and Claus still marveled at their continually changing world and the fact that every experience was new even to them with every soul that they shared it with. They never tired of the ineffable views they encountered, and they were happy to share it all with their granddaughter.

Mari turned to Lilly, who had been watching her granddaughter with pride.

"It's so much more than I ever imagined," Mari said, or rather thought, becoming more accustomed to the telepathic process. "The scenery is spectacular, and I love the animals. I'm not used to seeing so many different species sharing the same areas, but they're certainly peaceful with one another."

Lilly shifted on the seat to face Mari more directly. "The one legacy that I worked to leave your mother, and her siblings was to appreciate the beauty that is always around us. I'm pleased that your mother has continued that legacy and helped you to see that part of yourself. The scenes are striking here, and the peace is for all of us to grow in.

"That appreciation has helped me through some pretty dark times," Mari shared with her grandmother. "I remember missing you, but I would think about your goodness to draw you near me. Mom said that she could feel your presence when she took the time to appreciate the things you enjoyed. When I'd do the same, I would be comforted after you left us."

"You sometimes paid attention when we gave those hints from this side. At your memorial, it was relatively easy for you to be with your loved ones. You will find that it gets more difficult as you get used to this world. We are beings of a higher vibration here and we need to lower that vibration to get to the Earth level."

"I can relate to that," Mari commented. "I do feel that lightness, but it still seems that I'm trying to shake off the lower energies. Does that take some time?"

"That can depend on the soul and the way that it leaves physical life," Lilly answered. "There have been times when a soul is released before a traumatic event like an airplane or automobile accident. It may or may not take much time at all for that one to adjust to being here. Then there are those who suffer for long periods who are in a coma or kept on drugs because of a severe illness until they pass. That can be a blessing because, while their bodies seem to be at rest, their souls are visiting over here and beginning their transition until they are ready to release their physical bodies. They sometimes assimilate here a little faster."

"This carriage ride makes me feel that I'm traveling slowly into this world. Does that mean that it will be more difficult for me to be with those still over there?"

"You can give it a try if you like," answered Lilly. "In fact, now is a good time. Your parents are planning that move to Hood Canal."

"That's right. I almost forgot," said Mari. "My mom told me that I would be in my new home on June 21st. Now that means something else to me. That was the day that I passed over here. This feels more like home than any place I've ever lived."

"Good observation," Lilly commented. "Right now, your little sis, Natalie is deciding if she wants to move with them. She could use a little input from her big sister. I'm going to tell you the situation so this first time out you won't have to stay too long in that atmosphere."

Eight

"As you know, Natalie just graduated from high school, and she is feeling grown up and wants to make a decision that would be in her best interest. She's had an offer to stay where she is and stay with a friend. Her friends are important to her, but maybe for the wrong reasons. Her spirit guide has informed me that she could use a little help. I have a copy of that portion of her life chart that was shared with me."

Lilly reached under her apron bib and pulled out a parchment scroll and carefully unrolled it for Mari to see. They studied it together as the carriage continued through a glen with Claus's capable guidance. Mari took the information in and eventually nodded knowingly to her grandmother.

"Okay, I got it," she said. "How do I get to her?"

"She is in her room, and she's just come from being with your mother, who was very melancholy. They are feeling the loss of you now that the party is over, and things have quieted down. You can imagine the setting, only expect it to be darker than you may remember. It's only the energy of grief. They are healing and they will be fine."

"Alright, I'll try," Mari said, as she closed her eyes. She tried to take herself to that place in her memory of Natalie's bedroom, but she could only see a darkness that she couldn't penetrate. Opening her eyes, she was back in the carriage with Lilly.

"See what I mean?" said Lilly. "It gets more difficult, and I apologize. I forgot to tell you that you need to surround yourself with a white light that will protect you, but it will also brighten the dense atmosphere there. Try to concentrate on pulling your aura into your body and pushing it down into your legs. That's a method I use for lowering my vibration to the Earth level."

"Got it," Mari said, determined to make it work. She closed her eyes again, and imagined a pure, bright white light surrounding her. She also saw her aura as a sparkling light blue, and taking deep breaths, she mentally pulled the energy of it in through her skin each time she inhaled. She found it increasingly unpleasant for her mind to push it down into her spirit body, but she was determined to succeed.

As she continued the process, she couldn't help thinking, "It's no wonder spiritual visits to loved ones in the physical aren't more prevalent. This is difficult and unpleasant. Even painful!"

But even though she was experiencing something that she could only describe as ethereal agony; she tried to ignore it and keep her focus on her objective. She really loved her little sis and wanted so much to be of help to her in a way that she never could have in that life.

When she finally arrived at her destination, she only had to move through a vaporous veil to sit beside Natalie on her bed. She put her arm around her younger sister and felt her sadness and confusion.

This was truly a crossroad for Natalie, and Mari wanted so much to help her in her decision. But she knew instinctively that all she could do was ask the right questions.

Natalie accepted the warmth and tenderness that she had no clue was coming from her big sister's loving heart. But her soul did hear the softly spoken words, "You have a loving and giving spirit. Who needs that more right now?"

"My Mom," Natalie said out loud as tears welled up in her eyes.

"One last thing," Mari added, feeling a gentle pull back to the other side. "Think about school. There's a good community college near that new home."

"Good job!" exclaimed Lilly. Mari appeared back in the carriage with an electrical pop. "Just as you left, she got up and went to tell your mother that she wanted to move with her and your dad. It's amazing how just a few appropriate words at the right time can help a soul decide to be diverted. Thank God, literally, that she was willing to listen and that your parents let it be her decision. That's powerful. She's going to do just fine with your help now and then."

"You're so right," sighed Mari. "That is powerful, and I feel blessed to be able to help."

Lilly smiled, "It is a blessing to be able to help in ways that we couldn't even imagine when we were back there. You're a good little gardener. You planted just the right seeds. You didn't notice," she continued, "but I was there with you. That's how I knew what happened after you left. I've been doing this for some time now and I'm getting pretty good at it. It will still get tougher for you for a while, but the love makes it worthwhile."

"Thank you," Mari replied. "It was good to be with Natalie."

Lilly smiled. "I know you're still concerned about your family but remember that you need to release the idea of time. They will join you here eventually and it will seem like none of you ever left."

With that the two ladies snuggled down into the plush cushions to enjoy the rest of the ride. Claus looked back to check on them and smiled as they chatted and laughed continually. The family affection in the atmosphere was touching him too.

Nine

The carriage slowed as they came to what Earth Mari would have called "an enchanted forest." She had never been to the redwoods in California, but here they were before her, regal and awe inspiring, jutting up from the forest floor and soaring up into the sky like the spires of a grand woodland cathedral. The atmosphere was one of quiet reverence. Even the birds sang a song of muted admiration. These gentle giants impressed Mari with even more respect for the wonders of nature.

The enormous trees cast no shadows, as the subtle light of their own bright morning rays warmed the floor of the forest. Mari and her grandparents rode through it all quietly, as if to avoid disturbing the fairy and elfin spirits who, Mari imagined, certainly must be residing there.

The touring spirits meandered from the forest and traveled again through more pastoral scenes. The carriage rolled down a slope and around a bend where they felt a fresh sea breeze before coming upon a rugged and raw seashore. Mari marveled at how the vibrant blue of the sea contrasted with the bright white foam, created by waves that collided rhythmically with rocks on the shore.

She turned to Lilly and said with a great sigh, "Thank you for letting me see places that I never got to see during life."

"We're doing our part to help you remember your home here," she replied. "The beauty found on Earth is a reminder for those who are there of their true celestial home.

"Eventually you'll know that you went into that life with a blueprint or chart that was your spirit's plan. You wrote it, with guidance, before you crossed over, and it was your personal plan for learning and growing as a spiritual being. All of that will come back to you as you adjust to being here. We'll help you when we can, but your spirit guide will be more valuable to you. She's been with you throughout your life, and now she's preparing to help you assimilate into this side."

"Do you mean I haven't done that yet?" Mari asked. "I crossed over with the white light and all that, you met me and now I'm here. I guess that is a little simplistic, but it's what I recall reading about. It's all so strangely familiar." She paused then continued, "In fact, I'm getting the impression that I have been on other life adventures. And what is this about spirit guides? I've heard the term. You had mentioned Natalie's spirit guide."

"Many of us have been through multiple lives," Lilly answered, "and we have guides who help us along the way. You can think of guides as emissaries for Higher Power. Often, they are confused with guardian angels. Angels are something entirely different. God would never let us go to Earth without a substantial support system. The guides are souls who have lived lives on Earth and are familiar with the trials we face when we go there. They can be a huge help when we are willing to listen, and they stay with us throughout our lives. Take your time and rely on those who are here to help you. Right now, let yourself be in this moment. Your adventures aren't over yet." Lilly smiled and patted Mari's knee.

The two ladies sat back and relaxed once more into the ride and watched as more shoreline views passed before them. Mari's thoughts were jumbled and a bit confusing. From her grandmother's hints, she knew that there was more she needed to go through here. She was trying to figure out the implications when she heard a very distinct and familiar voice say to her, "Don't bother with any of that now, silly girl. That is for us to deal with when the time is right. We are with you, as always, so relax into the gifts of this moment."

Somewhere deep inside, Mari recognized the voice of her spirit guide. Memories welled up of playing with a special friend she referred to as Saria when she was very small. Mari's mom, Suzi, would hear her daughter talking while she played in a room alone. When she asked her who she was talking to, Mari would answer, "It's my friend, Saria." Suzi couldn't imagine where her clever daughter had ever heard such a name, but she would just respond, "Well that's nice. Have fun." Her motherly instincts told her that her daughter's imaginary friend was a good thing and not to tamper with it.

As Mari grew and the world got more complicated and all too real, Saria faded from her consciously, but she had remained a vital part of her guidance system that attempted to keep her on track. Now a special peace washed over Mari as she recognized the affection in that voice. She remembered the voice nagging at her later as a troubled teen, struggling to come to terms with difficulties in her life. This was, indeed, the spirit guide that she knew and could trust.

Ten

Claus pulled on the reins guiding Ez into a turn that put them into a long, winding country lane, leading to a cluster of cedars. The carriage glided as if floating on thin air even though the lane had the rustic look of a cracked and pitted road. Ez seemed right at home as she turned again into a long driveway that meandered through fields of enchanting wildflowers. An adorable cottage was revealed among the tall, heavily branched trees. There was no shadow from the trees, or from anything else for that matter. All things appeared to be made of light itself. Even the cottage glowed outwardly with an aura in the same shade of pink light that radiated from the essence of Lilly's love.

Mari took in the visage of the little white cottage. It had a ranch-style front porch with ivy growing up its posts, and it was furnished with an old-fashioned porch swing. The front steps led directly to a simple pink door that welcomed visitors with the promise of comfort and care. Everything had the inviting appearance of unhampered newness. Even the steps looked fresh and new.

"This has to be my grandmother's home," Mari thought. She remembered that every home Lilly had lived in had been brightened by her love for flowers. The yard around the cottage showed that Lilly must have found her seventh heaven in creating her surroundings. The yard, its colors and musical undertones gave Mari a new understanding of the phrase "symphony of color." It was like merging herself into a light-emanating Thomas Kincade painting.

As they drew closer, she could see more clearly the individual flowers that she knew had been Lilly's favorites on Earth. The purple and yellow pansies with their bright faces, the petunias with ruffled skirts, and dusty miller with its leaves of powdery gray that looked like fairy wings. Violets, primroses, snapdragons, hollyhocks and, of course, roses of many hues made the scene burst with color.

Among them were new, incredible looking flowers that Mari didn't recognize. Some grew in glorious tall clusters with large petals that had the appearance of iridescent peacock feathers, while others grew close to the ground with dainty white daisy-like flowers, having centers that glistened with a sparkle like diamond chips. Between them were green, thickly leafed plants that had a powder pink flower with inner petals that looked like thin, green slices of kiwi.

So much that Mari was seeing was familiar to her, and yet combined with unexpected details. She was comfortable and beginning to feel peace, but there was so much more, and her hungering soul was starting to grasp that this was just the beginning.

Claus pulled on the reigns and Ezmeralda swished her proud Arabian tail in response as they stopped at the gate of the white picket fence that surrounded the cottage. The fence was obviously a decorative touch, because just then a family of pure white rabbits casually sauntered through its pickets, as if the solid fence post weren't even there.

Claus removed his hat and turned to his passengers. He asked Lilly, "Well, Dear, shall I see you ladies to your door, or do you think it's time to remind this young lady of our preferred way to travel from one spot to another?"

With a good-natured smile, Lilly brought Mari into her own thought of the porch swing. Immediately, Mari found herself seated on the swing beside her grandmother and Dolly. Surprise showed on Mari's face as she exclaimed, "Well beam me up, Scotty!"

Her grandparents laughed, relieved that Mari was beginning to relax enough to find her charming wit.

"Well, Ez and I will be off," Claus called from the carriage. "We'll see you at another time. There's a lot we can show you, but we'll wait until you are ready. I can be with you anytime you need me, Mari. Just send me a thought, I'll be there."

With a wave of his hat, Claus, Ez and the carriage vanished from the scene, leaving behind the faint essence of their auras in the atmosphere.

"Oh my," Mari exclaimed. She was staring at the spot where they had once stood. "Where did they go?"

"Home," was Lilly's simple answer.

Lilly laid her arm across her granddaughter's shoulders. The light in her eyes sparkled. Lilly was grateful for all those family souls who were such a huge part of her being and she was especially thankful for those who had been on this side to help her cross over. Many of them were moving on in their chosen paths. Some had crossed over to other incarnations, while others chose to further their growth and learning on this plane to be available to serve where they were needed.

Eleven

Suzi finished her house chores for the day. She even baked bread and made soup for dinner. It was a full day. Mitch was settled in his chair with his Kindle, so she decided to take some time for a phone call.

The deck was a peaceful place to have a conversation, and it was a nice cool evening. She sat on a deck chair and put her feet up on the matching stool and dialed her cousin, Deirdre.

"Well, hello, Cuz," Deirdre answered right away when Suzi's name came up on her phone. "How are you holding up?" she asked.

"Pretty well, I guess," Suzi replied. "Things are settling into normal routines. I'm finding myself with time that I didn't know I had since I don't have to spend so much time at the hospital. But I would gladly do it again for Mari."

They exchanged basic information on how each family was doing. Nothing was new, so the conversation became serious.

"If you can," said Dee, "I'd like to know more about what happened. Mari was a special young lady. We connected for sure when I was out there in Washington for that visit.

"Oh sure," Suzi began. "I can do that. Well, let's see. I went up to her room to help her get settled in bed for the night. I took care of her IV and made sure that she was comfortable. She did seem extra tired but, other than that, there were no problems that I could see.

"I was tired too, so I tucked her in, kissed her forehead and turned to leave. My mind was on getting up early the next morning to take her for her dialysis treatment. She was a trooper to go through all that. I know that it was making her weary. Recently there were complications with her veins collapsing making access difficult, so we weren't looking forward to that session.

"When I got to the doorway, I swear that there was something or someone invisible blocking me from going through. An angel, my mother's spirit. I don't know, but it was real. I paused, then turned to Mari and said, "Good night, sweetie. I love you.

She tried to sit up on her elbow in bed and smile. Then she said, "I love you too, Mom."

Suzi had to pause her story. The tears were trying to start flowing.

"Those were her last words to me, then I was allowed to continue on my way through the door," she said with a tearful catch in her throat. "I can still hear her voice saying those words. "I love you too, Mom. They will always echo in my soul."

"Doesn't get more powerful than that," Dee responded. "How special and beautiful. I'm glad you had that moment with her. So, when did you know something happened?" she asked.

"Something took place during the night. It was sometime in the early morning. I woke up and thought I had heard the intercom on Mari's bedside. I started to get up, but for some reason, I paused. I felt a hand on my shoulder and turned to Mitch, but he was sleeping soundly. Then I heard, "You are going to need all the sleep you can get right now." I had been concerned but a strange peace came over my whole body and I was lowered back onto the pillow and fell into a deep sleep until the alarm went off at five in the morning. Again, that could have been an angel, or my mother's spirit, but looking back now, I'm pretty sure it was Mari looking out for me as she passed."

"I can see her doing that," said Dee, "but I'm sure there was another spirit involved also. I think it was your dad, Uncle Claus. Mari has been with your mom, but now your dad is with her also. He is a big part of her transition on the Other Side.

"I know you are close to all your children, but you and Mari have a special bond. You had been through so much together. Your lives have been intertwined for at least the last few years. She told me how special you are to her."

"That's nice to hear," said Suzi. "It means a lot. I do miss her."

Twelve

When Mari had first crossed over, she had learned from Lilly a few of the stories about other family members who were on this side. She had never known many of them, but as a child, her mom and dad had piqued her curiosity with stories from family history. Especially interesting were the times when they would look through family albums and boxes of pictures. She loved putting faces to family history. The thought occurred to her how important it is to do that, so we have a reference when we arrive on this side. It just might make it easier. It certainly did for her.

Lilly went on to explain that her mother, Mari's great grandmother Lenora, had been among those who helped Mari decide on this last incarnation. Lenora was now aiding another grandchild on Earth. "That granddaughter went into the physical with the difficult challenge of what is referred to there as "psychic abilities", said Lilly. "Lenora has her hands full with that one. Deirdre is stuck in a world where her talents are difficult to define yet she wants so much to be of service." Dee and Mari had been close. Deirdre had given Mari a compelling spiritual perspective to life that made her think there could be a higher purpose for her suffering.

Lilly's father, Mari's great grandfather, had so far chosen to remain on the spirit side to expand his creations in the arts, but was considering making himself available as a spirit guide for an art student who had chosen to cross over soon. That student is very gifted. His talent and purpose are to create works of art that would depict scenes that his spirit's memory had from this dimension. People wouldn't know exactly what it was, but his work would move them in a way that comforted their souls. It would remind their souls of this dimension that is their true home.

Mari also learned that Lilly was attending a special school in preparation for a life of service of her choosing. It would not be an easy choice. There are so many areas in which to grow.

Mari was the first immediate family member to join Lilly in this dimension and Mari needed Lilly's help to adjust. A part of Lilly remembered the changes and difficult work during her own transition. She wanted to make it easier for her granddaughter, but it wasn't her path. All she could do for this precious one was to stay bonded and be available to her. At this point Lilly was grateful for all the assistance that she could draw upon. She knew that when it was complete, Mari could know the "peace that passes understanding," which is the very essence of life here in her new home.

"I would guess that Ezmeralda has returned to her peaceful pastures," said Lilly. "Claus has most likely returned home where he has fabulous gardens and greenhouses that you can visit when you're ready. I know he'd be thrilled to share them with you. But for now, won't you let me be your hostess? I think you'll be comfortable here for a while."

"I can't imagine any place I'd rather be," Mari answered

She felt a swirling around her and found that they had left the porch swing and were now on a comfortable sofa in Lilly's living room. The sofa was upholstered with a crisp chintz fabric that had a white background and bright red poppies with green foliage. She could feel the grandmother she knew so well in every detail of the surroundings. The lush houseplants, knickknacks (including Redbirds) and the red rocking chair were just like Mari remembered. The most important thing that she sensed was the essence of this woman that was reflected within the entire room that Lilly had created. "Homey" was the best word that would come to her. She really did feel at home. This must be her grandmother's version of her very own mansion in the sky.

"This is the home that I'm most comfortable in for now," said Lilly. "I'm sure you notice that I like to surround myself with some of the things from my most recent life, but that old brown sofa had to go. Remember that old thing? In fact, I think I'm ready for something besides poppies."

Immediately the sofa transformed, small pink and red geraniums declaring Lilly's fondness for that flower. Mari was getting used to the magical changes that could occur in her new environment. She smiled with approval of the new choice.

Mari's thoughts suddenly returned to when she was 18 and had just moved into her first apartment, two blocks from her parents' home.

Her furnishings were the bare essential hand-me-downs to get her by. It was a traumatic time, and her bleak environment only emphasized her loneliness. She had wanted this apartment and the chance to grow up and try to get a handle on her life. She remembered sitting in her apartment thinking back through her medical trials.

Diabetes was a devastating blow to a preteen girl with so much optimism. Everyone around her, the medical staff and family, wanted her to learn that she could control the disease with the medical techniques that were available, but she could only feel it controlling her. She was strong-willed and desperate to get the upper hand, but her confused young emotions overrode the practical guidance she was receiving.

She reviewed the time she had returned to her sixth-grade class after the first hospital stay. Her teacher had already explained to the students why she had been absent. Something had changed. Mari was too young to analyze whether her friends had changed or if it was just her perceptions of them that had changed. All they could do was to try to be normal and wait to see how Mari handled it herself. She interpreted their reactions as rejection. She retreated into herself and found her solace and comfort in the companionship of books. In the drama of her situation, she could stand alongside Scarlett O'Hara viewing her own young life in the burned-out ruins of Tara.

She had been so young. Mari was beginning to realize how important family is in our lives. She knew they were there for her and doing all they could to help her, and she loved them all. But she felt alone in her adolescent confusion, and she internalized it. Getting her blood sugar under control and her physical symptoms in balance were the priority but she was also in the throes of her preteen emotions. Her thinking processes were so clouded because of the uncontrolled blood sugars that she was in a persistent fog. She wanted to do things the right way, but the insulin shots and the blood sugar testing were confusing to her normally intelligent mind. With the fog of fear hovering around her, the love of her family couldn't dispel the fear of abandonment and loss of control that haunted her.

"Future" was just a word to her. A darkness was created in her young life, and she was afraid that one more step would plunge her into permanent despair.

From the diagnosis of diabetes at age twelve until she was sixteen, multiple doctors treated her physical symptoms only in terms of disease. They thought she had what is referred to as "Brittle" diabetes. It wasn't until she encountered Dr. Ed Benson in the endocrine medicine department at Virginia Mason Hospital that the reality of the situation revealed itself. After reviewing her history and visiting a very ill, and much too thin, Mari, he was the first one to see beyond the obvious diabetes.

Standing in the stark, antiseptic hallway outside her daughter's hospital room, Suzi was presented with the information that Mari had an eating disorder, anorexia nervosa, that was seriously affecting her health and complicating the diabetes. Suzi couldn't deny it. Suddenly so much made sense. The symptoms that he was describing were telling a great deal about Mari's story and Suzi was bombarded by the realization. Mari had been a slightly overweight preteen when she was stunned by the diabetes diagnosis. The pressure began for Mari to lose weight to help control the diabetes, as if she were not already feeling the social stigma of being overweight.

"She's too intelligent for her own good," explained Dr. Benson. "She is using her diet and manipulating her insulin to keep herself in a state of ketosis to not only prevent her body from gaining weight but also to make her lose weight. That has deadly consequences. Her body won't be able to handle the imbalance very long."

By now, Suzi was educated enough about diabetes to know that ketosis meant that her child's body was a fat burning furnace beginning to burn the more essential cells of muscle and organs. Her life was being threatened by not just one, but two devastating disorders. At this point, anorexia was just beginning to be recognized as a growing phenomenon in the medical community. There was little information available about it at the time. Mari's parents read the books that were available and agreed that psychiatric help was essential.

Overcome by the pain of the memory, Mari laid her head in the lap of her loving grandmother. Lilly stroked the young woman's soft honey-colored curls and knew that her granddaughter's spiritual healing had begun. Mari had much to relive in the growth into her essential self. She couldn't move on and use the valuable gift of knowledge she had been given in this recent life without finding an understanding of it. Lilly reached out into the ethers for help.

Thirteen

Mari awoke to the firm pressure of a hand on her shoulder. She was still in the heavenly surroundings of her grandmother's home, but apparently, they weren't alone. She sat up and turned to find a strangely familiar face looking down at her. The face glowed with a brilliant smile that lit up the person's aura with the warmest sky blue she had ever seen. A smooth melody blended with those in Mari's spirit and washed her with peace. She knew instantly that she had not been sitting alone in the coldness of her first apartment so long ago. This face had been an unseen part of that scene. It was Saria, her spirit guide, who had always been with her, loving and trying to guide her in every step she took. If only she could have recognized that fact earlier, it could have made a difference.

"I'll just slip out for a bit," whispered Lilly, "so you two can have some time together." She disappeared as the room faded from around them and Mari found herself in a wall-free atmosphere empty of adornment, full of pure light. They were alone on the sofa, surrounded by gentleness and calm.

"I'm so glad to see you," Mari said through her tears of mixed emotions.

"I feel like I've been looking for you since I was a child, and I didn't even know what I was looking for until I saw your face just now. I'm beginning to remember a lot."

"Take it easy, Kid," replied Saria in a voice of no-nonsense familiarity. "It's a relief for me to finally deal with you face to face. We've been through a lot together. Earth is such a cranky place for me as well as for you. The nasty negativity on that level starts to work on a soul as soon as it jumps in."

Mari found herself warming to Saria's relaxed and casual persona.

"We went into that life together," Saria continued, "but by the time you were about three, I was fading from your physical eyes. I was still there but just really faded. You're going to be remembering a lot now so let's not rush it."

"Oh," Mari said a little sad, "I wish I had known that you were there."

"Your soul knew," Saria responded. "That's the important thing. That whole Earth thing can be a pisser. I know it was my choice to work with you, but it wasn't a picnic. To begin with, instead of looking for me, you would have been better off looking for your own true self. I'm just the guidance system. You're the rocket. My job has been to try to keep you on track. Now we'll be figuring out how we did. One could say the course is over and it's time for finals, then we get our grades."

Mari was totally fascinated with Saria and found herself uncharacteristically speechless. She could only sit there and stare at her with numerous questions swimming through her mind.

"I know you have a zillion questions because you're zinging the thoughts to me all at once. First let's go to someplace where we can be comfortable and take our time. Oh drat! Silly me! I still forget that we don't have to worry about time. I'm still shaking off that whole Earth thing, too. I guess I'm a little groggy."

"I'm beginning to like this "beam me up" stuff," Mari said. "Where are we going now?"

"You choose this time, Sweety," said Saria. "I'm just along for the ride."

"How do I do that?" she asked her friend. "I can't imagine where I'd like to go."

Saria threw back her head in a hearty laugh. "You are a kick in the pants, Kid," she said with a huge grin. "With all you've been through, you still think you can't make a decision. I'll be glad when your spirit memory kicks into gear again. For practice until then, just think of a place. You've been doing a version of that when you've visited your loved ones, but this is easier. You don't have to go through that lower vibration stuff. We'll stay on this side of the veil. Think of a spot where you have enjoyed quiet time, then imagine us there."

Mari didn't have to think very long. She did her best and deepest thinking after she received treatment at the hospital. The ketosis, with her out of whack blood sugars, kept her mind in a fog until the staff at Virginia Mason Hospital got her brittle diabetes back to where she could think clearly.

Once when Mari was recuperating, Hara, her nurse who was about the same age, had a short break so she found a wheelchair and took her patient and friend for a tour of the hospital.

Mari especially enjoyed visiting the nursery and seeing all the newborns. She and Hara stood and watched them for some time. The thought of coming in new like that and having a whole unknown future ahead made Mari a little melancholy that she couldn't do that. Just start over. If only she could go back and have the chance to undo some sadness in her life.

Their tour ended at the roof garden where they sat in the welcome warmth of the sun. They had a nice visit until Hara was due back on the floor and Mari was ready for a rest. It was the first of many hours she would spend with others or just by herself on the roof garden. It seemed to take her away from her troubles or maybe allow her to wallow in them, depending on her mood. She could see now that she hadn't ever been there alone.

"Not my first choice," commented Saria when they found themselves on a bench on the hospital roof garden, "but it will do. See? Deciding doesn't have to be so tough. And traveling here couldn't be easier. It's like a horse flipping a fly off its ear." She rose and walked to the waist-high concrete wall to investigate what was over the side. She was giving Mari a minute to take it all in."

Mari was lovely, sitting on the bench, still in her garden attire with the undulating pastel flowers. Saria knew from personal experience that these environmental switches took some getting used to.

Mari had so many memories of spending time here. Most of them were pretty bleak, but others were of relief to escape the hospital atmosphere. The surroundings were rather sparsely planted with a few evergreens in aged pots, furnished with a couple picnic tables, benches and wooden chairs. A used ash tray showed that it was a haven for the smokers in the building. City-dwelling birds pecked around on the deck in search of dropped snack morsels of leftovers from the lunch crowd.

This was the place where Mari would try to sort out why she was in the hospital and what she was going to do next. At least it wasn't the antiseptic atmosphere of her stark room. She would feel relieved to finally be able to leave her bed. She had to maneuver the wheeled pole that held her IV apparatus, but it was worth it for a change of scenery. And she really was trying to deal with her mixed emotions and get her life back on track.

Fourteen

The concrete railing overlooked the emergency entrance to the hospital. Saria's attention took notice of a screaming siren that was announcing the arrival of an ambulance. Attendants in white coats rushed to wheel a gurney through the automatic doors. She knew instinctively that it was a dire situation and nodded her concern to the other spirit guide that was arriving with the patient. Knowing that all was in good hands, she gave a salute to that guide, sending out bursts of helpful energy to those below, like sparks from fireworks on the fourth of July.

This was the first chance Mari had to take in the luminescent presence of the one who had been her loving guide. Saria seemed to have a physical body but also a translucent glow of inner light that set her apart from the dimness of the reality that surrounded them. Mari could see that the ethereal and physical worlds were overlapping on the same plane but with the light diffusing veil between them. She felt a part of both worlds, still trying to shake off the "Earth thing."

Saria was rather tall and carried herself with confidence. Mari hadn't taken notice before that her guide was dressed in a style that looked like she had just walked off the set of Little House on the Prairie but had left the bonnet behind. She wore a plain muslin blouse with a brown A-line skirt that hung loosely to her mid-calf. Her black boots appeared comfortable, but they had seen better days. Long chestnut hair was pulled back tightly to Saria's head into a large bun that rested on the back of her neck. The essence of this soul was all about comfort.

She was not a genteel woman. Instead, she appeared to be a tough, no-nonsense, lively person. Her facial features were hard and well weathered but the love and friendship she emanated to Mari were warm and real. Mari wasn't used to instantly trusting this deeply. This spirit was so different than what she would have imagined her personal guide to be, but she was ready to go wherever Saria would take her.

"Would it help if I strapped on my six shooter and cowgirl hat?" asked Saria with an amused smile as she returned to Mari's side on the bench. "I can feel you trying to decide where I'm from. Question marks are shooting out of your aura like asteroids on a clear August night."

Mari let out an amused chuckle. "You're fabulous," she said out loud, aware of where she was and the amazing magical intuitive powers of those in this new life. It was like being in the fairy tales she had loved having read to her as she curled up on her parents' laps as a child, but this was remarkably real and wonderful. She indeed did have so many questions that she didn't know where to start.

"Let's start with me," Saria answered the unasked, first question. "You're seeing me as I appeared in my last incarnation on Earth and like most guides, I've had many lives and some of them I've lived in that dimension. I was a cattle driver's hand until I was struck by lightning on horseback while on watch one night in Colorado near the Oklahoma border. Bit the dust, white light and all that. Yes, I was of the feminine gender at that time," she said as she continued to address the mental questions from Mari. "But I was somewhat ahead of those times. Independent women with a spirit of adventure were not encouraged. I just couldn't sit still in another St. Louis tea party or cotillion. Those damned hoop skirts and corsets were not fit for the human physique. I had enough spirit and guts at fifteen to steal one of my brothers' pair of pants, hop on a horse and find the nearest cattle drive headed for Denver. At the time I didn't know what made me do it. I just had to. Now I know that it was part of my spiritual plan to get me to here, now, with you."

Mari was captivated as she listened to this story of Saria's past. She found it interesting, also, that her spirit guide had come from Missouri, where her grandmother had been born and spent her young years before moving to the Northwest.

"I had to fight to be accepted to ride along on that drive," she continued. "Those fool men were like sailors who thought women were bad luck on the trip. But I had been raised on a ranch near St. Louis, a middle child with four sisters and just one brother. Ranch hands were needed on a cattle ranch, and I loved critters, the outdoors and hard work. So, I spent most of my time in the pastures and barns working alongside the hired hands preparing to join a drive someday. You could say I was a tomboy.

"My mother started trying to make me a lady when I was twelve, but she gave up totally when I was fourteen and a half. She had me all dolled up to meet an acquaintance of hers with eligible sons. She was rightfully worried about my future. Well, we were just sitting down to one of her fancy teas when I heard a calf in a nearby field howling and crying something awful. It was separated from its mother and stuck in a mud hole in a place where a mountain lion had been spotted. It didn't take me long to jump up and run across those fancy lawns, ripping off that frilly skirt. With pantaloons flapping in the breeze, I carried that calf on my shoulders back to its mother. That's when my mother threw up her hands in frustration and let me be. I tell you: I just loved those critters, and I took better care of them than any of the other ranch hands."

Mari smiled as she imagined the comical scene Saria was describing. She certainly appeared strong enough in body and mind, as well as spirit, for it to be true.

"I knew I had to try to move on somehow. I just wasn't learning anything new in that place. The West was for me. That's when I joined the cattle drive."

"I held my own with the other cow hands. It was tough but as soon as I knocked old drunken Pete on his ass and sent him packing for getting fresh, they let me alone and gave me some responsibilities. Finally, they trusted me enough to sit watch at night.

"One evening a freak thunderstorm came up with flash floods and all." She frowned and shook her head at the memory. "Some heifers got separated from the herd and were running toward the river and I rode off after them. Damned if lightning didn't just fry me to pieces. The next morning at daylight, the others found my dead horse with charred holes in the saddle, still steaming.

"I brought the spirit of that old nag over to this side with me and found her a pasture of her own. We still get together and have a laugh about that time and reminisce about when we'd done a life together in Persia during its heyday," Saria went on as Mari sat wide eyed in fascination.

"I was a kid then," Saria continued rambling, her demeaner more peaceful and reflective. As she did, Mari could see another softer, more serene Middle Eastern face appear as a transparent vapor over the more rugged one. "I had the gift of direction, and helped our group of Bedouins in the desert. Shayla, our spiritual and family leader, gave me the name Saria. It means fearless guide. The name stuck and helped me find direction on this side. That's when I decided to serve as a spirit guide."

Mari had a mental picture of an Arabian desert scene out of the stories of Aladdin. She could have sworn she felt a warm, dry desert breeze across her face as she listened to her charming friend.

Saria continued, "With spirit guides and souls who go to Earth, the ones having the toughest times are either the newest to the situation or the oldest. In our cases, you're my first challenge and you're an old soul on the Earth plane. The inexperienced ones are naïve and tend to want to take on too much, and some experienced souls just want to get it over with quickly.

The elders convinced us we were ready for that little twist. I didn't wet my pants about it, but you fought the idea and didn't want to go back to that darn place. Finally, you came around and admitted that it fit your soul's purpose. That should answer another of those question marks shoot'n out of you. You did go in with a plan. You don't remember it now, but it will come back to you. Don't rush it."

Mari relaxed a little and was enthralled by the different facets of this fascinating creature. She was happy that Saria had always been an important part of her life.

Fifteen

Mari's brow furrowed. She was a little confused about her growing memory of her birth. Saria knew that it was time for some explanation.

"Ok, Kid," Saria said, "just so you have an idea of what to expect, we do review our last life to figure out if we've learned anything. In other words, your life will flash before your eyes, but not like many expect. You've already experienced that it can come to you in flashes as you travel through your memories. And it's not necessarily in order, but you'll see it all, and it'll take, well, what you still call time. When you've been through it, you'll know your whole blueprint that you made before you passed into that life. You certainly were the architect of that go round, but you'll see how, in that screwed up place, your mind and free will can really mess with that design. You can darned well give up all that "judgment" stuff because there is no one harder on us than ourselves. We're the ones who tend to judge. Not the loving God who gave us free will to learn and grow. And those are the final questions you'll ask yourself. Did you learn? Did you grow?"

This added to the questions that Mari already had, including an especially big one, What's next?

"I'm available to you always to help when I can. So are your kin on this side. Your birth is a good place to start, but you will find that you jump around a bit. That's ok. You'll get it all eventually. When you look back at the experience, it'll seem like a single second of memory and, in the big scheme of things, it is."

Their solitude in the roof garden was interrupted by the sudden opening of the heavy door from the hospital corridor. Two nurses strolled past them and sat at a nearby table. Mari was surprised to recognize them, and she remembered that they worked in the dialysis unit where she had gone often for treatments because of her failing kidneys.

Again, she saw that this world of spirit was superimposed over the lower vibration of their world. The similarities in the surroundings were apparent, but she and Saria were elevated in a realm that existed a few feet above the physical. It was like overlapping transparencies that were misaligned. It made perfect sense that when sightings of other world beings were reported, they appeared to be floating. The nurses' appearances were slightly muted through the veil and Mari felt she was looking through a filtering lens.

One nurse was short with springy brunette curls capping her head. Mari knew her as Kitty. She could see that Kitty's aura glowed with soft lavender. The other, June, was taller with long straight auburn hair. Her green aura appeared to be going dim in the small of her back.

"Don't get your tether twisted, Kid," Saria said, interrupting Mari's thoughts. "You really are on the hospital roof garden with them, but you are in a different reality, or dimension. They probably can't see us. Some can, but it is rare. People like your sweet second-cousin Dee sometimes do, as you know. They're in physical reality where those abilities get drowned out by the blasted confusion that is so strong on Earth. Sorry if I'm nagging about it. Still shaking it off. It's because of that negativity that we decide to go there. Supposedly we learn faster because of it. Let's see how far along these two are."

Saria, deciding on the sly to give a demonstration of the thin veil between worlds, stood and placed her hands on her hips where imaginary holsters would have rested and stared intensely at their visitors. With a swift, Annie Oakley draw, her hands flipped to reveal a pink balloon in her left and a pin in her right hand that hit the balloon with a blast that sounded like it could have come from a cannon. It caused Mari's astral body to jump three feet off the bench. The nurses hardly moved. The spirit guide turned to her student and burst out with a hardy laugh at the sight of Mari floating there in shock.

"You... really... should see your...face," She exclaimed between fits of laughter. "I plum forgot.... you weren't... accustomed to the idea... of... of... antigravity yet. Oh... Oh...I haven't enjoyed a good knee slapper like that for some time," she continued as she gained control and lowered Mari to the bench with a flap of her hand. "Gravity! Think about it. The notion of dragging people down. It's part of that old Earth lower energy."

Mari could recall quite a few times in her life she would have appreciated the lift of a good, antigravity float.

"Did ya notice the little brunette jump just a bit?" the spirit guide asked with a satisfied grin.

"No," replied Mari. "I was too busy floating," she said, her eyes shooting Saria more than a hint of sarcasm.

"Well, that one has potential if she doesn't let her insights into her patients' needs get to her. She tends to take on that kind of energy. Her guide is making her aware of it as a problem for her, but old fear is in the way, as usual. The redhead is a healer, but she doesn't know it. It's subtle and she's using it without realizing what she's doing. She also takes on her patients' energies and feels too much of the pain herself. The job is getting harder for her. We can tell by the effect on her aura at her lower back area. She wants to be of service, but she doesn't realize yet that just her kind words have helped many of them to heal."

"Well now, where were we?" Saria asked as she sat back down next to Mari.

As she shook herself back into the moment, Mari returned to the thoughts of her life and how she came to be here.

"You were discussing the review of my life," Mari reminded her guide. "I have to say, I have a memory of being in a place like a waiting room with a viewing screen. It's like I was deciding who on the screen would be my parents. There were sections on the screen showing the choices. I felt a lot like I was picking a university to go to and who my teachers would be."

"That's about right," said Saria. "You were in the place where we prepare to exit this spirit world. We go there when we've decided to go into another life. There we work with the elders, who are like counselors, to create a plan. You're on the right track now. You can start to explore that life you just left. I'll leave you with your memories, but a part of me is always with you. I'm just a cattle call away. I can be at your side with the speed of a thought. Happy trails!"

With that Saria was abruptly gone as the roof garden scene faded from around Mari. She was alarmed that her guide had left but found herself surrounded by the veil of loving white light that she recognized as the power that had transported her spirit to this magical place.

Sixteen

Suzi hadn't spoken to Dee for a while, so it was time for another phone call. These were special times for them both. They considered themselves soul sisters and their conversations could go in any direction.

"The other day I was remembering," Suzi interjected into their conversation, "the first time I saw you."

"Oh really," Dee responded. "When was that?"

"It was during my first time visiting Missouri. I was fifteen and my dad had died, and my mom wanted to see her family. You were living in an older house in St. Peters. We arrived at your house and were introduced to your parents then your brother and sister. You were off somewhere with a friend. While the adults were visiting, I excused myself and went to the bathroom. It had one of those old hook and eye locks and, being a private teenager, in an unfamiliar situation, I am certain that I locked the door. I did my business, then was washing my hands and checking my appearance in the mirror when the door burst open. There you were, standing in the middle of the doorway, staring at me with a strange kind of intensity.

"'Uhmmm,' I stammered. 'Do you need the bathroom?'

"'No,' you answered. 'I just wanted to see you.' No smile or 'How do you do?' Just that intense stare. Your eyes were captivating even at that young age. You then just closed the door and went on your way. I remember wondering what that was all about. It was so strange.

"I've never forgotten that chance encounter. I suppose it sort of set the tone for our future relationship."

"I really don't remember it," Dee responded. "I must have been one strange kid."

"I guess it was just for me," said Suzi. "The beginning of an unconventional friendship. You got my attention."

"We've certainly come a long way from that," Dee offered. "We've been through some stuff together. There are no regrets on my part. How are you doing now that things are getting back to normal? Or are they?"

"I'm doing fine," Suzi replied. "But I do have something weighing on me."

"Spill it, Girlfriend," said Deirdre.

Suzi took a deep breath then said, "The last time Mari was in the hospital, we talked about her writing her story. She was open to it but wasn't sure she would be able to do it. I think she knew her time was limited. She was getting weaker.

"I don't know what came over me, but I opened my mouth and said, "If you can't do it, then I promise you I will." I shocked myself and it was like I was out of my body when I heard those words come out of me. I have never used the word promise with my children. It felt like I was doing some weird kind of channeling. Now I can't shake it off."

"That's interesting," Dee responded. "Have you ever done any serious writing?"

"God, no!" Suzi exclaimed. "I hated it in school. That's why I'm in shock that I even said that."

"I think you need to try it," said Dee. "And don't be surprised if Mari helps you. I see her behind you with her hand on your shoulder. She is smiling and winks at me."

"Ok," Suzi said. "I can at least try just for her. I'll keep you posted on that. Now I really need a glass of wine. I'll talk to you another time," Suzi signed off.

Deirdre hung up on her end, winked back at her vision of Mari's spirit, and did a thumbs up then said, "Mission accomplished."

Seventeen

Mari was at peace as she took in the beauty of the white light that surrounded her. In the mists she could make out the outlines of beautiful white roses, as if she were looking at some three-dimensional, heavenly wallpaper.

Her natural curiosity guided her to a spot in that light where a golden yellow glow was beginning to appear. She was drawn to it and the sweet humming that was emanating from it. She wasn't sure if she was gravitating toward the vivid color or if it was moving toward her, but she felt herself slowly merging into it.

The yellow deepened to a darker hue until it was a brilliant orange light, flowing around her that shocked her with a feeling of wild and erratic emotions that instantly took the place of the peace in which she had been floating. Mari was startled and confused as the orange light condensed, pressing harder and harder. Emotions became like balls of hail that were pelting her with feelings of disappointment, rejection, as well as joy all at once. They were attaching to her melting and dissolving into her essence. The orange light around her was pulsating with human emotion as she absorbed the energy, evolving into an Earthly emotional being. Each one was like an electrical current that was creating then throwing hail at her along with bold flashes of lightning. What had started as angelic humming was now the booming thunder of an emotional storm.

The emotion of fear started showing its ugly head. Mari began to get angry at the attack and that anger helped her to find her own strong will and determination not to let the storm get the best of her.

Instead of caving into the onslaught of pure emotions, she instinctively imagined herself wrapped in that loving protective white shield.

The thunderheads of emotions that Mari had just been gestalted through left her confused but she was able to clear her head enough to recognize that her spirit was occupying a developing physical body. It was about four months after its conception. She was aware that she had chosen to be here but memory of how and why was lost to her at this point. She knew that there was some reason and purpose in this incarnation even if she wasn't aware of it now. She could only be in the moment as she calmed down and let herself feel the nurturing moisture and warmth of her cocoon.

She knew instinctively that the vessel in which she rested was the body of that mother she had chosen before this incarnation. Mari sent the white light of her own essence to communicate her love and gratitude. With constrained movement, she gave an outward push with the new muscles of her growing extremities to confirm to her mother that she was there. She could sense her mother's delight at knowing that the quickening of life had finally begun within her. Her mother caressed her outer shell, that was the growing belly that had come to life. Along with the crimson flowing through the burgundy veins, came the soft pink light of mother love that surrounded and flowed through Mari, putting her at ease in the cradle of Suzi's womb.

The pregnancy seemed to be going well, and her new body was developing as expected. Each moment was an adventure and every new cell that made her more human fascinated Mari. The quietly muffled voices and sounds that vibrated to her tiny ears were delightful and she was anxious to experience that awaiting world. She had come here to learn, and she was starting already.

The bond between mother and child was a powerful thing for them both. They knew that the potential for mutual growth was great. They were aware that this new adventure into life would have trials, but it was worth the journey.

Mari was deep into her study of her developing body when she began to feel the constriction of her precious space. The pregnancy was ending in its second trimester. This took the form of a backache for Suzi. Mari began to feel frustrated and then alarmed because she knew it was more, but was not able to let her mother know. This was the first pregnancy for Suzi. She was young and had expected labor to be more of an abdominal contraction. This was so different than she had imagined labor to be that she was caught unaware.

As the constriction got worse for Mari, the back pain increased for Suzi until it finally became full blown labor, and Mari started seeing the orange glow of what she thought were thunderheads again as she was being forced into the birth canal. Mari had become accustomed to the powerful hormones and emotions that came to her through the blood that she shared with her mother. But she didn't know panic. It hit her so hard that it not only was a physical and emotional pain, but also a spiritual pain.

This was horribly wrong. Mari's physical body was unresponsive and quiet. Her spirit cried out in excruciating pain as it was forced from the warm comfort of the bodily existence that she was now separated from. The infant was born prematurely on December 12 but could not be brought to draw a first breath.

Mari was spared the orange furor of the emotional storm as she was pulled quickly through this time. Her focus was behind her on the receding image of the tiny premature baby that had almost been her vehicle into the physical world. The question of how it happened would never be answered fully for her or her mother. Premature births are often a mystery to everyone involved.

She covered her face with her hands as tears of anguish flooded from her. She mourned for the fabulous potential gone to waste and the horrible separation from the mother she had chosen and loved.

The reversing process had pulled her from the stormy orange light into a golden light where Mari was comforted and gently calmed and then, finally, into the loving white light where she could lower her hands from her eyes. The pain still existed but the tears flowed less as she became aware of the satiny smoothness on which she was lying, surrounded by a flowing mist. She was in a room where the transparent walls and floor looked like the smooth inside of a faceted crystal goblet. The ceiling was like stained glass that glowed with chakra colors the sent beams into her body to rebalance those energy centers and rainbows flowed around her. She was completely alone and drained. Her thoughts and her soul were dulled and dim with grief for the lost chance to experience life. From deep inside she managed to force out the faint cry "Saria!"

A soft whisper filled the atmosphere. "I said I could be with you at the speed of a thought," it spoke to her heart, "but in truth, I never left you."

Mari looked up into the loving eyes of the face that she knew so well now, though it was softer and framed by a white satin scarf. Complimented by a white silk robe that suggested her Middle Eastern persona, Saria was seated beside Mari on a brocade lounging chaise.Mari's ethereal body was weak from the stress and upheaval that she had been through. Her spirit guide knew that this would all pass and be forgotten, but at this moment, it was her responsibility to facilitate Mari's spiritual health. Soft pillows materialized on the chaise and Saria raised Mari's head and slid the pillows under it. Gently she rubbed Mari's forehead. As she would lift her hand, she was pulling forth the energy of the grief and pain that took the form of a dark mass that she shook from her hand. It splattered onto the crystal floor where it rolled into a black ball and disappeared into a puff of mist. She repeated the process until Mari's body relaxed and she slept peacefully covered with the coolness of a soft green blanket of light.

Saria was exhausted from her efforts, but she beamed with gratitude for the strength given to her to help this precious one with whom she had the privilege to experience and learn so much. She closed her eyes and relaxed as they both were bathed in the glow of a golden beam.

Eighteen

"I just had to call you," said Deirdre. "This morning, I was in an office building and stepped into an elevator with an attractive young woman and started getting information for her. I introduced myself and told her what I do, and I asked her about her boyfriend."

"That surprises me," said Suzi. "You usually don't just randomly offer you insights."

"I know, right," Dee replied. "I'm not sure what came over me. She was all gaga over him and how wonderful he is. I got brave and asked her if she knew he was unfaithful. She got all huffy and said emphatically, 'Oh absolutely not! You're wrong! He would never be unfaithful.' "So, I had to ask, 'Then why aren't you two together?' and she answered sarcastically, 'Well, he is still married.'

"Luckily the elevator stopped, and I got out just in time to not have a laughing fit. Look at the stupidity I put up with having this, so called, ability."

Suzi hadn't had a good laugh like this one in a while.

"I see your point," she said when she caught her breath from laughing so hard. "It must bite to be you.

"I don't know what I'd do without your phone calls," said Suzi to her favorite cousin. "You keep me grounded and elevated at the same time."

"I do what I can," replied Deirdre. "You do the same for me. Anything new in your world? Any writing happening?"

"No. I can't seem to get my mind around it," said Suzi in frustration. "I'm no literary genius and I find it intimidating. I still can't believe I got myself into doing it. Maybe I need to find someone who has that talent. I could tell them everything and they could write it. Too bad Mari couldn't do it. She was pretty good at writing in school."

"You may have hit on something there," offered Dee. "I'm not sure what I'll get, but I'll explore it with Mari if you like. She communicates with me every now and then."

"Oh sure," said Suzi. "I value any input. I'm just too blocked to be any good.

"On another subject, did I ever tell you that I had a miscarriage before I had Mari?"

"I don't believe you did," answered Dee. "What was that all about?"

"Well," Suzi began, "I was just thinking about it the yesterday. It was on December 12, exactly one year before Mari was born on the same date. As soon as I realized the coincidence, I knew at that moment that the same soul had come back to me. Mari's soul was that determined to be a part of my life."

"That's awesome," said Dee. "I've never heard of that happening, but I don't see why not. I know she could be that stubborn."

Suzi smiled in agreement and said, "I'm grateful that she is. For all that we've been through, I'm glad that I got to be her mother."

"You still are," said Dee, "and now she is grateful as well, and available to help you in ways she never could have in physical life."

"Thank you for that," replied Suzi. "I welcome her help."

Nineteen

Mari surprised herself when she awoke abruptly. A little drained, she was full of energy and questions. She couldn't be more pleased to find herself back in her grandmother's lovely peaceful cottage, Lilly and Saria standing over her with anxious looks.

"Okaaay," she began as she sat up on the sofa. She was totally aware of what happened to her before her visit to the crystal room. "Which one of you would like to fill me in on what that was all about?"

Saria, now back in her cowgirl persona, stepped out cautiously from behind Lilly, feeling a little guilty, and said softly, "That would be me, Kid. The guide. Remember?"

With a determined glint in her eye, Mari stared into the sheepish brown eyes of her spirit guide. "Oh, I remember everything," she replied with a newfound sternness. "Mind sharing with me just what happened back there? And what's with the room where we ended up?"

"All right now," interjected Lilly with cheerful relief. "I can relax. You're getting better. I'll just excuse myself, yet again, and go make some tea." She gave Mari a loving pat on the knee and turned, leaving the room.

Mari and Saria forced grins to each other and relaxed. Lilly was so dear to them both.

Saria sat down in the red rocking chair, opposite her confused kindred spirit and studied her carefully to be comfortable that she was indeed on the mend. "Well," she started with caution, "I'll have to take some blame here. I let you go on into your memories without giving you the most important information of all. I had forgotten how new you were to being back here. Believe me, I heard it from the elders on that little bit of brain lag. Once I got you settled in recovery, the crystal healing room, as we call it, they summoned me for a talk. Don't think I didn't thank God for their gentle, understanding natures. Did I mention that I'm new to the spirit guide thing?"

Mari gave her a low, serious, through-the-eyebrows stare.

"Okay. Don't answer that." Saria continued, "Before you try again, let me remind you that you aren't, for your own good, supposed to "relive" your memories. It's not necessary. Just watch from a safe distance and observe. You can get hit by that heavy stuff all over again. It was hard enough the first time as you went through it all and tougher if you make yourself do it again. Guess you found that out. Can't believe you dove in like that. That's pretty brave if you ask me.

"The elders could see that I was upset, so they said that there was the chance that it was supposed to happen that way. We checked your chart and conferred with your mom's spirit guide. You had a hard time making the decision to go in the first place, so panic hit you in a soft spot. It was real, all right. And it did happen that way."

"Hold on a minute." Mari raised her hand in protest. She expressed her frustration and disbelief, spiced with a little anger. "Are you telling me that I died before I was even born? That was my mother, Suzi. I chose her and she was my mother for twenty-five years. You can't mean that something happened to erase all that. I'm here now as a twenty-five-year-old ethereal body or spirit or whatever we're calling me now."

"Maybe I can help," said Lilly returning to the room and setting a tea tray on the round dining table. "Let's sit and discuss it over tea."

Saria and Mari looked at each other incredulously, that Lilly could be so nonchalant.

"Oh, come on you two," she chided. "Don't make it more than it is. Mari just needs some explanations. I think it would be best if we relaxed with refreshment, and some girl talk. Mari, I have something I want you to try. It's dinglebell tea. It's been developed here, and it's said to help the spirit after its energy has been zapped. When that happens, you can end up a little dingy, thus the name. Right now, you're a good test subject."

"You're right, Gramma," said Mari as she calmed down. She joined Lilly at the table that was draped with a delicate Chantilly Lace tablecloth. "I guess I can't expect all my questions to be answered at once. I do need to settle down a bit. Saria, please join us and we'll have a good talk. And relax. You're a dear and worthy guide. I just need to be brought up to date."

"Well, you know I'm not so fond of tea parties," she responded, "but if you'll pardon me while I change, I'll make an exception for y'all."

Before they could give their pardons, Lilly and Mari watched Saria's clothing change before their eyes. Intertwining, swirling veils of gossamer transformed her functional prairie look to elegant robes and scarf. The dark tan of her weathered cowgirl skin transformed to the soft olive of her Bedouin persona but still with those wonderful chestnut eyes revealing the same familiar soul.

"There, that's better," she said in a gentler, more graceful voice. "The fearless guide's name fits me better this way and the attire is far more appropriate for tea."

She glided gracefully across the room and sat with the others around the lovely table. Mari was in awe of her chameleon-like abilities and intrigued by the idea of adapting to different personas to fit a given situation. But she had to smile at herself. We sort of do that naturally at times with our personalities on Earth.

"Now," Lilly said to Mari while she poured the dinglebell tea into delicate floral teacups, "I can see how your experience had you all flummoxed. I can help because I was there. Your mother did have a baby prematurely on December 12th, one year before you were born. If you think about it, I'm sure she mentioned it to you sometime. She was six months pregnant. It was an emergency delivery at a small country hospital. There was no time to get her to the larger hospital where they had the proper instruments to handle preemie deliveries. The doctor did all he could, but he didn't have equipment small enough to help the baby to breathe on its own. Suzi, as well as the rest of us, were devastated by the loss. It took her a while to get over the emptiness. You were a big part of her life. A few months later she was thrilled to find that she was pregnant again, but she was nervous about it until she passed the six-month point. Then she relaxed, trusting that all was okay this time, and on December 12 the following year, you were born. She realized right away that the date was the same but exactly a year later, and she knew in her heart that you were the same spirit that had been the other baby. Her instincts were right on. Your strong will and love for her made that beautiful reunion happen. The two of you did bond during that first time and that bond was a source of strength for you both."

"What you experienced both times," interjected Saria, "is called transference of the soul. That's when the soul bonds with the developing child. Over here, there is no set rule when it happens. It is all up to the soul, and its needs in that event. That is all part of the plan that a soul makes using free will and personal choices concerning its physical life."

"Well, that is a relief," Mari sighed. "And I think I do remember her mentioning one time that she had a miscarriage, but she didn't dwell on it, so I forgot about it."

"You were a welcome new arrival for our entire family that second time around. The previous loss had been a heart-wrenching disappointment. Your Aunt Dawn was a troubled teenager who suffered with depression ever since her father, Claus, died. Your entrance into her life brought her new hope. She nicknamed you Janie and would dress you up cute. She told me later that she would take you places and pretend that you were hers."

"This was all during the Vietnam War era. It was a bad time for us all. Your Uncle Joseph was in the Philippines on a Navy ship. Every day he saw the horrid casualties of war that we only heard about on the news. Uncle George was in the Air Force Reserves, ready to be called to active duty at any time, and there were many other relatives and friends who were also fighting over there. We lived daily with the fear of loss, so new life meant everything to us then. What a precious gift you were."

"Thank you for clearing that up, Gramma." Mari's relief was palpable as she sipped her tea. Lilly's explanation was helping her to come to terms with and understand her experience. It was a lot to take in and she looked forward to a time that she might release the vulnerability that she had apparently carried over here. Her hope was that this orientation could eventually be looked back on as a fleeting task. She needed to know if she would be allowed to stay in this new home where she felt peaceful acceptance.

Across the table, Saria watched Mari as she listened to her grandmother continue her stories of the infant and child that Mari had been. She reflected on how important a loving grandparent can be to a grandchild. Their time together was special, and a grandparent's patience and experience were able to do a lot toward healing.

Saria was there to guide Mari on the spiritual level, and she was grateful to Lilly for filling in the memory gaps. As she watched them, Mari's love for her grandmother was evident as their auras reached out toward each other, their spirit bodies touched with delicate hints of rainbows, as from light through a faceted crystal. It's beautiful to watch spirits reaching out and touching in this existence. The energy that they create can extend beyond the heavens and into the physical world to exude a feeling of peace.

Saria continued to stay quietly transfixed by the beauty in the scene until Mari turned to her.

"You were there, too, weren't you Saria?" she asked. Mari understood more about the trauma of what she and her family had gone through with the loss of her first attempted incarnation into that family.

"Yes, Dear," Saria answered, still in her reserved persona. "It was my honor and, I must say, a relief to see you successfully move into a new life. With that next merging, your courage was inspirational."

"What you experienced that first time with the colors, was your spirit traveling to the infant body through your mother's chakra system. The chakras are the body's energy centers, or vortexes, that are represented by the colors of the rainbow. They are not usually visible in the physical world, but they can affect physical vitality. Some people are very sensitive if they are out of balance."

"The chakras begin with red as the lowest or first chakra at the root of the spine. Going upward in the body, the next is orange, then yellow, green, blue, indigo, and the last, purple with white light above the crown."

"You entered your second time, during the beginning of the infant's second trimester, through the third yellow chakra and held fast as you went down through the emotional storms of the second, orange that filled you with powerful human emotions. You rested in the first, red chakra and comforted your mother with gentle movement as she fought the fear of the loss of another pregnancy. Then at the beginning of the third trimester, when she finally relaxed, you did something wonderful. You allowed your spirit to travel back up through that energy system to the green of the fourth, the heart chakra, where the two of you healed from the first pregnancy. You bonded even more with your gentle caresses of love to her heart."

"You and Suzi became a team," Saria continued, "and we celebrated your birth on this side with a gathering hosted by your spirit family for your guides and angels who tended you and helped you across. It was a great party."

"And Mari, I want to thank you for including me in your birth experiences. You and I both elevated to new levels of learning because of it. I hadn't been too clear on why the elders thought we would be good together, but I admired your strong will and determination and was glad that we were encouraged to work together."

"Well," Mari thoughtfully interjected, "the rest was certainly a bit of a roller coaster ride. But I guess once you're in the seat with a cherished friend, you know that if you just hold on tight and maybe even close your eyes sometimes, you'll find some fun together. I hope you were there for the fun parts, too."

"I most certainly was," answered Saria, "and to be a guide I had to develop the ability to bilocate. I stay active on this side, but I can also be with you fully as your guide. Even though you didn't physically see me, I was there feeling and experiencing right along with you. I'll be doing that here also.

"I was sometimes a gentle thought, a ringing in your ear, or a feather-light touch on your arm. Sometimes you were so surrounded by a gray fog that I had to jump and shout to get your attention. Once, when you were sitting on the river bench deep into your thoughts, your thinking was getting too heavy for me, so I thought I'd be playful. I made a bubble that floated by you out of nowhere. It was fun watching the surprised look on your face as you tried to figure out where it came from. It's a good trick to distract a spirit."

Twenty

"I want to go back to your question about the crystal room that you experienced after your first attempt," Saria continued. "I'm the one who took you to it. You had absorbed so much negativity in that event that you needed rest. The room is a recovery cocoon of sorts. It's a place for the overwrought spirit to go and be tended by its guides and caring angels who bring God's healing love. It allows you to float in the perfection of that love between worlds so you can regain the strength to continue. When we choose a plan for incarnating, we receive the support of the entire heavens. A good comparison is a boxer who climbs the ropes into the ring, but his coach and crew are there between rounds to help and tend to his needs, keeping his strength up as his fans cheer him on to victory.

"The crystal room was also your sanctuary when you were twelve and in the throes of a diabetic coma. That's where you spent time with your grandfather, Claus. All of us here knew that your experiences would touch and help heal many spirits who were struggling with the physical world. You are one of many in this era who have been conduits to quietly continue the works of another child of God, Yeshua, whom you knew as Jesus of Nazareth. His messages, like "Seek ye first the Kingdom of Heaven" to name just one, are continued in the trials of many who don't even realize the source of their strength as they climb into that boxing ring that is life and take on the challenges there. Your mother shared with you the notion that 'God doesn't give us more than we can handle.' She was right. Whole legions are available to assist from this side."

"I'm grateful for you both," Mari said with a sigh. "Thank you for your patience with me and for the explanations. I'm okay with that memory now and the learning from it has elevated me," she added. "I'm more comfortable to call on the help that is available, but will all my memories come so abruptly?"

"That is a matter of choice, like most things here," Saria answered. "At this point you can choose whether to take them intermittently, as you've experienced so far. Or you can choose to visit the library, with its Hall of Records, where I can be with you, and we can view your life together. It's certainly a quick way to get it done all at once but it's up to you. Take your time. It's good to be in a learning frame of mind."

As Saria spoke, Mari closed her eyes and allowed the words and the memories to be absorbed along with the healing warmth of the dinglebell tea. She felt tingles of electric-like energy that flow through the body when the spirit recognizes truth. Slowly she opened her eyes as she realized she was beginning to float above her cushioned chair, and Saria and Lilly were quietly watching her with smiles of amusement.

"And you should be aware," added Lilly, "that we learn more about our own experiences faster, if we allow ourselves to realize the effect we had on others and feel how they managed to deal with us. It can be tough to get that double hit of emotions, but it accelerates our learning by a hundred-fold. The decision is yours to make along the way. In the meantime, are you ready for more tea?"

"No, but thank you," Mari replied. "And thank you for answering so many questions at once. The tea seems to have done its job. It was wonderful. I don't think I've ever tasted anything like it."

"I'm not surprised," Lilly commented as she patted her granddaughter's hand. "And your grandfather will be pleased to hear that. You see, he developed it in the laboratories at his ranch."

"Laboratories?" asked Mari with a quizzical look. "I had only pictured his home as a place with gardens of fruits, vegetables, flowers and, of course Ez. Now I'm really intrigued."

Lilly was bubbling with pleasure and pride for Mari, and it showed in her aura. She had known on Earth that this child was a scholar in the making. Now Lilly could see that Mari's natural curiosity could fully bloom in the presence of pure light and love. She couldn't be happier about the wonders that were in store for Mari.

"Oh, yes, Dear!" Lilly answered. "It's a wonderful place. There's all that and so much more. But I especially enjoy the produce from Claus's gardens. Some of them you'll recognize but there are some things that are quite exotic in their look and taste. Your tea was a new idea from his herb garden. He developed it just before you arrived, and now he's working with that formula for a spirit guide who will be taking the seed of the idea to someone on Earth to help those who could use it there. Things are evolving here also. One way we help those of Earth to evolve with us is by sharing new developments and ideas that originate on this side."

She leaned close to Mari and, with eyes wide in anticipation, continued, "I understand that there are some exciting things in the works that will help those on that side to be more in touch with this side. A new energy is forming there now and the potential for spiritual growth is increasing. Claus has decided to work with it on this side and I'm studying to find where I may be of service."

"It sounds like I chose a good time to return here," said Mari. I can't wait to explore it all. I've heard enough to want to start with Grandpa's gardens. I was too ill to get my driver's license on Earth. I know that I can go anywhere by just a thought, but it would be fun to travel there in a pretty red sports convertible."

A smooth, sable brown, leather-covered steering wheel appeared before her. With her mouth open in surprise and her eyes twinkling, her attention darted from Lilly to Saria. They, in unison, smiled, raised a hand and wiggled their fingers with a parting wave.

As the tea party faded from her vision and her awareness, Mari could barely hear her companions' enthusiastic, "Have fun!"

Part Two

REDBIRD'S
SACRED PROMISE

Twenty-one

Mari found herself surrounded by the sweet smell of new leather as she settled in the driver's seat of a passionate red sports car. It hummed to her in anticipation of possible adventures.

The supple leather upholstery fit her new body beautifully, but felt a little unusual. She rubbed its delicate surface to decide what the difference was. It was firm, but oh, so soft. Her hand enjoyed the rich smoothness, and she realized with relief that the precious animals here would never need to be killed for their flesh. This was an otherworldly material, with a richness that was far superior to the leather goods on Earth. The idea of a fabric like this couldn't get to Earth fast enough for her. Evolutional thinking was needed there as far as her animal friends were concerned.

Satisfied for the moment with just sitting in this new car, Mari let her hands caress the "leather" of the steering wheel. Suddenly she had a flash of memory, and then also remembered Saria's warning to keep a distance while observing, to avoid getting lost.

Heeding Saria's advice, she placed herself above this memory that had escaped her until just this moment, no doubt brought on by the familiar feel of the driver's seat. In the memory, Mari was behind the wheel of an old clunker that her dad had bought from a friend for her to learn to drive in. It would have been hers if she had gotten the hang of it.

She was driving down the road near her home and her mother was yelling, "SLOW DOWN. YOU'RE GOING TOO FAST FOR THE TURN!"

From above, Mari observed her spirit guide, Saria, appear in time to grab her hands to help her jerk the wheel, avoiding a high dirt bank that loomed before them. She had almost driven them off the road. Saria guided her to a place where Mari could safely pull over.

Suzi could see on Mari's face the fear that was gripping Mari at that moment. Mari wanted so badly to learn to drive and enjoy that freedom, but the ugly fear sent her into panic. It teased her with false images of accidents and her parents' disappointment. She was frozen in the coldness of that paranoia and her lack of self-confidence.

She was sixteen and the uncontrolled diabetes that had been with her for four years made her mind vulnerable to negative thoughts that bombarded her constantly. Her discernment was way off track.

As she returned her thoughts to being in the shiny red convertible, Mari's white-knuckle grip on the new leather steering wheel loosened and the fear that had overtaken her in her previous life vanished. She realized she had been in a body that was overwhelmed with an accumulation of sensations and fears, limiting her experience of freedom. She was intelligent. Mastering driving required a presence that she was not able to achieve. She remembered that when the incident happened, it had thrown her into an even deeper emotional depression.

She sat still, enjoying the complete comfort of the little red car seat that was obviously made for her, and remembered Saria's words. "We learn more about our own experiences if we open ourselves to know the effect we have on others and let ourselves feel how they felt."

Fully aware that it was her choice to do so, Mari let herself go back into that memory, but this time she let herself explore Suzi's feelings through it all.

As her mother yelled at her in panic, Mari felt Suzi's apprehension for her daughters. Not only for Mari, but also Natalie who was riding in the back seat. The alarm she was experiencing was a mother's excruciating anxiety about harm coming to any of her children. It was very powerful. Mari couldn't remember ever feeling anything like it, even with all the terrible fears she had confronted in her life. She was relieved that her connection with this maternal alarm was brief as she watched Saria bring the car to safety. She also felt the powerful intensity of her mother's sigh of relief.

Suzi had hoped that learning to drive would give Mari some much-needed confidence and a sense of independence. But the panic in her daughter's face told her that Mari wasn't ready.

All those motherly emotions surfaced in that flash of a second and Mari saw in her mother's memory that by now Suzi had lost count of the number of times that she had stood over Mari in emergency rooms as she was treated for severe ketoacidosis, on the edge of a coma. It was hard when the nurse would ask her to leave as the doctor pierced Mari's frail body with needles to inject insulin and hooked her up to life-saving machines. Suzi would be led to a waiting room where she could only imagine what was happening to her precious Mari.

Suzi tried to pray and hoped that God would hear her desperate but distracted pleas. She kept an open ear in case the doctor came to her with the dreaded news that the tired and weak heart of her child had given up. A part of her knew that this was going to happen someday. It was an instinct that she tried not to dwell on. When a healthy child is born, it just doesn't seem right that the parent should have to face the possibility of outliving that child.

Mari saw Suzi's many memories in different emergency waiting rooms in Northwest hospitals, including a family vacation on the Oregon Coast. The first time at the small hospital in their mountain home in North Bend, she found the waiting area had a tiny chapel with a remarkable stained-glass window that took up an entire wall. It had huge flowers in beautiful shades of blue. For having no religious theme, the blues of the window penetrated her spirit as the sunlight danced in the tiny chapel. She felt a sense of balance and warmth as if God were touching her and helping her to release Mari's fate to powers that were beyond her maternal love.

Mari gave her head a shake to bring herself out of her observations of those memories that had once seemed rather insignificant in the grand theme of her life. She knew how a situation could, in a flash of a second, bring powerful feelings and memories back to her mother. She understood Saria's warning that to allow ourselves to feel another's reactions to our choices could be tough, but now she had a clearer idea of the emotions that her mother had kept to herself in her efforts to just be a good mother. She had been trying to save her daughter's life the only way she felt that she could at the time. Just as strongly, Mari had observed and learned how Suzi felt the same bond with each of her children. Mother love is so very powerful. No wonder we need to know and feel the mother essence of God.

Mari felt herself grow deeper into the knowledge of how her life had progressed. The seed of purpose in reliving it all was firmly planted in her now. She decided for certain that she would soon opt to review the rest of her life in a faster manner. It made sense that it was time to get the review behind her to move on. She was getting impatient to have it over.

"And with so much ahead," she said aloud to herself, "what am I doing sitting here?"
She took a deep breath to release the lingering images of that memory and relax into the glories of her present environment.

Twenty-two

With this refreshed attitude, her thoughts created a road that began to materialize before her. Fear was unnecessary and she was pleased to find that driving was natural to her. How could it not be when all she had to do was mentally urge the car forward?

The road was not any old blacktop road. Like everything else here, it had its own special qualities. It appeared to be a smooth line within nature that glowed around her. As she thought of moving the car forward, the road would glow in welcome and as she journeyed on it would sparkle as if it were strewn with glitter or maybe fairy dust.

The trip to her grandfather's home was grand with some views that she remembered from the carriage ride. She enjoyed the animals peacefully at home in the fields, woods and streams that she passed. She even spotted a herd of sheep with a sheepherder guiding the pure white animals over a hill. She did a double take as she realized that he was holding a staff and had a halo just like the one in a picture of Jesus that she had seen as a child.

Mari thought to herself, "Could it be?" She liked the idea that Jesus, another child of God, would be quietly present here, peacefully tending to his flock in the distance. This scene would have caused her to screech to a halt on the physical side, but here it made her smile with approval.

She could see for herself what her grandmother had alluded to about the crossing over experience. Lilly and others had met her with a rousing welcome. What Lilly had taught Mari at the time was that each soul is met within their personal frame of reference. For some there are phases of assimilating into this world. Our loved ones want us to take what time we need to be at ease as we get accustomed to the immenseness and magic of this new existence.

What Mari was seeing was so much like her home in Washington State. She continually encountered what she was familiar with from her last incarnation as she traveled this divine world. Her impression was that it was very much like a family trip across the state to visit relatives in Idaho, only now there was so much more to see. She was excited that sometime she might visit other sectors where she could meet once again that wonderful little Buddhist neighbor boy and close friend she'd known in the fourth grade. She wondered what had happened to him. She missed him.

What a remarkable place this was where true diversity could be a reality. Lilly had told her, "Instead of the sectors being places of discrimination, they are more like the instrumental sections of an orchestra with God as the conductor. There is no reason for competition or dissention. It's all about soul comfort. They all work in cooperation to make this existence beautiful and harmonious when they come together and assimilate into the totality of the spiritual symphony."

Lilly had gone on to comment, "The only barriers that exist between those souls still on Earth are the fabrication of humankind."

Mari had no idea how to get to Claus's home, but the car easily traveled onward as more roadways kept magically appearing before her. She watched the scenery as the little car purred in response to her urgings. The landscape resembled Earth, yet it was more impressive than she was used to. Her new sight had the ability to not only see the overall scene, but her eyes could zoom into even the intricacy of the tiniest wildflower along the way. She was getting accustomed to the fact that this was home and that things here were exactly as they were supposed to be.

Nature was truly pure and untouched. Colors were brilliant with melodies hinting of glories that Mari had only imagined while listening to her simple stereo. Music resonated in the atmosphere around her, swept over her like Vivaldi's "Seasons," then changed to the magnificence of Mozart as she deftly rounded a hill and viewed glorious purple and white mountains in the distance. The beautiful green foothills welcomed her.

The car seemed to have a mind of its own so she could simply enjoy the warm mountain breeze around her that exuded the presence of eternal summer. She hadn't felt this sense of freedom since she sailed through the trees on dad's homemade cable swing, or raced down the icy hill on the old red rider sled. Those were memories that she was anxious to revisit.

The road ahead was taking Mari over a hilltop that gently sloped down into a lush valley divided by a meandering river that reminded her of her Snoqualmie Valley home on Earth.

One large farm filled the entire valley. The fields were rich with many colors combining to create the hum of a country tune. At first, she couldn't think of the name of the song until she began hearing the words and melody being sung by John Denver. "Take me home, country road," came in loud and clear, "to the place where I belong." She understood his words more clearly than ever.

She could make out the roof of a farmhouse surrounded by trees with billowing canopies. Then she noticed several conventional red barns and huge, long greenhouses along the river's edge. The greenhouses were a sight to behold. The architecture was that of traditional greenhouses with green glass walls, but the rooftops were clear, and they shimmered like glittering sunlight on the surface of a lake. Their straight lines were occasionally interrupted by crystalline faceted domes that glistened like massive sparkling diamonds.

Twenty-three

As Mari rode down the hillside, she could see acres of tomato plants heavy with their brilliant red fruit, cornstalks rich with the silk of abundant corncobs, poles of bean plants and rows of multicolored foliage of different root vegetables.

Her view was like many fertile Earthly valleys but the glow of the colors and the vibration that emanated from them could only exist in this reality. It could have been anyone's valley and farm, but Mari felt her grandfather nearby. Her confirmation came as the car eased into the valley. It turned into a graveled driveway that led to a farmhouse past a luxurious grassy field. There she spotted Ezmeralda grazing in an unfenced pasture. The lovely white horse raised her head and nodded a welcome to Mari, who waved in return.

In a tightly strung pea patch, Mari caught a glimpse of a glowing blue green light emanating from within one of the rows. Nature here was incredible, but even more extraordinary when enhanced by the light of a spirit's aura.

She drove closer and could see that the colorful light she had seen was Claus's beautiful aura. He was bent down to tend the sturdy string that provided a place for the reaching tendrils to grow. He stood up just before she stopped on the edge of the field and walked over to greet her.

He had changed since she had seen him last. He was no longer dressed in his woodsman costume from the carriage ride. Now he was a simple farmer with baggy gray pants and a blue plaid shirt. He looked natural and at home in his horticultural environment. His head sported a baseball cap that he took off and slapped it across his knee to dust it off. He obviously gained pleasure from his work.

But it wasn't the clothes that Mari noticed first. He was a younger version of the grandpa she was getting to know, and he had a much brighter aura than before. His features were defined in the youthful face with the handsome, long straight line of his regal nose topping a big toothy grin upon seeing his granddaughter. Although he almost looked like a different person, she knew him right away. Her connection to him was very real.

"I've been watching for you," Claus said as the car stopped where he stood. "Can I bum a ride to the house?"

"I'd love the company," Mari replied. "Keep in mind that I'm new to driving. Luckily this car has a mind of its own."

"Well, it's not just a cute little car," he commented as he opened the door and slid into the passenger seat. "It's smart, too. The road appeared just as I was finishing my work in the pea patch."

It wasn't only her active imagination that made her see the road appear as she drove along. Mari turned and looked behind at the rolling green hills where there was no road to be seen anywhere.

Claus gave her a grin and said, "We aren't even there yet, and I can feel the questions already. You always have been an inquisitive soul. No, we don't have roads here. We usually move by thought but sometimes we enjoy the feeling of a vehicle beneath us and create the roads as we go along. It's a more leisurely way to travel and we can enjoy the scenery along the way. Journeys by thought leave out a lot and there is so much to see. I have a favorite blue pickup truck, and your grandmother shows up sometimes in a pink jeep convertible that suits her light spirit."

Mari remembered her grandmother kidding about getting a pink jeep to get around. She had seen one on the old TV show, Fantasy Island, that she watched when the grandchildren were visiting. She smiled at the imagined vision of her grandmother motoring along in her fancy pink jeep.

Claus brought her out of the memory before she slid deeper into it. He pointed ahead and said, "Motor on whenever you're ready. My home awaits you and I've been eager to share it with you."

Twenty-four

Claus led the way up the steps to his porch and opened the door, which squeaked just enough to add to the character of the farmhouse. As she walked through the doorway, she felt as though Claus had opened his very soul to her, into a space that somehow collected and embodied and exuded his special energy. She remembered how her mother and father built their homes with the features they enjoyed. When they moved in, the house would fill with the family's energy and make it a home. The homes that her grandparents shared with her here were almost like living things that complemented the simple essence of their creators.

They walked into a spacious living room. It was furnished with large, overstuffed furniture that looked comfortable and inviting. The pictures that decorated the walls were mostly mountain scenery except for one that caught Mari's attention. She crossed the room where The Falconer was hung.

"I loved this look for you on the carriage ride," she said turning to Claus, who was standing beside her. "But I would know you anywhere now. And this home is really you. I like it."

"I'm glad you do." Claus put his arm around his granddaughter's shoulder. "This picture has meant a lot to me. I'm glad your mother found it. It took some prodding on my part, but she finally heard me and went back for it. That trip had some good moments. I especially enjoyed the sunrise walks on the beach with your mom. She thought she was alone in her thoughts, but we had some good communication going. One morning, as she gazed out on the horizon, she had a vision of one drop of water falling into the ocean. I showed her the understanding that a single event can be small in the big scheme of things, and she was reminded of her universal connectedness."

"I'm so glad you were there for her," Mari smiled. "On the carriage ride, Grandma helped me to visit Natalie, but she said that it gets harder to do as we get into the higher vibrations here. Do you find that to be the case? Can we do something about it?"

"Yes, and yes," he answered both questions, "but there's lots to tell you about and even more to show you. First let's get comfortable. How would you like a nice round table discussion in a cozy farm kitchen?"

Before she could answer, Mari found herself seated at a small round table with a red and white checkered tablecloth. The center was adorned with a small vase of yellow daisies. She looked around and observed the simple ambiance of the kitchen. Its tall cabinets were painted soft yellow and went all the way to the high ceiling. The sparkling clear glass in the upper cabinets revealed all the accoutrements a farmer would need to live comfortably, including several shelves of beautifully hand preserved fruits and vegetables in mason jars.

"Lilly did those up for me from the produce from my gardens and orchards," Claus said in answer to the unasked question. "She always got a lot of pleasure from canning and making preserves and she still does. Even though we can create wondrous things here, many of us go back to simple pleasures that give us joy.

"You may have noticed that here our bodies don't require food as we did with a physical body, but some of us do enjoy the pleasure occasionally. Those preserves taste great but are mostly just pretty to look at. And food doesn't really need to be preserved. It's just an activity that Lilly enjoys.

"To answer another future question that I can feel coming on, Lilly and I were married in our lives, and we are kindred spirits still. But we are also individual spirits with our own personal tastes. Marriage is honored here with that special connection that happens on that side and can grow stronger with time. We spend a lot of time together and enjoy each other's company and each other's homes.

"Sometimes I enjoy a mountain cabin, or I might stay in an apartment in the city if I want to partake of activities there and enjoy the energy of the city. When Lilly arrived, I shared this home with her until she was ready to create her own surroundings. With the ability to bilocate, we are together much of the time but we're individuals just the same. You'll understand better as you become more comfortable here."

"Wow!" exclaimed Mari. "I have so much to get used to. I'm shedding a lot of my old ideas, but with the love that is obvious between you and Gramma, I can understand what you're saying. I suppose that's what's meant by being together in spirit. I think I understand that part.

"One thing I do need to ask about," Mari went on, "is the fact that I recognized you even though you appear so much more youthful than I remember in the carriage. I'm finding out that we can have many appearances, depending on circumstances, but this change is strikingly different."

Claus took a deep breath and relaxed, thinking that he had his hands full with this one. He had helped others assimilate to this side, but Mari was the precocious one. She was a beautiful challenge.

Twenty-five

"It would do us both well," he started gently, "to remind you that time isn't an influence here. We use the word but it's more about experience. You've surely heard that by now. The answers you seek will come to you eventually, and in different ways. Some you'll find on your own journey through the memories of your experiences, while others need explanations from those of us who have been here longer.

"To answer your question about my appearance, age is not relevant here. We are all spirits existing in the way we were created by God with our own creative input. The best example I can give you in relation to Earth is that many of us function at about the physical age of thirty Earth years. But even that is a choice. I chose to greet you with the falconer persona so you could relate to me through your mother. Now that you are comfortable with my essence," he continued, "I can be with you as more of my true spirit self. Your spirit knows me, even though we've never met in physicality, from visits with you over the years. This brings us to some other questions you have."

Mari sat quietly to take in her grandfather's words. It wasn't her nature to be at a loss for words, but many of her questions were being answered. Deep in thought, she rested her elbows on the table and gently rubbed her forehead with her index finger as she had in moments of concentration on the other side. After she sighed, Claus lifted her delicate chin with a loving hand. She saw truth and caring in his eyes as he telepathically reminded her that she did, indeed, have the capacity to understand and function in the world of spirit. He sent her a mental message of reassurance that she knew she could trust.

When he was sure she was ready to move on, Claus continued. "I've been with all my loved ones, who are still in physical life, at times I can help them, mostly when they have difficult decisions to make or if they need comfort. Our love that we leave with them, and their love that we bring here with us, keeps us bonded and able to pass through the veil that diminishes us from their awareness. We visit them mostly in their dream state. That's when their spirits are the most available to us. The dream state helps them to process their Earth experiences, and we can help them sort some of that out. From this side, we're able to help them in ways we never could while we were there. It's a privilege to be of service to them and to their guides. But sometimes we merely pop in to say, 'Hi.'

"What's really great," Claus said as he sat back in his chair with his face flashing an amused grin, "is to follow them around in their daily tasks and just when they are relaxed into something mundane and least expecting it, we can give them a little spirit nudge of a thought or an idea. They're not usually sure where it came from. For some people, like Suzi, who are open minded enough, it creates a physical tingling that releases energy from their chakras. This creates sparks that we can see, and they can only feel. It tells us that they get it."

"Mind you," said Claus, seriously, "we don't do this only for a lark. It's an important way to relay information. Some great advances have been passed on to humankind from this side in those moments of inspiration.

"On a lighter note, it can just be a non-intoxicating way to give a spirit a lift. Too many people abuse drugs or alcohol to do that. They don't know that those artificial "solutions" sadly separate them from us, and the experience of a real and true spiritual high. It's such a waste of precious time when they choose to try to function on those negative earthly paths. But we still never give up on them."

Mari listened intently to her grandfather's words. He was very kind and nonjudgemental and had a gentle way about him as he spoke. Claus's concern for those he loved was apparent. He could see that Mari was opening her consciousness to the influence that she and other spirits could have on people who were still in physical life.

"Good point to bring up," said Claus picking up on her thought. "The one big rule that we must bear in mind is to not interfere with the gift of personal choice. We don't like to watch our loved ones make difficult choices. But they all have their private blueprints or plans for that side, and some choose to be diverted on paths that are more difficult. It's a lot like choosing college courses in construction management when your actual degree should be in art history. There is always the added knowledge and experience to be gained and applied later but one is diverted from a swifter and clearer path to their intended goals.

"Then again, there are some whose choice of blueprint is to be an example. They go to that side with special guidance and protection from this side. A historic and powerful example that you're aware of, is the life of Jesus. His example reminds us that we are all God's children and, in his story, we can relate and find that higher part of ourselves."

Twenty-six

"Grandpa," interrupted Mari, "on my way here I saw a man in a field with some sheep who reminded me so much of a picture of Jesus that I saw when I was very young."

"Like the other avatars, he is with us here often," Claus explained. "He appeared to you because he is your Christian reference to God. But don't be surprised if you see Buddha, Shiva, or Mohammad and others. They appear in many profound ways. Most of us can bi-locate and even tri-locate. They can be in many places at once. We communicate with them and other spiritual leaders on many levels and they're always available to assist us, no matter what side of existence we are on. We are their emissaries for you for now since you are comfortable with us as your family members. But like we've been telling you, everyone can have their own unique experience."

Mari remembered a dream that she had not long before she released her physical self. She was moving along a path when Christ appeared before her with his arms open wide, waiting for her. She awoke totally at peace and the vision stayed with her and gave her comfort in those last days.

Now she recognized that she was part of a huge universe and that her loving God surely had made room for all children.

"But Grandpa," queried Mari, "I've always been so confused about the different spiritual leaders who influenced that world. There is so much controversy over whose message we should listen to."

"You're right." Claus replied. "First remember that we are all children of God. The avatars are a gift from God. They chose to go there because, while we're there in that lower vibrational atmosphere, we need to be reminded of the existence of our higher selves. Those leaders take on human form so they can truly understand and connect to us. They know our infirmities and trials, including cultural influences. They not only influence us while we're in the physical world, but they also help those of us on this side to stay aware of what it's like to live on Earth. This is a pretty great place to exist, so we sometimes need to be reminded. I've been here for some time now, so I go to the seminars that are put on by those leaders. We need to jog our memories as we grow here, also. It helps us to stay connected and be of service to others."

"That helps me to understand why they go there," Mari said, "but why is it so messed up and misunderstood over there?"

He had to think about that one for a second then replied, "Well, that's a big question. I'd have to say that we get bombarded there with the concerns and difficulties of life and it's good to have someone come along and remind us of the bigger picture of our purpose. The avatars inspire us to demonstrate how to live that life to get through it so that all comes out for higher good. They remind us to seek God and in God, we can find that Divine Source within our own higher selves. It's too bad, but some people live in the negative energy. They take divine inspirations and twist them with their warped egos to play on others' fears and confusion. A big test there is to be able to see past all those negative influences and find a positive truth that keeps you on track. Many call that faith. It comes down to God's love and wishes for good for all the children and for that world."

"Grandpa," Mari said with much love and gratitude, "I have to say that talking, or rather listening, to you is such a comfort. Have you always been so wise?"

He couldn't help but smile at her innocence. "I wish!" he laughed. "I've struggled like everyone else over there, but I've been here for a while and have chosen not to incarnate again, at least for now. And I've worked with a lot of souls coming home and I guess that's helped me to gain some knowledge along the way. And like everyone else here, I work to continually evolve. Thanks for the compliment, but you'll find others just as, if not more, helpful."

Claus watched the colors in Mari's aura show healing and more natural light as she began to feel and understand her spirituality. The blues of balance were merging and showing more brilliant hues with fingers of sparkling gold that come with understanding. Claus was grateful for his own guidance system in dealing with and healing this delicate soul.

"You were there with very powerful help," he continued. "Even Saria was specially chosen for her own strength. She has demonstrated an ability to keep herself at bay when you chose your most difficult path. The eating disorder was a wrinkle that we hadn't seen coming when we were trying to help you deal with diabetes. You somehow latched onto that negative idea. We could only send our love and try to help you when we could. We could see then that there must be an example element in your plan. We aren't always made aware of all the elements of your plan.

"The more difficult someone is to understand, the more knowledge is available to those who make the effort to do so. You dug a deep hole for yourself, and we could only protect your soul and continue to nudge you on by reminding you of your chosen goals.

"Wow," Claus suddenly exclaimed, sitting back. He shook his head and released himself from Mari's intense stare. "That bit of conversation covered more than I intended. The point was to be about not interfering in a person's choices. You don't have to deal with all that other stuff now. What was your original question?"

Mari was so into her grandfather's discussion that she had to pull her attention away with a deep breath and pause to remember. He had given her a lot to absorb and think about.

"Oh yes!" she finally said. "I was wondering about visiting those who are still on the other side. I'm concerned about my family. I know that my leaving wasn't exactly a big surprise. Mom knew that the chances were that she would outlive me, but I'm not sure she was really prepared in her heart. She was cool getting the party ready, but I would like to see if she and the others are getting on okay."

"You can do that," he responded with caution, "but if you approve, I'll go along until you get a little stronger.

"Good idea, Grandpa."

"It's not easy for us," Claus warned. "Your grandma probably showed you that they function on a lower vibration than we do, so we must lower our frequency to get through the veil between worlds unless we are called to service in an emergency. Their dreams are an available avenue for us to get through to them. There are some people there who can intuitively raise their sensory vibrations to see and hear us."

"That might be how Deirdre does it," Mari realized. She had many memories of special times with her clairvoyant cousin.

"She is great that way, but even she gets blocked and needs to study her dreams," Claus said. "But your mom isn't on that vibration yet, so we'll try the dream path with her. You sit tight and I'll check the situation over there."

Twenty-seven

Mari watched as Claus muted his essence. His aura quickly became a darker shade, then faded from her sight. The magic of this world was becoming commonplace but was amazing at the same time. She didn't feel at all alone as she waited for him to return. She smiled serenely to herself as she remembered spending time with Dee.

Mari and Dee lounged on the comfy sofa in Mari's apartment. It was December, near Mari's twenty-fifth birthday. Deirdre was visiting from Missouri, and it was near her birthday, too. Suzi had tickets to take them both to Seattle to see the stage production of *The Phantom of the Opera* in a couple days. Mari loved the music from the show, and she could identify with the reclusive Phantom.

Even with the special plans, this was not a good time for Mari. The complications from her illness were getting more serious. Her kidneys had failed, and she was going to dialysis three times a week. She was ill but determined to make it to The Phantom and not have to go to the hospital for her birthday instead.

The conversation was light. Dee and Mari were planning their big evening out, sharing their girly enthusiasm about what to wear and how to do their hair. Dee was a mature woman with a good sense of her inner ingenue that reveled in simple fun. The two had become very close in recent years and were happy to be celebrating their birthdays together.

After a lull in the conversation, Mari's demeanor shifted. She began telling Dee about a recent trip with her mom and their moods turned serious.

"Mom took me to Hood Canal and showed me the new house," Mari said, lacking the enthusiasm that one would have expected.

"I've heard about it," Dee started cautiously, sensing that Mari had something to get off her mind. "How is the construction coming along?"

"Well, it's getting done," Mari hesitated. "The house is framed and mom showed me where all the rooms will be and gave me an idea of what it will be like when it's finished."

"Yeah? And? Come on, Girl," chided Dee, patiently waiting for her to get to the issue that her intuition told her was really on Mari's mind. "Spit it out. What's on your mind?"

"You know me too well," Mari said slowly, trying to get her thoughts into words.

Quiet conversations with Dee had the potential to turn into a real experience. Her abilities seemed to take people to a higher place where communication could happen on an unexpected level. Her presence and openness seemed to give voice to one's own higher self, and her patience assisted in helping seekers to discover their own truth. Mari felt her spirit needed to vent and Dee's gentle energy was making it easy.

"I know I'll never live there," Mari said with a self-assured softness to her voice. "I knew it in my heart the whole time we were there, and I know it now. Mom took me downstairs and showed me where I would have my own apartment. They even plan on vinyl floors so I can move around with my IV pole. I know it will be nice, but I just couldn't connect with it all."

She hesitated to gather her strength. "To put it bluntly, I don't think I will live to see it completed. It's just that I don't see myself living there and it doesn't feel like a part of me. I really want to move with them so I can stay with my family. It breaks my heart to know that they will be moving, but I know I won't be going. I'm not sure how or why that will happen, but I'm afraid that I won't live that long. I really don't want to die!"

There! She'd said it. And in her very soul, she knew it was true. Her intellect knew that she should be really upset and emotional, but instead there was a serene calmness that came over her as she and Dee paused in silence.

Dee marveled at the luminous vision unfolding before her as Mari's aura merged from the grayness of illness to fingers of fluttering blue and pink light, in beams of purest white. She kept watching her, convinced that Mari was about to levitate from the sofa. Even with her sensibilities and innumerable spiritual experiences, she knew it was a privilege to witness such a glorious sight.

"You know," Dee tenderly reminded Mari, "I've been visited by your grandmother, my Aunt Lilly, since she has become more comfortable on the other side."

"Yes," Mari answered. "I remember you telling me so."

"Well," Dee said smiling and looking a little behind Mari, "she is with us now and she is here to comfort you and let you know that she and others will be there for you when you need them. She is smiling and glowing with so much love for you. It's really a beautiful sight. She says that you're not quite finished here yet." Then Dee paused, listening. "And that's all I'm getting for now."

"Thank you, Dee," whispered Mari, "and Grandma, too." She sat in silence and wonder with a veil of peace surrounding her.

Twenty-eight

With a sudden electrical "pop" and faint sparks, Claus was back in his seat at the table.

"I'm pleased to report that your mom has fallen asleep reading on her sofa. She's really tired because she had trouble sleeping earlier. Her grief and longing to be with you have kept her awake at night and struggling to function during the day. She has been looking for signs from you, but she is healing from her perceived loss of her child. She is doing okay, considering.

"In her dream, I've planted the idea that someone is trying to reach her. Her mind is telling her she is at a party and that there is a phone call for her. Her dream state is relaxed and peaceful so it's a good time to go. Even in her alert state, she's been hoping for a visit from you ever since the memorial party."

"Oh good," Mari beamed. "I'm ready too."

"Well then," Claus began, "this is the best way I can describe what you must do. At least it works for me. When you hum to a favorite song, you are matching the vibration of your hum to that of the music. You're aware of the colors that are associated with those pulsations so you can use that image also. To lower your vibration to that of physical life, you need to feel the frequency of your body's energy and then concentrate on lowering it, as with biofeedback. Or it can be like lowering your voice octave. That sums up my method. You can see how it works for you."

That sounded easy enough to Mari, but the lower vibrations were becoming foreign and uncomfortable to her evolving existence. She struggled to get command of the sensations that were swirling through her until she remembered *The Phantom of the Opera* and *The Music of the Night*. She closed her eyes, concentrating on the totality of that hauntingly melancholy melody that helped her to achieve a resonance that felt dense, heavy and even painful like she remembered.

"There!" exclaimed Claus as Mari's aura darkened like his had earlier. "You've got it. Now we'll go back together."

Mari felt herself fade from Claus's kitchen. With an electrical pop, she opened her eyes to find herself standing near her mother. Suzi's shoulders moved slowly and rhythmically as she lay in quiet slumber on the sofa covered with a striped crocheted blanket. Her eyes were still swollen from crying herself to sleep.

Mari wanted to go to her mother and hug her and feel that hug in return, but Claus kept a mental hold on her at a distance.

Then suddenly he exclaimed, "Oh great!" He explained, "In her dream she had left the party, and her mind has her driving into a war zone. This kid has always been fighting wars in her dreams. It's a past life memory that she's having trouble shaking off. I'll have to go in and divert her away from that fantasy. She even sees tanks rolling down the road she's on. At least she is still looking for the young woman who is trying to reach her. I guess she thinks that you are there in that battle zone and she needs to be your rescuer. She hasn't let go of that idea yet. It'll do her good to know you are ok. I'll just interject some roadblocks and go in as a friendly policeman and send her on a detour."

He closed his eyes and gave an I Dream of Jeannie nod to clear up Suzi's dream state confusion, then motioned Mari to sit on the sofa next to Suzi.

"Her subconscious is with you now," he whispered to Mari.

As Suzi lay in deep sleep, Mari's eyes grew in wonder as her mother's ethereal body slowly separated from her physical form and rose to a sitting position. In her dream, she was sitting with the daughter that her heart was aching to see again. Mari looked wonderful and relief washed over them both, bringing much-needed peace. Suzi could see the radiant pink aura of love all around her daughter as she raised her hands and held Mari's beautiful face that showed no sign of the illness that she had known so well in her child.

"Look for me now, Mom," Mari planted into Suzi's mind. Then she rose and watched her mother long enough to know that a tremendous healing had taken place for them both in that short visit. She could see the luminous pink energy of love they shared leaping from Suzi's palms that had held Mari's face.

Claus was beaming with pride at what his two loved ones had accomplished. He would never cease to be amazed by the amount of healing that could come from such a fleeting moment of souls touching. Mari watched as Suzi woke up and looked at her hands where she could still feel the lingering softness of her daughter's face.

"That was beautiful," he whispered to Mari. She melted into his arms as the scene faded from around them.

Twenty-nine

"Well, hello, Cuz," said Deirdre when she answered her phone. "I was just going to call you."

"Yeah, great minds think alike," Suzi said. "I had to call you. I just had the most amazing dream."

"I had one, too," said Dee. "You go first."

"Ok. I was tired and fell asleep on the sofa. My dream was kind of all over the place. I was looking for Mari in some strange scenarios and I had the feeling that she was looking for me. Then she ended up sitting with me where I was sleeping. I took her face in my hands, then she said, 'Look for me now, mom.'

"I swear to you that I can still hear her voice and feel the energy of her face in my hands. They are vibrating with her essence. I miss her so much."

"That's one for the book," commented Dee. "I'm so glad you got to experience her like that. What a beautiful healing for you both, though I hear the sorrow, too. What a powerful connection. I know it must be hard, but how is the writing going?"

"Certainly nothing I can brag about," answered Suzi. "I've experimented with different story lines but I'm still not sure what kind of story to tell. Nothing flows. At least I'm finding that I can put a sentence together. I'll call that progress.

"I so want to do this for Mari, but I feel I'm out of my element with this. I am usually pretty creative, but this has me stumped. I have so many regrets that I wasn't better at writing in school and that I didn't keep a diary when Mari was here. I have so many blocks. Maybe I'm afraid of reliving all of it. I'm not ready for that pain. I could use Mari's help."

"Now that you and Mari have found each other through the veil," said Dee, "maybe things will open up for you."

"I'll hold on to that thought," said Suzi. "Now tell me about your dream."

"Oh yeah," started Dee. "I was only observing but, to sum it up, I saw Mari with your dad, Claus. They were in a garden, then they were actually flying over a green valley. I often have dreams of flying. This gives me hope that it can happen.

"Mari was happy to be with him. I know she never got to meet him in life, but he is a big part of her evolution over there."

"I'll take comfort in that," said Suzi. "He was a kind and gentle man. I think he had something to do with my dream also."

Thirty

Details slowly materialized as Claus and Mari found they were standing, once again, in his farm kitchen.

"I'd hoped that I could show you my little spread before we did all that, but now is just as good a time. How would you like a tour of the grounds while we clear our heads?"

Mari smiled. "I bow to your wisdom and wishes, Kind Sir," she said with a dramatic flair as she bowed respectfully. She so loved his spirit.

Her spirit was even lighter now that she knew that her mom was indeed mending from her loss and that Suzi's healing would surely help the rest of the family to cope. She smiled remembering her dad teasingly telling her and her siblings, "If Momma ain't happy, ain't nobody happy."

Claus held his bent elbow to his granddaughter and said, "Then shall we proceed to the gardens, Madam?"

The lushness that met them off the back porch was just too incredible for mere words. Claus and Mari could feel themselves being pulled into the splendor of the gardens that surrounded the farmhouse. Abundance everywhere vibrated with wonder and magic.

Mari gasped, held her left hand to her heart and clutched Claus's elbow as they, literally, floated into the many amazing hues of green that filled the air around them. The gardens had an aura of life that welcomed the pair with undulating caresses. They glided into a narrow path that appeared ahead and meandered through a thicket formed by the leaves and branches and as they strolled on, vines grew like trees with brown trunks that twisted within the dense underbrush that was growing upward, forming a verdurous leafy canopy.

Their spirits lifted and they began to sail through the green tunnel, noticing occasional sparkles of jewel-toned flowers. It was like a lush tropical forest, in an atmosphere that was pleasant and comfortable, and not humid at all. It appeared that plants from many different worlds coexisted happily as they reveled in diversification.

Tiny yellow birds flitted through the leaves of the canopy and sang a sweet song of welcome. The leaves of the underbrush rustled with activity and Mari caught sight of a family of creamy light brown rabbits darting through the thick vegetation. The smallest of the family stopped and looked up to watch the two ethereal bodies float through the treetops. The little bunny gave Mari a wink of recognition before it scurried on with the others. She had known him as Peanut Butter, and he had been her much loved pet at one time. She was happy to see him here.

Mari felt a quiet reverence for this fantasy forest. She didn't want to disturb the natural sounds of the symphony that they were floating through, so her comments and questions took the form of thought waves. Her response to the magnificence around her was more than she could put into words, but Claus felt the pleasure that glowed in her aura.

"How is it possible," Mari asked in hushed waves of thought, "for vegetation this thick to let in so much light to allow it all to grow? It should be dark in here, but it seems even brighter than the open air."

Claus placed his hand on hers, which still held tightly to his elbow. Gliding through the fairytale wonder of the emerging moss edged path his thoughts to her were also hushed. "Plants here emit their own light in a way that resembles our auras. You can see it now with your more sensitive vision."

"I'm a little confused about our senses," Mari thought back to him. "Without our physical senses, how is it that I am getting the blended aromas of the freshness of the plants. and muskiness from the moss and the soil? It's even more pleasant than I remember from our home in North Bend."

"You might say we have a memory of our senses," Claus answered. "We are beings of thought, memory and communication. You are remembering the experiences of your physical senses that are a part of you. Everything here is more enhanced than over there. This is only one garden experience that I created. If you hold on tight, we'll move on. There's more to see."

"I could just stay in here forever," said Mari, feeling the welcoming vibrations of the plant life. "It's hard to imagine anything more."

She held tightly to Claus's elbow with both hands and the path ended before them. She felt a lightness overcome her and looked down as they rose through an opening in the canopy. The rush of the thick green around them became thinner until Mari found herself rising and sliding over rich fields of herbs. She could detect the fragrance of something that was like a blend of peppermint and spearmint with a touch of vanilla. Some of the herbs and other plants had colorful flowers, and were planted in patterns on the fields below as if Higher Power had laid a natural, multihued heavenly quilt over the land.

Thirty-one

Fear had imbued Mari's physical existence, making this experience of freedom particularly sweet. It was a feeling that pulsated within her very being as she and her grandfather sailed and hovered above the vastness of his fields. Aviary friends of many colors were flying in circles around and between them. It felt like independence and newfound liberty.

As they flew, Mari began to notice more deeply what felt so good to her in that moment. The physical and emotional absence of fear amazed her. It gave her a lightness that allowed her to fly with the warm air currents in a dance of free expression. In fact, she felt so safe in that moment, she knew she could dare a mental journey to her previous life, and she explored a memory of her first airplane experience.

It was winter, just after the holidays, when the family moved into the unfinished house on the hill. Not long after the move, Mari's dad, Mitch, received word that the company he worked for had a major job in American Samoa. In the past he and Suzi had discussed the possibility of foreign work in the construction industry and vowed that if the opportunity were presented to them, they would go. Mitch's father had turned down work abroad and he realized later that his family had missed valuable learning experiences.

After looking into what they would need to know about that South Pacific culture and their living conditions, Mitch and Suzi decided they were ready for the adventure. The company was flying the entire family to those Polynesian islands that lie about halfway between New Zealand and Tahiti.

Mari and her siblings were excited with their parents about the adventure, and Mari, being the oldest, had a million questions, but there wasn't much time. The whole house had to be packed, items sorted into "storage" or "sell/giveaway" or "take," and there wasn't much space for "stuff" on this adventure. They said goodbye to their neighbors and the friends and acquaintances that crossed their paths in the short time left on the mainland, and then released themselves into the world like the Swiss Family Robinson, sailing the high seas of the unknown.

It was a fourteen-hour flight to the islands, with stops in San Francisco and Honolulu. For Mari and her two siblings, Suzi packed special carry-on bags filled with coloring books, storybooks, small toys, dolls, and snacks. This was a real adventure for a family that hadn't traveled much at all, and it was their very first plane ride together.

Suzi and Mitch tucked a seat belt snuggly around each child and gave them a peck on the cheek, then prepared themselves for take-off. The children looked especially small in the seats of the Boeing 747. Suzi smiled at each one individually and wondered what their young imaginations would gain from the adventure that lay ahead for them. They were each excited in their own way.

Four-year-old Natalie was wide-eyed in the excitement that swirled around the whole family. George, at age six, was caught up in the anticipation of a ride in this huge airplane. Mari, age nine, was trying on a sophisticated demeanor as she chatted with the cheerful flight attendant who was pinning a winged TWA pin on each child in honor of their first airplane ride. Suzi and Mitch were ready to be proud of their children for taking this move so well, and for being adaptable to new experiences.

The passengers, including some other company employees and their family members, were all settled. The pilot came over the intercom and announced that they were ready for takeoff. As the engines became louder and louder, Mari suddenly felt the overwhelm of the reality that this was more than a ride in the family car. The whole family was leaving everything they knew. Additionally, she was old enough to know that this overgrown tin can was going to be shot into the sky by those thundering engines, and her young mind and active imagination remembered stories of plane crashes on the news and in movies.

The roar of the engines filled her mind, and fear started gripping her at her toes and flowing through her body as the plane gained speed on the runway.

Suddenly Mari started talking, and in fact the words that formed comments and questions flowed from her at a speed that matched the jet engines beneath them. Mari's father, who was sitting beside her, didn't have time to answer a question before another would come out. As the plane lifted and she felt inertia forcing her body deeper into the seat, Mari talked so fast she could barely catch her breath.

George, who sat on the other side of her, giggled and exclaimed, "Oh cool!" as he enjoyed the best roller coaster ride he had ever been on. Natalie, dwarfed by the big seat and clutching her Strawberry Shortcake doll, looked up and smiled a big smile at Suzi, who sat on the other side of her and George.

As the plane leveled off, Mari realized that all the family eyes were on her. She was unloading everything that came to her mind. The verbal flow couldn't be ignored.

"What's the weather going to be like when we get there, Dad? I hope it's nice. My teacher said that it's tropical there. What does tropical mean? I guess that's palm trees and all. Are we going to start school right away? I'm going to miss Mr. Sorenson. He's a good teacher. I wonder if I can get straight A's again in Samoa. I'm glad some other kids who are coming with us will go to school, too. Mom said we'll have to wear uniforms there. Can we go swimming? I want to do that right away. Isn't it funny that today it's winter here and tomorrow we'll be in summer? Is it really hot there?"

Mari's parents began to look visibly concerned about their daughter, who was now breaking out with beads of sweat on her brow and eyes like big blue saucers. Mitch put his arm around her and patted her hand, trying to calm her. Suzi had heard about panic attacks, but never considered that her oldest daughter, who was so capable and dependable, would be vulnerable to panic. She realized that she had neglected to inform the children about the rush of a plane taking off. She leaned forward and spoke softly to Mari to let her know that all was okay.

Thirty-two

The plane leveled off. Mari caught her breath, and with her parents' assurance, the verbal outpouring of internalized questions and fears finally calmed down. She was still too excited to read the book she had packed, but she did finally explore the bag of goodies that the flight attendant brought. Suzi dreaded the take-off from the San Francisco airport looming before them, as well as the one from Hawaii. However, now that they had been through the shock and panic of that first lift-off, Mari managed the next one by holding her breath through the experience. By the time they took off from Honolulu, Mari was a seasoned traveler.

The rest of the flight was the long leg of it. By now it was late at night, and one by one, the children dropped off to sleep while their parents tried to be comfortable and rest also. They had switched seats periodically and now Suzi was by the window with Mari beside her. When she wasn't dozing, Suzi would look out the window and see nothing but blackness, until she would spot the distant lights of ships on the ocean below. She tried to imagine flying without fear, but she couldn't get past the vulnerability of the physical body in this world. She smiled to herself as she was given a glimmer of a spirit memory of flying that her mind interpreted as imagination. Mari stirred beside her, and Suzi put her arm around her.

"What 'cha looking at, Mom?" Mari asked, looking up with her sleepy face.

Suzi pulled Mari closer into a tender hug and answered, "Just enjoying the view, Hon. I can see ships below us. They look so tiny. One is really lit up. It must be a cruise ship."

Mari's curiosity got through her sleepiness, and she leaned over her mother's lap to look. Suzi was pleased to watch her child work through her fears even though she would rather take it on herself and spare these innocent ones the pain.

As she sat back in her seat, Mari snuggled in with her mom and they both took a snooze for most of the rest of the flight.

This became a precious memory for Mari. She was missing that physical closeness of shared love and affection.

This memory only took the flash of a second, but in that brief instant, Mari relived her whole Samoan experience at the same time she was taking in her grandfather's farm, and she and Claus continued to glide toward the green houses.

She remembered the Samoan school where she and George picked up some of the language, although lessons were in English. Mom never had trouble finding her children in a sea of tapa print uniforms. They were the only children at the school with blonde hair. It was interesting to be a minority in a foreign land, particularly in a place that felt safe, with people who were welcoming.

The family spent quite a bit of time in the clinic there because George kept getting ear infections from swimming so much in the warm ocean. The children in particular seemed to be vulnerable to local viruses, and had occasionally suffered flu-like symptoms for which they could not quite identify the source. Later, one of Mari's doctors suggested that she perhaps had contracted a virus that had attacked her pancreas and brought on the juvenile diabetes, but they would never know for sure if that was the case.

Thirty-three

Now Mari's natural curiosity was taking in the wonder of the colors and sounds of Claus's amazing valley, including the sparkling river that meandered through it. She spotted the greenhouses that were a marvelous green that she thought leaned more toward blue tones. Claus and Mari slowed as they approached them, passing over the tops of the patches of varied vegetation and animals romping playfully in the lush pastures. The greenhouses were flanked by orchards lush with fruit that ended near the massive forests of the foothills beyond them.

"By the way," said Claus to Mari as they again found their footing on the fertile ground. They were standing on the edge of a squash patch that had huge orange and purple striped vegetables shaped like pyramids. "This is another way we can travel here. I wanted you to see the overview of my little spread."

"One thing about it," said Mari with a sweet grin, "I must say, you so know how to give a girl's spirit a lift."

Claus smiled. He took Mari's hand, leading her to an intricately carved bench that appeared on the edge of the garden. The wood was as dark as ebony and had carvings that went up the thick legs and across the high back of winged animals flying above exotic treetops. The glassy smooth seat of the bench looked hard, but it gave slightly as they sat on it, with a softness almost like upholstery that formed to their spirit bodies and made them completely comfortable. Mari thought briefly of a time she would have jumped in shock at this, but she was becoming accustomed to these little surprises in the kingdom that she was beginning to think of as home.

"Mom shared with me stories of your bountiful gardens," said Mari. "They helped the family through some hard times. She said that she and her siblings would sell your produce to local grocery stores and that it would give them a little money to put toward a few clothes for the coming school year. Your hard work was appreciated. It was even harder for them after you died. Mom often said to me that she misses you even more the older she gets. She has so much she would like to share with you. When she remembers your smile, she can feel your love."

"Well, I appreciate hearing that, "said Claus.

They were seated in front of what seemed to be the main building with its huge, barn-looking, plum-purple door. The building was about five stories tall and was flanked by shorter, just as beautiful, structures. Mari blinked as she focused on the buildings and realized the walls weren't flatly painted a blue green, but instead they were subtle trompe l'oeil pictures of grand forests, orchards and gardens with marble fountains and statues of angels. The paintings were done in the style of impressionists like Monet and Van Gough, and they vibrated with a life of their own. The blue skies that were depicted were dotted with soft white clouds with edges that were touched with the soft pinks of a celestial sunrise.

The walls of the buildings appeared solid and strong, but they were translucent, like many other things here, transmitting a light of their own from within as if they were stained glass panels in an exquisite Tiffany window. Mari turned to her grandfather with eyes that glowed from absorbing the wonder before her.

"When Gramma mentioned your gardens," she began in a soft voice full of awe, "I never, in my most vivid dreams, imagined something so grand, let alone having you to share it with me."

"Get used to it, Little One," he responded, still smiling to be at his granddaughter's side. "This is merely a sample of the things to experience here. Greatness is everywhere yet simplicity is its essence. My gardens are a part of me. On Earth, the last time around for me, I was the closest to feeling at home when I was in my simple gardens there, working in the soil. Creating all this was my best healing when I returned home here. Some spirits come over with the literal idea of streets paved with gold. Well, one man's gold is another man's soil. I feel like I'm working with the symbolic equivalent of gold. This is natural, life-giving soil that enables me, and those who help me, to do some of God's work in the plant world.

"These greenhouses are where we have duplicated Earth's atmosphere and growing conditions. And the murals on the walls were indeed done by the noted artists who took the impressionist movement to Earth. Each one of them has visited here and put their own personal touches on the walls. I think it works because they were all in harmony within that movement. Their egos enjoyed the competition to decorate the walls, and each one tried to outdo the other. You'll probably see later that Van Gough went a little excentric on the far wall of building C. It's especially beautiful with the ethereal materials they must work with here."

"Van Gough? Really?" asked Mari. She was impressed by Claus's casual references to names that he seemed to think were just some buddies who would pop in occasionally.

"That may sound a little grand or unbelievable if we were sitting on a park bench on Earth," he continued, "but it's ordinary here. Your grandmother has struck up quite a friendship with the spirit who was known on Earth as Betsy Ross. They have tea often and do the most amazing embroidery work together. We're all equals here, and we enjoy sharing talents. It's interesting how on Earth humans think they must give fame and notoriety to those who are doing the job that they went there to do. But then," he thought again, "I guess if others weren't made aware of the work, they couldn't learn by their example. Yes," he smiled as he answered his own conundrum, "on second thought, I guess it does work. Fame can serve a purpose on Earth."

Mari was embarrassed to realize that she was staring down her nose at her grandfather, giving him quite a view of her tonsils. She snapped her jaw shut, shook her head and came out of her trance-like state.

"Oh wow!" she gasped and caught her breath. "That's interesting. I guess on Earth I never stopped to imagine what this side would really be like. I always thought that just floating around on a cloud playing a harp sounded boring. I like that we have actual, down in the dirt work to do here. You've inspired me to start a little garden of my own as soon as I can."

"That is If I am allowed to stay after my review. On Earth I was barely able to take care of myself let alone nurture even a simple house plant. Mom gave me a potted shamrock, and it didn't take long for it to wither and die. It must have picked up on all my negative energy."

Claus stood and looked at Mari with such love and pride that she thought she could see tears in his eyes. He comforted her with a thought. "Here the only tears are those of joy, love, and knee-slapping laughter. We love our work, but we know how to play, also.

"Now," he said, "we'd better wind up this tour with a visit inside so you can get into creating that garden of your own."

He stood tall and offered his elbow again. With the skill of a seasoned thespian, he said, "Madam, may we proceed?"

Mari giggled a little as she stood, took the offered elbow and said grandly, "Sir Claus, I would be utterly charmed."

At that moment they were startled by a fluffy gray mouse that darted from under the bench. The merry creature was being chased by an exquisite white cat with China blue eyes. Mari was concerned about what would happen if the cat caught the mouse.

"Don't worry, Dear," said Claus. "Here the game of cat and mouse is just that. It's only a game of tag that they enjoy. Next time you see them, the mouse will, most likely, be chasing the cat. They have a good time here too."

Mari was relieved and a little shy that she hadn't realized that herself. The whole balance of nature and food chain things were Earthly concerns.

Claus's facial expression grew serious, and he leaned close to his granddaughter and suggested, "Before we go into the greenhouse, how about if we ask someone to join us? I am thinking of Saria. She could help. You see, as I mentioned before, we have successfully recreated Earth's atmosphere in these buildings. That means negativity is part of it. You're recovering from that so it would be good to have your spirit guide visible by your side."

A little puzzled at what it all meant, Mari trusted Claus and as quickly as she thought it, Saria appeared at her side, her flowing garments billowing delicately around her.

Thirty-four

"Not to worry, Little One," Saria said in greeting Mari. "You're in good hands with your grandfather, but I always enjoy seeing his work in progress." She smiled across at him, took the elbow of Mari's other arm, and with a light skip, the three of them stepped onto a yellow brick road that playfully became visible ahead of them. A corny joke, but Mari appreciated it.

Huge purple doors opened automatically for them with only a whisper of a sound, and they stepped onto the gleaming white granite floor of a reception room. The space was round and had a magnificent crystal chandelier suspended in midair above them. The sparkling crystals hung from a gold frame and shone with inner light that projected specks of prismatic colors all around them.

Through the clear glass walls that enclosed the space, Mari could see more gardens with paths. They were much like the lush gardens that she had been through with Claus, but these were dull by comparison. She watched a scant and barely perceptible gray fog drift through the atmosphere of the paths, and she detected distant, morose low tones of energy. They reminded Mari of her visit to Natalie, and the darkness of the energy of grief.

She started to panic as a feeling of fear and dread flowed around and through her. She began to feel faint, but Saria's hold on her arm kept her steady. Her old familiar Earth pain started to envelop her, and it showed on her face and in her aura.

Releasing her arms, Saria and Claus stepped away from Mari with questioning looks on their faces. Mari was aware of a thought that passed between them, that she was still sensitive to the effects of Earth's atmosphere.

"It's not a problem," comforted Saria with a soothing smile. "You only need a little protection. Just close your eyes and see yourself surrounded by a pure white light. You don't need protection with us by your side, but it will make you feel more comfortable."

She did as her trusted companion suggested. As the white light swirled up and around her body, she felt even more insulated by the positive energy that had been prevalent since she arrived in the spirit world.

"Oh, thank you," she sighed. "That was a traumatic experience. My whole body felt assaulted by a familiar heaviness that I hope to never experience again."

"Very good!" exclaimed Saria. She turned to Claus with relieved pride. "She's remembering how it's done."

Mari gave them an amused, but slightly frustrated look. "You two do tend to coddle me. I appreciate your concerns and reminders, but do you really have to be so anxious about me in this world?"

"Ok," answered Saria, getting her point. "We can lighten up. It's just that some souls carry a lot of their Earthly anxieties over here until they process it all. It's temporary. I must admit that you seem to be coming along fine for the most part."

"And your point is well taken," Mari replied. "Let's get on with it then. This is all so fascinating."

Claus and Saria motioned her to and through one of the clear glass walls that opened as they approached. She was stunned that it happened so casually, but then, why not. She was becoming accustomed to the simplicity of their movements and appreciating not having the density of a physical body.

A familiar downward pull gripped the three of them. It gave Mari a flashback feeling of gravity that was a fact on Earth, but she knew that she no longer needed to be concerned about it. Reminding herself that she and her companions were spirits visiting another dimension of the artificial Earth's atmosphere, she eased into it without the need for the accompanying fear that defined that world.

She glanced down and observed that they were on a gray flagstone path that was leading into an enclosed forest. It seemed like the one that she and her siblings had romped through in their adventures on the other side, but it didn't have the luminosity of inner light that she had become familiar with outside these buildings. Mari knew that she was inside the greenhouse, but the roof seemed to disappear above the tall trees. She could smell pungent soil and the musky dampness of the shaded forest. The distant cry of a raven sounded lifeless, and depressing compared to the lilting music of the birds outside this encased forest. She thought about the homesickness for the beauty and peace of the spirit world, that was so prevalent in those who were still in their physical state. Her grandfather had done a marvelous job of setting up this facility. It was almost too real.

"We've done some important work here," said Claus as they proceeded to glide down the path. "I've chosen to remain on this side to both learn and teach. As things progress on Earth, we try to keep a step ahead so we can give the souls who are there the information they need to influence the physical and spiritual evolution that is steadily progressing there."

As he said it, Saria and Mari found they had entered a section of this building that was like the garden nursery store that Mari had visited with her grandmother in her recent life. As far as she could see there were many rows of potted plants at different stages of growth. Some were familiar, but most were new varieties that were reacting to the thick atmosphere of their heavy environment. The weaker ones seemed to be exhausted, trying to get the proper nourishment from the simulated sunlight that was dim compared to the inner light of plants she had seen in the spirit dimension. She thought of the radiance and music of the flowers outside Lilly's cozy spirit cottage.

It saddened her to see the ailing plants and she became concerned that she was feeling a negative emotion, until she remembered that she was in the atmosphere of Earth where sadness wasn't strange to her at all. An old familiar weakness started to come over her, but the white light around her responded instantly and intensified to give her additional strength.

"It's ok, Love," Saria said gently. "You're just susceptible to these conditions. If you weren't strong enough to overcome it, you wouldn't be here at all."

Thirty-five

Mari was seeing and hearing the lower tones of energy that came from the gray mist in the air of this place. She was about to send a barrage of questions to Claus and Saria, when she was distracted by an intense lavender light that she spotted out of the corner of her eye in the next row of plants. Her keen alertness was riveted to a vaporous apparition that was being hinted at, but not quite taking full form. She thought she recognized something in the beauty of the light that was flowing toward her, despite the grayness around it. She was about to remark on it to her companions when a tender voice stopped her.

"Hush for now, Mari," the voice said. "They can't see me. This is only for you."

The light slowly faded, leaving her curious and intrigued. She tried to hold that sensation, as it faded with the apparition, but only a void remained in its place, sparking an unusual longing in her heart, touched with grace beyond description.

Mari felt like she had been lifted to another place, and had to shake her head to bring herself back to her tour guides. She found them in a serious discussion about the work Claus was doing.

"That one snuck in on us," Claus was saying to Saria. "But we will be sending some clarity on AIDS soon. It's a little tough to get through to scientists there because of the confusing information permeating the discussions about it. A thick current of emotions surrounds the whole issue. The labs in another sector have a cure figured out and have sent it on but they haven't found it over there yet. It's another 'can't find the forest for all the trees' situation."

"I remember," Mari interjected into the conversation as if she hadn't skipped a beat, "how upset I was when the doctors told me that they wanted to test me for the AIDS virus, just to rule it out as a possibility, since I had had blood transfusions. Just the idea was horrendous to think about until the tests came back negative. I was relieved."

"That's a good example of emotional experiences there," commented Saria. "We're being careful with your transition because you had such a heavy dose of them that your aura is still cleansing. In that chart that you wrote for yourself, you were hit hard and fast with a lot of different emotions in a relatively short life."

She let that sink in for Mari and turned to Claus and asked, "So what specific conditions are you working on at this site?"

His endearing grin lightened the mood. "I think you ladies may be interested in the experiments in the next section," he said with a gallant bow toward a giant arched door, with a beautiful Tiffany-stained glass garden scene that appeared to their left. "After you," he invited as the door slowly receded into the wall.

Saria and Mari poked their heads into the charming and slightly lighter surroundings of a picturesque and expertly manicured English garden. They walked under an arch formed by vines that were heavy with bell-shaped flowers, an amazing amethyst shade with ruffled pink edges.

"Welcome to our dinglebell garden, Ladies," said Claus with delight and pride in his voice. "This has been especially fun and rewarding project for me."

At once, Mari recognized the scent as the one that had drifted from the wonderful steaming tea she had enjoyed in her grandmother's parlor. She inhaled deeply and let it fill her senses.

"I should have known that tea had come from such a beautiful flower," she said. "Is there a story behind it?"

"I'm pretty proud of that one," Claus began. "You may remember when your mother had an especially difficult time. She was under an unusual amount of stress with several deaths in the family, running her own business and frustrated with your condition. She had what is referred to on that side as a nervous breakdown. Here we call it a spiritual emergence. Her emerging spirit was caught up in a tornado of emotions that could only be controlled by the limited medications known to help at the time. Our efforts from this side were supportive but I became aware that it didn't have to be so tough on someone in that situation. Earth has a lot of questions and we're helping from here on the answers.

"I left her in the care of her spirit guide and other loved ones from this side to come here where my assistants and I worked on developing a better treatment for souls in an emergency. We worked steadily on the project and found it more complicated than we had anticipated. I had to clear my head, so I went to a favorite meditation spot in a rain forest near here.

"Sitting on my usual boulder," he continued his story, "I was enjoying the amazing exotic plants that were around me. The environment in the rare forest is a unique inspiration, and I was admiring a favorite flower I had planted there sometime previously, when a tiny vine sprouted before my eyes. I knew at once that I had been given my answer. I brought a cutting back here where we have been strengthening it genetically so it can be propagated on Earth.

"I'm pleased to report that it has been of help to many souls here. Particularly those who have come over by way of trauma or have had experiences like yours when you started to process your memories. By the way, your aura has improved since I first met you with the carriage. I hope the tea helped your healing."

"It did," answered Mari. "I felt better with just the sweet aroma of it. My question now is, how do you get it to the other side?"

"That's an important step," Claus said. He smiled and led his companions under another arch. They moved through groomed topiaries and simple stone paths with low boxwood hedges. The sensory pleasures were divine here, but still not as intense as Mari remembered from outside the greenhouses.

"I have an assistant who is considering incarnating soon," he continued. "He'll take the knowledge with him. The challenge will come when he must rise above the outside influences that he'll face so he can remember it all as he grows in the right situation. But that's part of his plan. Then he'll have to prove what he already knows as truth to those less enlightened on the other side. A good guidance and protective system will be available to him. He's working on a blueprint with the elders now."

Mari was fascinated with Claus's story and the idea of working on a plan to reincarnate.

"The mission is clear, but the obstacle has to do with how this discovery is to be used. The properties of the plant will be either used as a beneficial healing substance or misused as an illegal drug. There are huge dark obstacles in both arenas. The higher good for humankind has already been determined but human choice makes it a matter of physical timing. It's a limitation that we accept when we go to that side for the experiences to be gained. All of us who support him try to help with the construction of his chart, but personal choices are honored here, too. We should be seeing Mario soon."

The mere mention of the name sparked something very deep in Mari. "Mario," she whispered to herself, and it instantly took on musical notes with a colorful lavender to purple spectrum. Was the name a memory? If it was, then it was not from her previous life's world that she was, hopefully, leaving behind. She found that a void in her spirit was beginning to fill as the mysterious voice came to her and simply said, "It's more. Just more."

She was grateful that her grandfather and spirit guide proceeded quietly through the lovely garden, allowing her to collect her thoughts and inhale the heady herbal scents that permeated this section. Her new elevated sense of smell made her able to distinguish between familiar aromatic scents of sage and rosemary intermingled with unfamiliar ones, and the gentler essences of the flowers that grew among the herbs.

Realizing that she was beginning to levitate, Mari breathed deeply and lowered herself back to the path. As she looked down at the muffled green grasses of the tea garden, she longed for the brilliantly verdant hills that she had seen on the trip here in her sporty red car. The greens there had sparkled more than emeralds in the sunlight of a jewelry store window. Here the artificial atmosphere of this building dulled the colors and made her long for the outside. It reminded her of the pervasive loneliness that the souls on Earth feel for the pleasures of their heavenly home. As real as it felt to her now, she thought how being on Earth must be what it feels like to be lonely and away at college. With that thought, she saw a vision of a student focusing on a calendar with the date June 21, the day she died, circled in red, with the word Graduation!

Claus and Saria had reached the massive door at the other end of the garden when Mari caught up to them. She experienced a feeling of "déjà vu" as they entered a white room that had every appearance of a horticultural laboratory. Milling among the tables were light beings of all shapes and sizes whose auras gave off hints of color. They were the only distinct hues in this dull environment besides the grays and muted blues and greens of the various plants that they were working with.

"We have fun with my gardens," Claus announced, "but here is where we do some serious and highly rewarding work."

With an inquiring look, Mari shot a mental question to him. "Have I been here before?"

"I was wondering if you would pick up on that," he grinned in answer. "You have been a most valued assistant here. It's no coincidence that you were fascinated with the medical world that you were immersed in. As a kid you even talked about being a veterinarian or doctor someday. You were feeling a calling that was a goal of your work on this side. We're glad to have you back."

"Now I really like that idea," she said. "I don't have a memory of it now, but I love the idea of working with you. What did I do here?"

"You're getting ahead of us again, Dear," cautioned Saria. "For now, I can tell you that you have worked here as a student toward later goals. This will all come back to you after you've had your review. Will it suffice to know that some of your work had a lot to do with not only diabetes research, but also anorexia?"

Mari was at a loss for a response, but the tears that welled up in her big blue eyes spoke volumes. She managed to get out a mental "Thank you!" that wasn't even necessary because her heart chakra radiated with a healing that encircled and caressed Claus and Saria in a spiritual hug. She remembered the frustration of not being physically able to do any meaningful work in life. Her mom had been very insightful when she tried to convince Mari that on some level, with her experiences, she was indeed working very hard. Now she reveled in the idea that her suffering and maybe even what she saw as her bad decisions could possibly serve a useful purpose.

Thirty-six

Mari fell lightly into a vignette of foggy past memory and emotions, cataloguing various decisions, mapping myriad forks in the road, trying to discern which might be "intended" and which might be "veering off the path." Suddenly the energy of another entity appeared in their midst and surprised her back to her present reality. Mari's heart leaped, but her companions just continued their conversation about work on the spirit side.

With her awareness locked into a bubble of sorts, she took in the vision before her. She felt a transformation of spirit that she didn't quite understand as the new energy flowed to and through her, before it took form. She was hearing and feeling mysterious, angelic music that was coming from the soft lavender aura of the light of a masculine being, resonating with a tone that she found familiar. From somewhere, she remembered the incredibly intense ocean blue eyes that were smiling at her from the misty vision of only one face, with features that were gentle yet strong, full of inner knowledge and confidence. Finally, the masculine energy began to take on a recognizable physique and he was beaming at her.

He was not especially tall, but Mari had to tilt her head back slightly to take in his features. The peaceful lavender of his aura now glittered with gold and deep purple emanating from his trim etheric form. His garment reminded her of her brother's karate uniform, but this tunic was trimmed with gold and silver threads braided in a flowing leaf design embroidered on the edge. It was held at the waist with a gold and silver braided cord that was casually tied, tassels dangling loosely. Subtle auburn and golden highlights from his straight, ash-blonde hair shone in the tight plait that sat at the back of his neck.

Mari studied this amazing spirit with more than simple curiosity. She found that same void in her soul, that had revealed itself earlier, was beginning to reach out to the essence of this spirit that stood before her when the words, "Patience, my friend," reverberated within her. He hadn't moved his lips, but she knew that the familiar distant voice had come from him.

"And I'm especially proud of the results she's had with the infant souls who need special care when they return," Saria was explaining to Claus. "That first incarnation that she tried with Suzi gave her the experience of their struggles. Now she can make our jobs easier by using that knowledge. And your musical talents," Saria added, stopping mid-sentence as she turned to Mari, who was staring at a spot next to her.

Mari blinked and a man appeared in that place. He was the same man, but without the intensity of the one who had stood there the instant before. He was now wearing a simple white lab coat over blue jeans and he was smiling at Mari, a flash of lavender sparkle reaching to her from behind his blue eyes.

"Mario!" exclaimed Saria. "I was hoping we would see you here. Care to add anything to our visitors' tour?"

There was that name again. Mari found an internal connection to the sound of it.

"I'd be honored," he replied, his deeply sonorous voice vibrating with an oboe-like quality. "I've been waiting for this opportunity to welcome you back, Mari," he said through a tender inviting smile. "I hope you remember all of this soon. We could use your help," he added, his gaze casual but still intent on her. She was perfectly at ease with this one who seemed to know her very well.

"But I really can't add much," he went on, crossing his arms across his chest as he spoke to all three of them. "The rest of the operation is typical of an Earth lab. The main goal here, is that we're trying to get plants that have been perfected here to live in Earth's atmosphere.

"In this section," Mario continued, as he glided his entourage to a long table full of lush plants, "we're working with a plant that was developed here that has large amounts of a special protein that can help some of the complicated diseases that are affecting those on Earth now and some that we have seen coming up. To illustrate how we work for the higher good, there are souls there who are now working to save the rainforests, as well as the planet in general. Those same rain forests, with their diverse vegetation, are a prime spot for the souls on this side to introduce these new developments to Earth. They're sort of like horticultural angels who are transitional beings who work on both sides. Those souls are running out of areas to work these developments into the varied and limited environments there."

"You have a question?" Mario addressed Mari's quizzical look.

A little tongue tied, Mari shyly asked, "As a matter of fact, how does science handle angels taking strange plants to Earth?"

"Ah, a good question," Mario began. "In another area here, in the world of spirit, is a place called the Hall of Earthly Science. There, entities are studying where Earth sciences are now in their evolution. They're also working on new science methods of working with those earth sciences. Their goal is to relay information to those on Earth. Some choose to incarnate and take the information with them.

"Work with children on that side is so important. They're finding many with special abilities that some refer to as Indigo Children. The Earth needs them to be open to their creativity so they can grow up to overcome the lower existence there. They need to work to share the knowledge and skills that they carried into that life.

"Well," Mario continued, turning to Claus, "this is a lot for Mari to take in right now, but that should suffice as an introduction to how we operate here."

"You're probably right," responded Claus, "and we should escort Mari out of here for now. She'll be ready to dive back in with all her new insights soon enough."

"Mari," said Mario, reaching for her responsive hand, "I couldn't be more pleased to see you again, but your grandfather is right. We'll meet again." He added, "We always do," in a mental whisper, then said out loud, "In fact, I am going to a concert soon. Is that something that you might enjoy?"

She found her voice again as she replied without hesitation, "That sounds wonderful. I'd love it."

"Great," Mario said. "I'll call for you when the time comes. Until then, I'll leave you to your capable guides and get back to work."

"Speaking of guides, Saria," he said to Mari's spirit guide, "It's been a pleasure to see you again. But you've been unusually quiet," he teased. "Did that white cat outside get your tongue?"

"No," answered the robed lady of the group with a sassy tilt to her head. "I'm learning to be a good guide and that means knowing when to shut up and learn more yourself."

With an easy laugh, Mario released Mari's hand, gave a slight bow and returned to light form as he joined the entities who were busy at the lab tables.

The encounter left Mari with a feeling of a strong connection to this place that gave her hope and a new confidence. Saria and Claus were smiling at her with what she observed as knowing grins.

Their surroundings changed at once and they were outside the greenhouse in the lighter existence of the welcoming spirit world. The white bubble that insulated Mari in the artificial atmosphere of the massive building was no longer necessary or visible, but she could still feel the tingling presence around her.

"Well," Claus said, breaking the momentary silence, "that was a sample of what some of us do here, and now you have an idea of your connection with me. And don't get me wrong. I'd love to just bring you back now, but patience is needed here, also."

Thirty-seven

Seatac airport was always a busy hub. So many people, so many journeys; a great place for people watching.

Suzi arrived just as Dee's plane was taxiing to the gate. She was excited to see her cousin. Times with Dee could prove interesting to say the least. Her presence could feel electric.

Something told Suzi to start this visit off right. When Dee came through the door she stopped and looked around for Suzi's familiar face. She was alarmed that she didn't recognize anyone. Suddenly, from behind her, she heard "Boo." She jumped and let out a yelp, and turned to see Suzi with a big grin and a mischievous twinkle in her eyes.

"Hey, Cuz," Suzi said with a wink.

"You got me, you rascal," said Dee through a fit of laughter.

After a heartfelt embrace, they looked around and saw people staring at them, wondering what the commotion was about. "Let's get out of here," said Suzi, as she grabbed Dee's carry-on.

Dee loved the Northwest's majestic mountains, saltwater views, and dense evergreen forests. She was relaxed on the ride to Suzi's new house on Hood Canal, and felt at home.

"So how are things in the psychic world?" asked Suzi.

"Always a part of me," Dee answered. "On this trip, I feel like I've brought an entire entourage with me. I can feel your mom, Gramma, Aunt Sadie, Mari and others tagging along. It never ceases to amaze me."

Suzi took Deirdre to her room and let her get settled in. It was a beautiful summer day, so they decided to sit on the deck and enjoy the view of Hood Canal and the Olympic mountains. Dee walked up to the open sliding door and began waving her arms about.

"What are you doing?" asked Suzi. "Are you trying to chase out the ghosts? That doesn't look like a very graceful way to do it."

"No, Silly," Dee replied. "I was trying to get out and I thought there was a screen door." After a good laugh, they got comfortable in lounge chairs.

"I've got one for you," said Suzi. "The other day I was lounging out here enjoying the sun and getting into spirit and meditating on the beauty of these mountains and the water. I remembered hearing that the beauty that we enjoy on Earth is one hundred times more beautiful on the Other Side.

"It was a perfectly still day. Warm and no breeze at all. I closed my eyes and tried to imagine a view on the Other Side, then felt an amazing swoosh pass over me as if it were from huge wings. When I opened my eyes, nothing was there, and the air was still perfectly still and there were no eagles or hawks anywhere. I felt like I had been visited by someone or something in spirit that appreciated my recognition of that world."

"That's certainly an experience to treasure," said Dee. "Sounds like you may have touched on a higher dimension."

"That could be," Suzi replied. "I'm sure I'll remember it."

"I've had situations that felt similar," said Dee. "When I was a child, I was in church, I was ignoring the priest, as usual, but I was suddenly overcome by an overpowering anointing of unconditional love. It was so powerful and awesome. Something like that stays with you for a lifetime.

"You should include your experience in your writing," offered Dee.

"Any progress on that front?"

"I have to say, no," answered Suzi. "At least nothing significant. It doesn't flow the way I'd like it to. I still play with different approaches, but so far nothing works. I guess I'm blocked."

Deirdre got quiet, then commented, "It may not be just you that is blocked. I'm given an image of Mari standing in a doorway. She is really beautiful and glowing with bright light all around her. But you are standing in front of her blocking her way. She wants to know why you are blocking her?"

"Oh, wow!" exclaimed Suzi. "That's certainly an image that makes a statement. I don't know. Maybe lack of confidence, ego, not tuning in enough, lack of trust, or just timing. I know I still have a fear of revisiting the pain of past struggles. I even start to panic when I remember the sights, sounds and smells of hospital stays. My heart aches when I visualize the many times Mari was on the verge of dying. A part of me just can't go back there. It's too hard and life seems to get in the way and offers too many distractions."

"I know you will get past all of this," said Dee. "I'm getting strong feelings that you are contracted to do it. You just need to get yourself out of the way and let Mari help you."

"Yeah, I know," said Suzi. "You're probably right, and I should pay attention. After all, I've heard you are psychic."

Thirty-eight

Mari was about to butt in with frustration when she heard the tooting of a horn behind her. She turned and was amused to see a pink jeep sporting a striped canopy with a dangly pink fringe. It was headed toward them on a road that materialized before their eyes. The driver, whom she knew instinctively was a much younger version of Lilly Mae, was leaning out of her windowless door, waving enthusiastically.

Mari laughed in delight at the sight and waved back along with her tour guides. With fringe swaying, the jeep slowed to a stop next to them and Lilly asked Mari excitedly, "How was it?"

Lilly had the same unmistakable, vibrant pink aura of grandmotherly love and her smile was as bright, or even brighter, than Mari remembered. Her eyes sparkled with the same spirit that she had known for the twenty-five years they had shared Earth-side.

"Never mind, I can see in your face that it was enjoyable and even enlightening," Lilly answered her own question. "Now if you're quite ready to move on, we have a party to attend. How about a ride in the peppermint mobile?"

"I'd love it and with everything so wonderful here," said Mari, "I wouldn't miss a party for anything."

"Run along with Lilly," said Claus as a cheerful dog with brown and black spots materialized at his feet. He bent down to give the dog a rousing pet. "I'll see you later. Pal, here, and I need to play for a while." He sent Mari off with a warm hug.

"I'll tag along, too, said Saria, "if you don't mind."

"Great!" Lilly said eagerly. "Hop aboard!"

The two women climbed into the fun and silly vehicle and transported themselves from the lushness of Claus's garden world returning, to Lilly's cozy cottage living room. Mari was still getting accustomed to traveling by teleporting and it left her a bit woozy.

"Oops," said Lilly. "Guess that was a little quick for you. Sit for a moment. You'll be fine."

"Yes," replied Mari as she lowered herself onto the sofa. "That was just a tad sudden, but I'm beginning to get used to teleporting. I have to say, it's a convenient way to go, but I do miss the ride and seeing the sights."

"You'll have lots of opportunities to enjoy the scenery, Hon," Saria expressed with limited concern. "You can travel to anywhere your heart desires. It's only limited by your imagination. But for now, your presence is desired here by a lot of souls who have been waiting patiently to greet you. This is your welcome home party."

Though shy that this event was in her honor, Mari was anxious to meet the other souls who would be coming. "Do I need to get ready for this party?" she asked.

"There is no need to," answered Lilly, "unless you wish to change your look."

"That might be fun," Mari said as she stood and held her chin, thinking about the possibilities. She decided on a classic Chanel look for herself with a tailored suit in a velvety beige with tan cording over an ivory silk blouse. A full gilded mirror appeared before her. She never ceased to be amazed at the vision of herself. She was beautiful and sophisticated and realized that she was beginning to look more mature. She had died at twenty-five, and had been curious how she would appear here if everyone had a countenance of less than thirty Earth years.

Thinking to herself, she marveled, "So this is what the mature Mari was meant to look like."

Her face was a bit fuller, with a peaceful softness, but the vivid sea-blue eyes were the same. She had a healthy color to her cheeks instead of her past pale complexion. The most startling change was her figure. Instead of straight boyishness with a slumped, old-lady posture, she now had the roundness of a womanly figure and a confident pose. She loved the open high-heeled tan shoes that hugged her feet, their thin feminine straps around her shapely ankles. Mari watched as she transformed her hair into a lovely chignon with wispy tendrils surrounding her face. She did a few turns to enjoy the vision in the mirror. The look was elegant, and she was pleased.

"Well," she announced to the others, "I guess I'm ready," even though she had no idea what to expect. Just then the mirror, which was much like the one she had stepped through in her old bedroom, ages ago, vanished from the room.

She turned and smiled when she saw the other two had done the girly thing as well and had also changed for the party. Lilly was now her youthful self, wearing an enchanting knee-length powder pink dress with a huge cabbage rose sewn on her shoulder. Saria was dressed in a long, dramatic indigo skirt with a snow-white Victorian lace blouse that made her smooth olive skin glow with sublime warmth.

"We feminine spirits love a chance to dress up here, too," said Saria when she saw the look on Mari's face. "And we do love any excuse for a party."

There was a knock and a slight hesitation before a man and woman appeared through the door like they were stepping from a portrait. Mari could not have been more pleased to see her paternal grandparents, Bruce and Bertha. They looked wonderful in their younger personage, and she recognized them instantly. In a flash, she was across the room and totally absorbed in what her mom and dad would have called a "Super Hug" with all three of them embracing at once. The warm greeting took her to a brief memory of her youth.

In the memory, Mari was about three years old, and she was with her parents. They were on a beach outing, feeding the ducks at a local lake. Suzi had saved old bread and baked goods specifically for their duck friends. It was a cool Northwest autumn day, but the weather didn't concern them. They were having a great time.

Mari was always cautious when first approaching the ducks, but their enthusiasm for their treats soon had her giggling until all the bread was gone. Then Mari played on the swings and other playground equipment.

When it was time to leave the beach retreat, Mitch bent down and Mari ran into his waiting arms to be lifted, swung around, and held in a loving hug. On this occasion, Suzi joined the enchanting embrace. She walked up to them and threw her arms around them both and declared it a "Super Hug."

After that incident, they would occasionally call out in moments of glee, "Super Hug!" and they would all embrace in their own special way.

Oh, how she sincerely missed those beautiful physical hugs. Or was it that she longed for time with her loved ones who were still over there. It gave her all the more reason to hope for a successful transition here so she could possibly get on with visiting in spirit.

"Wow!" was all Mari could say as the memory faded. The grandparent "super" hug relaxed and they stood apart to look at each other. "You guys look great! And it's wonderful to see you again. I've missed you so much."

"Wow to you, too," they said in unison enjoying the vision of their granddaughter's natural appearance.

"We're so excited to see you," said Bertha with a bright smile. "We've been preoccupied with some other of your relatives either coming to this side or needing help on the other side. But we knew that you were in good hands here."

Mari remembered that this grandfather had been one of eleven children, and that Bertha had been one of sixteen. With that many siblings of advanced ages on Earth, she could understand how busy they were. Many had crossed over recently and she could imagine them being busy helping on the sidelines on Earth with the complicated lives she remembered some of her cousins had. She was happy that these grandparents were there for those loved ones, and also thrilled that they could be with her now.

A quick flash of memory came to Mari. The last time she saw her gramma, Bertha; she was deep into the throws of Alzheimer's disease. Bertha smiled at Mari as she picked up on her thoughts.

"That's all behind me now," she reassured Mari. "My mind is sound and my memory intact. In fact, my experience has made me a good case study for those working on that problem from over here. They're starting to coordinate with the studies in the physical world. I believe you learned a little about that process on Claus's greenhouse tour. We've kept up on your travels since you've been here."

The three of them spent a little time catching up on family and recent events before more spirits joined those assembled. Many of them Mari recognized immediately; others she had to think about for a minute. As she greeted her guests, she watched the room magically expand to accommodate the many friends and relatives who were now residing in the spirit world.

The enlarged room made space for a profusion of flowers, including white roses, that suddenly materialized. Streamers decorated the room, along with tables of exotic, wonderful looking food and a dazzling array of sparkling glasses full of beverages. The buffet was an artful feast of tasty treats sculpted into animals, flowers and architectural marvels. What seemed to be intricate ice carvings were designed from pure crystal, gracing the center of each table. The party guests' ethereal bodies may not need refreshment, but they certainly knew how to enjoy the memories of their senses. More important, the room was filled with an atmosphere of love circling among every individual. Mari was blessed as she mingled with everyone present.

Her great-grandmother Lenora floated into view. Mari had met her when she was just a child and had corresponded with her over the years until Lenora passed over while Mari was still quite young. She had missed her letters but now she found out that she had been with Mari to help and guide her.

"Baby Doll," said Lenora, her love mixed with a good dose of exasperation, "you were one tough cookie. I'm glad to meet up with you here. I wish souls over there knew how hard it is to work with you all there. Why, I remember trying to get your attention, but you would just sink your stubborn nose deeper into a book, bless your heart. Luckily God gave those of us in your circle an extra helping of patience."

Mari gave her great-grandmother a big hug and said, "Well, thank you for trying."

More spirits arrived that Mari didn't distinguish right away until Saria whispered their names and relationships in her ear. However, she was immediately comfortable with each one of them and felt a familiarity with them all. She hadn't realized until now how badly she had missed being her social self instead of being locked into medical concerns. Mari needed this and she was having a ball.

She was thrilled to meet her great-great aunt Sarah Catherine, nicknamed Sadie. Mari's mom, Suzi, and grandma Lilly had always spoken so fondly of Aunt Sadie. Mari could see what they meant about Sadie's merry demeanor when she walked in wearing a big sunny smile, well-worn overalls and a funny, floppy straw hat. It was so cute of her to show up with exactly the look Mari recalled from a favorite photo of her.

Mari remembered when her mother was pregnant with Mari's first sibling. She wanted to name the child after Aunt Sadie, but as it turned out, Sarah Catherine wasn't such a good idea for a boy, so she chose the name George.

Aunt Sadie was elfishly charming, and Mari promised to spend some time with her soon. She had been in one of Mari's spiritual entourages, her soul circle. Being the comic in the group, Sadie would step in whenever Mari needed to be nudged to enjoy a little levity and let her wit raise her above the densities of that life.

She was also pleased to even meet, for the first time, her great- great grandmother Ida Mae, who had originally owned the stunning garnet brooch that had been passed down through several generations. Lilly had given it to Suzi as the last Earthly Christmas present to her daughter. Suzi treasured it as a symbol of the love of those who came before her. It made them a single collective of evolutionary souls who would always be connected.

Mari had to suppress a snicker when she met her grandpa Leonard. She remembered giggle fits with Deirdre when Dee would share stories about how he could clear a whole room of people with his flatulence.

Saria nudged Mari and assured her that he was relieved of that problem now then gently took Mari by the arm and escorted her through a door when they met a party of judicial, but friendly, looking beings. Three were men with handsome beards, each wearing matching brilliant white togas held at their shoulders with gleaming gold clasps. The other three were women with pure white hair, glowing complexions and welcoming smiles. With courtly respect and clear affection, Saria introduced Mari to the delegation of Elders who had assisted her in her choice and her plan to incarnate into her recent life. They all greeted her with warm smiles and reassuring handshakes that transmitted a love that made her feel cherished and at ease.

In a quick flash of memory, Mari caught a glimpse of herself sitting comfortably in a living room setting with these gentle beings, discussing her proposed life on earth. She didn't see any details, but she could see now how they fit into her story of the life that she had been about to experience.

As the Elders merged with the rest of those assembled, Mari felt a tap on her shoulder and turned to see a lovely woman with long, fawn brown hair and engaging hazel eyes. Mari felt that she should know her, but she was a bit perplexed.

"Well, hello Kiddo," she greeted Mari with a big smile. "I don't expect you to recognize me right now, but you knew me in that last life as Jane. I was your neighbor when you were about seven years old, but we are also friends here."

Thirty-nine

"Oh my!" Mari gasped as she remembered, in a flash of an instant, living in a Seattle suburb with her family. She was just seven, and for the first time, she had her own bedroom. It made her feel so grown up.

There were quite a few childhood memories from that period in her life. She recalled the time her dad, Mitch, had his tonsils out at Christmas, and the family learned how nice it was to have a quiet, relaxed holiday at home together, instead of traveling around to all the extended family events.

Her siblings, George and Natalie, enjoyed playing with their hot wheels in the cul-de-sac they lived in, and this place was also where Mari received her first bicycle. She remembered the family next door with four boys who were a real handful, remembering one summer day when their parents were gone and the oldest boy stood on the roof pouring gasoline into the rain gutter. Mitch caught them just before the younger ones struck a lighter at the bottom.

Two other events stood out in her mind about that summer. One was when her little sister, Natalie, who had just started to talk, saw a kitten run over by a car. It traumatized Natalie so badly that she stuttered severely for a month afterward. The kitten belonged to two girls who lived on the next street. That memory brought Mari to recall the second event.

Tears began to well up for Mari as she recalled one of the more public, and also very personal, tragic events of her young life.

In this quiet little neighborhood, Mari's family lived next door to two little girls, Jane and Cory. Mari and her siblings played with them a lot. They were terrific fun, and they had a great swing set. Mari and Jane were about the same age, and they were easy company for each other in the chaos of spontaneous games. Never bored, they spent countless hours in summer revelry.

One weekend Jane and Cory were excited because their family was planning a trip with their cousins in a new camper that belonged to their aunt and uncle. The four parents were in the house preparing for the trip while the cousins explored the new trailer.

Jane's cousin Mark found his father's rifle and intending it as a joke, pointed it at Jane. He hit the trigger. The safety was off. The gun was loaded.

Mari, as well as the entire neighborhood were in total shock. A cloud of the darkness of grief hovered over that house. The pain of tragic loss flowed through the family and out to all those who loved Jane. The parents became consumed by unfounded guilt and anger that they had allowed such a tragedy to happen. Finally, they could no longer stay in that house, and they moved from the neighborhood. Their lives had to go on without their beautiful Jane.

Mari's parents thought that, though still so young, she had handled news of Jane's sudden death quite well. She was understandably upset, but she internalized a lot of what she was feeling after her first experience with the finality of physical death. She was so young herself, and she had really loved her friend Jane, and she had trouble imagining life without her dear friend.

With this memory, Mari could recall many times through her life when questions about gun control legislation or details of an accidental shooting would arise in conversations or in the news. Something would put a terrible pull on her heart, but as soon as that feeling hit her, she thought she could sense a loving hand on her shoulder that would calm her.

Forty

"Welcome back," said Jane, as she and Mari enjoyed a heartfelt embrace.

"It's so great to see you!" exclaimed Mari. "You are so grown up, I can't believe that I actually recognize you, but I do."

Jane laughed and replied, "I know what you mean. It's pretty amazing when we first return. I was just a kid, and all these people were greeting me that I shouldn't have known, but I did. It was such a relief to get through the transition and have all the pieces fall into place so my life here could get back to this normal."

"So, there is such a thing as normal here?" Mari thought that the word seemed contradictory.

"Oh yeah," answered Jane. "But it's certainly never dull or mundane. I find life here as exciting or as peaceful as I need it to be. And what a relief it is to be rid of the time issues. For your friends like me, it's like you never left. We felt your absence and missed you, but that period goes quickly for us. And we were with you when you needed us."

"I know that now. Thank you." Mari recognized Jane as a cherished friend and kindred spirit. It felt great since she hadn't cultivated any real peer friendships in her last years. "I hope we'll get a chance to catch up soon. I love talking to you."

Jane took a quick glance around the room. "There's no real reason we can't slip out for a bit of girl talk now," she said with a conspiratorial raise of her eyebrow. "Everyone seems to be having a great time. They won't miss us."

"Sounds good to me," her co-conspirator replied.

They found themselves sharing a white carved marble bench in Lilly's fragrant, light filled rose garden. Mari stared at the little cottage that they had just left. Right now, it appeared to be the same size she remembered when she first saw it from the carriage. Having watched the room grow as everyone arrived at the party, she was surprised that the exterior of the house stayed the same. Surely spatial mechanics here were as irrelevant as the effects of time. She made a mental note to ask someone about it. For now, she was more interested in Jane and hoped that she could contribute something to her quest for personal answers.

"So, tell me more about us," she prompted Jane.

"First a toast," said Jane. A sparkling stemmed glass of bubbly champagne appeared in each of their hands. "To special friends who took on Earth and rose above it."

They touched their glasses, which responded with a cheerful ping. Mari remembered tasting champagne in her physical world, and she had to say that she liked the fanciful idea of it more than the taste. But as this aromatic bubbly wine rolled over her tongue, she was pleasantly surprised by the many layers of its marvelous essence. It was fruity and tart, but the effervescence teased her palate with the slightest hint of the sweetness of the grape.

Jane was amused as her friend's eyes opened wide, then rolled back in pleasure. "Yes, it is divine here, isn't it," she commented.

"Well," Mari answered, "there are no words to express the taste. I've never tasted anything so superb."

"And the best part is," said Jane, "there's no alcohol to be concerned about. There is absolutely no use for it here. Besides, these bodies wouldn't absorb it anyway. But it's a wonderful way to celebrate this occasion. If you think that was a treat," she held out her hand and a small gilt plate appeared with a beautiful mound of molded dark mahogany brown chocolate. "Try this!"

Mari hesitated, remembering the torture of being in the presence of something so decadent that was taboo for her diabetes. Tears came to her eyes when she remembered all of that was behind her now.

Even the physical pain associated with anorexia was a distant memory, but she remembered the awful guilt and fear that she experienced when she would allow herself to enjoy something so lovely and tasty.

"Oh, Honey," sympathized Jane, "it's ok now. Use it as an opportunity to release those old fears. Our main concern here is spiritual health. This is called a Mayan truffle." She held it up and admired the confection. "I thought you might enjoy it because it is something your mother has recently discovered at a shop near her home on the other side. She loves them. In fact," she said as another truffle appeared beside the first one, "I'm going to have one also. Join me my friend." She offered the dainty plate to Mari.

"It really is time to let go," Mari breathed a big sigh of release as she shook off her concerns and took the delectable looking treat. She lifted it to her mouth and inhaled a heady aroma of chocolate. Biting through the firm outer layer, her teeth slipped through the soft interior of the scrumptious treat.

"Mmmmm," she hummed as the richness grew in her mouth melting into a smooth burst of flavor that was more than she had ever experienced with chocolate.

With an audible deeply sonorous moan, she exclaimed, "Oh woooow! I always knew mom had good taste," and giggled as she added, "literally! These are sensational!"

"Oh yeah," Jane agreed, "and with the second bite you begin to feel the chili pepper."

So that was the mystery ingredient. Mari took another bite and allowed herself to slowly enjoy it until a sweet warmth began to tingle in the back of her mouth and on her tongue. If this was only a memory of her senses, as she had been told, then it was a very intense memory. That idea prompted her to refer to her recent Earth-side life. She thought of the things that were associated with those memories.

Forty-one

She pondered the idea of the five senses. Touch, taste, smell, sight and sound. Each one took Mari into specific memories, as well as the resonance of her emotional responses at those times.

When Mari thought of touch, she remembered when her brother had been born. She was three years old and felt the sensation of the amazing softness of a newborn's face.

When she was five, she experienced her first kitten snuggling into her warm embrace. And she would never forget the physical sensation of the caressing warmth of the sun as it broke through the clouds on a chilly Northwest day. During her hospital stays, that delicious solar warmth was especially welcome on the roof garden, when she had the desperate need to feel that touch of God.

For the sensation of taste, Mari remembered the earthy freshness of a sip of cold water from Denny Creek, high in the Cascade Mountains. The sweetness of crunching into a fresh picked apple from the Yakima Valley was a good memory, too. She decided that her favorites were the natural ones, but now the Mayan truffles were added to her list. Even though she was from espresso-stand-on-every-corner Seattle, she never developed a taste for coffee.

The scent of a summer evening, especially when driving past a freshly cut field of hay, or after a refreshing summer rain, always brought to her memory of the freedom of summer vacation. The pungent scents of fall brought back the excitement of returning to school, friends and the flutter of falling orange, red and golden leaves.

Her seeing senses were ignited with the memory of a sunset over Hood Canal that set the water on fire with a dazzling display of pink and orange against the purple silhouette of the Olympic Mountains. Then again, sunrise through the Cascade Mountains washing over the Snoqualmie Valley from Winery Hill was truly a glimpse of the pleasures and wonders of Heaven.

The memory of the delightful trill of a child's laughter and the purr of her kitten snuggling into her ear helped Mari recall her special gift of blended sensations seeing her own intimate prism of color in concert with music she heard. She remembered listening to classical music, especially Mozart, with her mother. For Mari it was like being in the heart of a kaleidoscope, each symphonic crescendo vibrating her soul with bursts of color and light. This is when she experienced a hint of the glories that must exist on the Other Side.

She didn't specifically remember much that she could say was of the sixth sense, besides the usual prediction of when a phone was going to ring or feeling a comforting presence that she couldn't see. A few days before she died, however, a knowing calm and peace descended upon her that even the doctors and nurses noticed. Blessed with a sense of completion, she experienced the sixth sense penetrating the veil between worlds. She was infused with the knowing that God uses all our senses as celestial communication to his beloved children to remind us of the delights of our true home.

That last night on Earth after Suzi had hurriedly seen to her daughter's needs for the night, Mari saw the faint vision of an angel halting Suzi in the doorway. Suzi stopped and turned to tell her daughter, "Sweet dreams. I love you."

"I love you too, Mom," were Mari's last, physical interaction with Suzi. The tender, sweet words would resonate lovingly in Suzi's mind and provide her with comforting peace for many years to come.

Forty-two

Mari meditated for a moment on the amazing power of physical senses. She thought that these positive sensory experiences could be "God moments" that bring the "peace that passes understanding" when they touch emotions, possibly because God created us to be an emotional experience. Our senses can help us to feel Gods presence beyond the veil that exists between worlds, no matter which side of it we are on.

Her meditation returned her to her grandmother's beautiful garden, the bench where she sat with Jane and the ambient sounds of the party. In that moment Mari could hear people laughing, glasses clinking, and a buzz of conversations. Lively music played in the background of this magical world with its grand vistas and sensory experiences.

"We're a good team," Jane informed Mari, referring to their relationship on the spiritual side of existence. "I'm looking forward to having you back when you're settled in."

"I'm sorry," Mari said, puzzled at the comment. "I'm still a little vague about some of the things I did here before I left. Please fill in those blanks for me."

"Oh sure," she replied. "I should have known you are still remembering. It seems like you just left. Anyway, besides your work with your grandfather, you and I work with children who are transitioning here. We both had traumatic experiences in our youth, you with your miscarriage then with all your medical problems, and me with the trauma of the shooting. Everyone brings valuable experience to the team that works in that sector. And it is rewarding to be of service there. I have really grown from the experience, and it's helped with my own healing. To watch those confused little souls cross the Rainbow Bridge and eventually return to being the mature souls that they truly are, keeps me on a spiritual high. It also prevents me from going back there any time soon."

"I'm with you there," said Mari. "I have to say right now I'm grateful for the experience, if that's what it took to get me here now, but I can't imagine going back any time soon. I actually start to feel physical pain at just the thought of going back."

"Yes, I know what you mean," Jane sympathized. "We could all see from this side how hard you were fighting that existence. You really seemed to feel trapped in a physical body."

"That's it!" Mari replied emphatically. "You've hit the nail on the head. That's exactly what I was feeling much of the time. And I really was fighting it. But at the same time, I held onto the notion that it was all for some good reason. That's what kept me going."

"All of us who go there feel that to some degree," said Jane, "but you did live it especially powerfully. I'm glad you're through all that now. It's a lot easier to get through to you here. What are you feeling now?"

"A real and true freedom and acceptance," answered Mari. "Like this is what I was longing for the whole time I was there. And now I have some pent-up energy, and I want to put what I learned to good use. Claus said that I work in his labs here, which sounds great, but what you are suggesting sounds wonderful also. I must be a busy girl."

"We all have the opportunity to be just as busy as we want and need to be, and "work" is as much a pleasure as recreation is," said Jane. "It's a comfortable balance, with no time issues, and stress is nonexistent. We are all free to do meaningful work. You're good with the kids. I always enjoyed helping you with the theatrical events that you organized. They provided the children with opportunities to role play the situations from which they were coming. You could take the simplest fairy tale and inject into it some elements of a psychodrama, but always with comedic twists. The kids loved it, and they were guided toward taking a lighter view of their circumstances."

Mari smiled to herself as she connected the relationship of her favorite activities as a physical being to her apparent work on this side. It warmed her heart that the simplest experiences from Earth could be so significant here, and it just made so much sense. She and Jane continued to have a splendid conversation, imparting a lot of information to Mari, and including plenty of girl talk that had them giggling with abandon.

Mari had made what she thought were friendships in life, but they were on a much different level than what she was responding to now. Those relationships usually turned out to be disappointing. Her medical and phycological conditions became too much for them to deal with. She usually ended up sad and alone.

This new experience, with Jane, was as simple as girlfriend time could get, and yet it was also a complex blending of kindred souls. She could guess that she and Jane had known each other through many previous lives.

This was all being contemplated in a lull in the conversation, as the two ladies finished their chocolates, and Mari gazed at the bubbles rising in her gracefully fluted glass.

Jane watched as her friend's essence began to dull a little with the questions forming in her mind. She decided to wait and see what was troubling Mari.

Finally, still staring intently at her glass, Mari expressed her thoughts. "Jane," she began hesitantly, "Why did we do it? Why did we go there and do what we did? I know there were people there with even tougher lives than ours but we both must have made some heavy choices about our own lessons. It can be so dark and negative there. The suffering is so prevalent and difficult to rise above."

"I can't speak for you as an individual," said Jane. "You still have much to explore from various sources. That is necessary because there are so many dimensions to our decision. There is meaning to every contact that we make in the physical world. Putting together a plan for life on Earth is a complex process even for here. We do not just think one day, 'Oh, I think I will go to Earth for a while.' Many other souls participate in our plan, and their purpose must coordinate with ours to attain higher good in that atmosphere.

"To narrow it down to our connection there, you and I were shown that with the Earth evolving like it is, the children that we were working with were coming back here with some heavy issues. We decided that the most immediate way for us to learn what we needed to help them was through firsthand experience. So, we each incorporated examples of these scenarios, and our connection to each other, into our plans.

"For example, you were working with Claus on plans to confront medical issues for your work with him. My time there was shorter, but I incarnated specifically to drive home issues of violence, safety, and gun controls. My reasons also crossed over with me to my existence here and included helping those who I left behind who were emotionally upset by my sudden death. I spent a lot of time comforting my family and friends, including you."

"Ok," Mari nodded in understanding. "That helps put it in perspective. It's almost overwhelming to think of all the souls on Earth that we encounter as part of our plan, but it does explain a lot. I remember sitting in the waiting room of the clinic on a difficult day, and how much it meant to me when I got a warm smile and words of encouragement from a stranger whose condition seemed worse than mine. That was powerful."

Jane nodded with appreciation of what Mari was saying. "That is so true. We are all souls on a mission there, and part of our job is to be support for each other. A simple gesture of understanding like that is part of it. Sometimes all we need is an expression of kindness from another soul to help us rise above whatever is attempting to drag us down. And there are certainly many downward tugs on us there."

Mari was still sensitive to even the suggestion of the lower energies of Earth, so she sat quietly for a moment to absorb the ideas Jane was offering. She remembered the grayness of the air in Claus's Earthly greenhouse atmosphere, but that also reminded her of another aspect of that tour.

Forty-three

Mari ventured shyly into a thought that was beginning to surface in her mind. "I met someone in Claus's lab who seemed interesting. He was introduced to me as Mario."

"Oh reeeealy," Jane teased with a sideward glance and a twinkle in her eye. "That was rather sudden. How did that go?"

"I'm not sure," answered Mari. "It was rather brief, but it had an impact on me. I'm intrigued and I know there is, at the very least, a connection there. He was a bit mysterious, and he seemed to know me quite well. So, you seem to know him. What can you tell me?"

"Well," she leaned in closely for serious girl talk, "I won't say much, but usually that kind of connection isn't made until later in transition. With the twinkle I see in your eye, that little sneak must have got to you on some level besides a simple introduction. Well, you know him, all right. Mario is great. We all have a lot of fun together."

"Did I hear my name?" came a familiar voice from a brilliant lavender ball of light that appeared before them.

"You know you did," chided Jane as she turned toward the vision of Mario emerging from the glow. "You may as well join us."

He settled himself on a bench that appeared opposite the two women. He and Mari shared shy smiles. "Thank you," he said. "I thought I'd better warn you. The two of you are beginning to be missed inside. They are moving the party out here."

As he said it, the double French doors to the garden burst open and the crowd emerged with a lively band in tow. Their music had a colorful Caribbean rhythm that had many of the festive group dancing cheerfully into the garden, stirring up the sweet and spicy fragrances of the many beautiful flowers.

"Thanks for the warning," said Mari still smiling at Mario. "This is starting to look like quite a party."

The music was intoxicating. Mari was ready to celebrate with these wonderful souls who had come to welcome her home. She had a brief memory of the touching memorial party that she left behind at her Earthly mountain home. It had been sweetly quiet and elegant, and appropriate for the healing of the loved ones she planned to revisit. But for now, she let go of all her cares, concerns, and questions for a while and let the music rise within her.

Mario stood and took Mari's hand, asking her to dance. A loving spiritual current ran between them as she rose from the bench. It felt so natural to be spontaneous with him, and they moved with cheerful freedom to the artistry of the musicians. One dance followed another, with the only interruptions being Mari's chances to dance with others, including her grandfathers and the Elders. She and Mario even joined a Conga line through the garden that seemed endless.

It did her so much good to feel the lightness and agility of her new body, experiencing bright, festive colors with the energetic music that filled the air. It created a variegated cloud of crimson, sun yellow, poppy orange, and vivid blues and purples that undulated with the Caribbean rhythm, emitting colorful beams that reflected in the auras of everyone assembled. They were all having a grand and colorful time.

Mari and Mario danced and laughed, thoroughly enjoying the party and each other. She had never known this type of attraction in physical life, but she knew that it was possible. She had watched others' relationships from a distance. On Earth she had only experienced a hopeless longing for the kind of closeness that she saw in the rare joining of soul mates. It had broken her heart, that her health kept her from meeting new people with whom she could possibly enjoy such special intimacy. She couldn't put this exactly into words, but the sensation of attraction now was wonderful and even familiar.

Finally, the music began to fade, and her friends and family started milling about, visiting again. Mario escorted Mari through the throng, stopping often to visit. The going was slow, and he was patient as she greeted those who wanted to welcome her and congratulate her on a successful journey from physical life. She still didn't recognize all that she accomplished, and felt chagrined by all the adoration. There were still so many more questions. Would she even be allowed to stay in this amazing existence?

Forty-four

As Mari made her way through the room, she took in the entire congregation of souls and was overcome with a feeling of oneness with everyone present. She could sense each soul's many attributes, and at the same time she felt the importance of each contribution toward the whole of a limitless collective purpose. It was so beautiful, and she was pleased to know that she, too, played an integral part. She wished for those still on Earth the ability to recognize other souls and know everyone is an evolving spirit, given a significant quest with their own set of complications, and yet they are all sharing in the experience. If they only knew the power of that kind of understanding, and the fact that even their thoughts have energy to promote good, Earth just might have a chance to evolve into a world of true and lasting peace and love: a glorious place for all souls to visit.

Maybe it was language that got in the way and could cause harm there. Mari thought that perhaps there was a seventh sense that had to do with the perception and interpretation of words. While individuals could physically hear the same words, each might react differently to them. An example appeared in another flash of memory, having to do with her first endocrinologist.

In this memory, Suzi and Mari were sitting in two comfortable chairs in front of a large, impressive desk, surrounded by shelves of neatly organized medical books. This doctor was supposed to be one of the nation's most renowned endocrinologists, specializing in juvenile diabetes. He had the dignified air of an experienced doctor and teacher, but he apparently hadn't mastered the skill of displaying any warmth or bedside manner.

This was their second visit with him. Mari sat respectfully as she listened to the same advice she had heard the first time. The lecture was heavy for a twelve-year-old girl with preteen emotions. It all had to do with control. While her mother, Suzi, listened to the suggested methods for helping her daughter deal with the disease, and even gain a measure of control over it, Mari's thoughts were fixed on the first part of the lecture, leaving her mind reeling with fears of the potentially devastating complications of blindness, lost limbs, heart disease, kidney disease, and early death. The terror that arose in her spirit kept her from hearing what to do about it. She held the tears in as long as she could. She was drowning in the overwhelming despair of losing control of her young and innocent body.

The doctor droned on as Suzi listened attentively, but Mari was oblivious to the words. The humming of emotions that was growing in her ears sounded to her like a helicopter landing on the roof above them. She began to audibly sob. Suzi turned to Mari and put her arm around her. Even she hadn't realized how deeply Mari was being affected by the gravity of the situation. She hadn't been surprised by a similar but milder reaction after the first visit, but she had hoped that Mari's intelligence and normally mature understanding was beginning to grasp it all by now. The motherly words of comfort and the logic of the procedures that would help her must have been lost in Mari's cloud of raw frustration and fear.

The doctor wound down his speech and gave Mari only a vague token of sympathy. Suzi, a little stunned by Mari's strong reaction, knew she had to cut the conversation short and get her out of there. She knew that the doctor was medically accurate, but she began to see that he was not relating to this child on a level that was comfortable for Mari. Even though he was regarded as one of the best in his field, it was clear that she would have to find another doctor who was more in tune to the psychological needs of a young girl. But the damage had been done, and Mari spent the rest of her short life dealing with the pain and fear that had been seared into her from that experience, along with even more confusion that was to come her way.

Suzi was relieved to get Mari out of that office, to love and try to comfort her. They never went back to him and heard not long afterwards that he had retired. The incident was dismissed, and they moved on to seek new medical help. Later, Suzi related the incident to Mari's psychiatrist. He shook his head and said sadly, "As doctors, we get caught up in our training to simply prolong life, and many times lose sight of helping patients to live a quality life, even if it is to be short."

Forty-five

Yes, words and thoughts are powerful. Mari knew that firsthand. As individuals we are quick to let our minds handle the interpretation, when maybe we should let our spirits be open to hearing what it is that we really need to know.

Take the word sunset. One person may perceive a bright and glorious sunset on Earth as a beautiful ending to their day while someone else may just see it as the darned sun in their eyes on their way home.

Mari was getting used to having these flashbacks at odd times, but she was growing weary of them. She was incredulous that she could visit with the party guests and still entertain such deep thoughts. It really was getting time to speed up the process and get on with life here, if that was indeed available to her.

Her attention came back to the wonderful party and Mario by her side. She was glad to be the reason for a festive celebration, and comfortable knowing that she belonged to such a lovely and diverse fellowship. She made sure that everyone knew that she honored them in return. She saw everyone as the individual evolving spirit that they are, and one was no better nor more important than another. Even with the peace so prevalent there, they were all seeking, growing souls, each one glorious and bathed in God's grace.

The earlier lively music had softened to a sweet melodic background, synchronizing to the hum of fading conversations as the party fervor slowed. Finally, those attending began to say their adieus. The gathering was great fun, and Mari enjoyed being acquainted with her extensive spiritual family that was always so generous with their loving support. She found it comfortable to see the members of her soul circle off to their own activities. The understanding that they were always available to her was beginning to sink in, and as she moved from one situation to another there was no anxiety or feeling of wanting to cling. The word "goodbye" had no meaning at all here.

Each event had a sense of completion, and yet it was part of the flow of her entire current of experience. It was like floating on a raft down the Snoqualmie River behind her family home, with the view changing around every bend.

The last few guests were leaving now, and Mario reminded Mari of their concert date as they said goodbye. He whispered a special "welcome back" with a feather touch of his lips on her ear, then faded away with the others. He left a new, warm violet glow in Mari's aura and a softly romantic melody in her heart.

Finally, it was just Mari, Lilly and Saria sitting together on the comfy sofa in the cozy living room that miraculously cleared and shrunk back to its original size. They chatted and laughed for some time about the party and all the soul connections that were made. It had been as uplifting for Lilly and Saria as it had been for the guest of honor.

"We do love our parties," commented Saria. "I enjoy quiet times with my friends as individuals, but there is a special energy when we come together in groups. It's like we're connecting to the divine as we relate to each other."

Mari thought about that for a minute then added, "It must be the love. I felt it in everyone."

"We're very much like instruments that resonate to God's love," summarized Lilly. "When we come together there's a lilting melody that touches each of us, with God and the angels humming along."

Forty-six

"What about God, Gramma?" Mari asked. "I've always had an image of God as a big celestial being in a huge golden recliner with family busy fussing with their everyday activities all around. I see this being smiling, resting from daily labors and enjoying their company. When any become weary, they can climb up onto that big lap and snuggle in the warmth and safety while they doze with the loveliest of dreams."

Lilly took her time answering. Wise souls have been trying to explain that one to inquisitive types for eternity.

"I'll try to explain things as I view them here. But first, we'll have to erase all the names that have been given to God's essence. Humankind needs to use names to attempt to encapsulate that essence with the restrictions of mental and religious frameworks. God never wanted us to label that essence. I fact, to say "Him" is a misnomer. What we talk about is an energy that is to be felt, not described or even named, let alone be a gender. We feel the essence of that energy through our senses until we know It with our souls."

"God is the ultimate of feminine and masculine energy. That means neither a He nor a She. But for conversation's sake we'll use 'Source.'" We can't truly know energy by merely a name. God is an experience that transcends the limits of language. To experience God is to know the Source that is all things, and that experience can be as simple as the wonder in the intricate details of a tiny flower, or the power of a piece of music that fills our heart and soul. It can be different for everyone, and those who know Source, as an experience, find it impossible to put it into words. Source energy exists in us and in all things. As Creator, the Godhead is our Mother and Father in One.

"God has many ways of showing us reality and we all have our imaginings about our experiences of God. As you are learning here, they can be more than imagination. There really is a place somewhere for you with that big recliner. We can take ourselves to the place where these scenes become reality. We recognize ourselves in God's love, and we recognize God's love in ourselves and in each other. God is the pure Source of love that transcends everything."

Lilly could see that she had Mari and Saria's attention, but her words felt a little lofty. Mari needed something a little more personal to relate to.

"I remember a time," Lilly continued with a far-off look, "when your mother and her siblings were school age children. We lived in a small Puget Sound navy town called Keyport. The house was old, but charming in the Craftsman style. In fact, now that I think of it, I sort of modeled this house like that one. I liked it there.

"Well, I was always the first one up in the mornings to see Claus off to work and the children off to school. I loved taking a few moments to myself to stand on the back porch that faced the harbor. I would inhale the moist morning sea air that refreshed my soul and made it ready for the day, as I tossed food scraps to the sea gulls that had become accustomed to my morning feedings. Claus would get a little peeved at me for attracting them because they would do their business all over the porch. And I'm not talking about little robin droppings. But I enjoyed my morning conversations with them. Their squawks filled the air with excitement, as if calling me into the day that lay ahead.

"One morning," Lilly continued her story with a big grin, "Claus strolled into the kitchen just as I came in the back door, and he woke up the whole house laughing. I was in shock, dripping with white seagull poop all over my dark hair. They really got me good.

"When Claus finally got himself under control, he just said, 'That'll show you. You must not have had enough bread for them today. Now are you going to keep feeding them?' Well, I did, but I learned to keep a big, wide-brimmed hat by the back door for my morning visits with my seagull friends.

"Anyway, I digressed there. I wanted to make the point that some mornings the fog was so thick I could barely see the neighboring houses. I was a little creeped out when I first experienced that dense Northwest waterfront fog. But as I stood there in the fine mist, a foghorn started calling to me from the harbor. I grew to love fog and the foghorn. That's when I would think of God, who was always out there somewhere watching and guiding us through the foggy times. In those moments I felt the experience of God, the Creator and Protector."

"Your grandmother is right," said Saria. "God is an experience more than a persona. Everyone is a part of an alliance with God in our quest for unity and an open dialogue with the Heavens. Scientists on Earth are defining life and energy down to the finest molecular particle, but someday they will have to define the energy that holds it all in sync."

"God has been known to appear here on rare occasions," added Lilly, "although that's not usually necessary. We don't need to give God a face. In fact, it can be an unnecessary distraction when it's more about Source energy. It occurs mostly depending on a soul's Earthly belief system for reference when they cross over. God attends to their needs in that situation. But even then, it is according to their perceptions. You've already found your visual place to go where you can feel Divine presence and those of us here know God is always with us. It's just nothing to stress about. In fact, it's quite the opposite. God, Source, Divine Energy, and All That Is, is the peace that we feel."

"I must say that I didn't notice feeling any stress about it," shared Mari. "Every step I take now is on a path filled with serenity of mind, heart and soul. But still I imagine it may be even more so when I've completed my transition here. Everything is leading me to the decision to do a more complete life review than the occasional memories that have been revealed to me since I arrived. I want to do it. I'm ready to move on and am ready to embrace life here if that is to be."

"I've been waiting for the decision from you," Saria interjected with reassurance and an element of relief. "We can do that whenever you say."

"Hold on just a second," Lilly interrupted. "I have a little something for Mari while we still have the hint of celebration in the air."

Mari couldn't imagine what it could possibly be. In this moment she felt that all her wants and needs had been met beyond her imagination.

"Well, we enjoy surprises here, too," Saria said.

Lilly held out her arms, palms up and in her hands appeared an exquisite ebony case glimmering with gold and silver inlay and a shiny gold handle. It was shoe box size but longer. It looked heavy, but Lilly held it out to Mari with ease.

"You gave this to Claus before you left. He's been keeping it for you. You obviously had a memory of it that you took to the other side, and I presented you with that Earthly one when you arrived here. This one is special. Claus asked me to give it to you after the party, and it is my pleasure to do so."

The case certainly was beautiful enough for Mari, but she sensed something amazing inside. "That must be the most beautiful case I've ever seen. I can't believe it's mine. You say that I left it here?"

"That's right," Saria joined the conversation. "And we're glad to be getting it back to you. You may ... Oh, just open it up."

Mari took the case carefully from Lilly. She set it on her lap and smiled lovingly and expectantly at her companions. The latch opened easily, then she lifted the golden handle. The inside was lined with luxuriant powder blue satin cushions on which lay a simple, but glowing, silver flute. All Mari could do was stare spellbound at the stunning, luminescent instrument. It had the appearance of one that she could imagine in the hands of an angel playing in a heavenly ensemble.

The flute she had played in the sixth-grade band was nice, but nothing like this one. Again, she was associating her experiences on Earth with what she was familiar with on this side. She had been drawn to play the flute there and enjoyed it immensely until illness, yet again, got in the way. She had even taken pleasure in practicing, and the meditative qualities that playing it held for her.

"And this is mine?" she finally asked in amazement.

"Of course," Lilly answered sweetly. "We've been holding it for you."

"Well, I'm at a loss for words," said Mari. "This is amazing. I thought that playing music was lost to me. Now I can enjoy it again, and it means so much more to me now."

She reached into the case and felt the wonderfully smooth metal vibrating to her touch as she gripped it and lifted it out. It was much lighter than her old flute, and the keys were polished to a glittering sheen. It felt marvelous to raise it to her lips and let her fingers play on the keys. Silver toned notes floated in the air and a bird-like trill swirled around the threesome, bringing shades of blue to their auras. Blue can be a color for balance, and Mari did, indeed, feel a restful evenness wash over her as she played just those few notes.

Lilly and Saria saw that this was a good thing for Mari. A thought passed between them and Lilly said, "Honey, you just go ahead and play to your heart's content. And you know by now that you can go anywhere you desire to be, by yourself if you like."

"You know," Mari said, realizing that they were right, "it is time for me to be alone for a bit, and I may be doing you both a favor since I haven't done this for what seems like, a long time. I'll get some practice in, then I'll play for you later."

"Then off with you," urged Saria, "and have fun."

Forty-seven

The day began at a slow pace. Suzi reviewed the list she had written the night before. She decided those things could surely wait. Instead, she picked up her phone and dialed Deirdre.

"I was just thinking about you," Dee said when she answered. "I want to thank you for the amazing visit I had with you in your beautiful new home. I hated to leave."

"I enjoyed it too," said Suzi. "You are welcome back anytime. I've given a lot of thought to your helpful suggestions about writing. I think Mari is trying to get to me. I came across her flute the other day and could almost hear her playing it."

"That's sweet," said Dee. "I'm certain she's enjoying it over there."

"So, what else do you think she is doing?" asked Suzi. "Maybe you can get some insights that will inspire me."

"Oh gosh," replied Dee. "Good question. Let me think for a minute. She is getting reacquainted with a lot of souls. Family, friends, and her spirit guide. She even has met a love interest that she has over there."

"That's amazing!" said Suzi. "I hope that's so. I'm happy for her if it is. She never had a boyfriend in her Earth life, and I know she felt like she missed out."

"Well, besides family and friends and her love interest, her work over there, yes, they do work but on a different level than here, has to do with helping children, who have come over the rainbow bridge, to acclimate to the world of spirit. I hear she is very good at it. She helps to make it fun for them so they can relax and move on. Other than that, she is learning a lot. She is beginning to be able to reach loved ones. Like she told you, 'Look for me now.'"

"I feel like her input for the writing is slow to come," said Suzi. "I get hints but no clarification. Maybe it's just my memories. My brain is trying to sort it out."

"The best thing I can suggest," offered Dee, "is to keep notes of your impressions. You never know how it might all fit together. On another subject," she whispered, "I'm sitting outside, and a pair of Redbirds just landed on a nearby bush. I'm going to be still and see if they will sing for me."

The cousins listened close, for the song of the Redbird.

"Oh, did you hear that? They are singing for us," said Dee.

"Yes," said Suzi. "I can. They are so lovely. I loved seeing them on visits there. I know my mom and our grandmother loved them. Why do you think they are so special?"

Dee replied, "I know Gramma used to tell me that if she had to come back into another life, she wanted to come back as a Redbird because they sing so pretty. I've heard it said that if a Redbird is near it means that our departed loved ones are nearby. I certainly like that idea.

"I recently had a dream where I was looking at a tree that was full of a whole flock of Redbirds. I wasn't sure if there was a meaning to it, but now I'm being told that it has to do with your writing. Each Redbird represents a chapter in the final book. There were a lot, so you better get busy."

"Oh great," said Suzi. "Now I'm getting pressure from the Redbirds. I had a lot to do today but now I think I'd better try to make some progress. I do write something resembling bits of random chapters that aren't cohesive yet. Like you said, they just might come together. As hard as this is for me, I'm experiencing some healing. I miss Mari terribly. I would go through it all again just to have her back. If only I could know that she is healing also."

"I don't think you need to worry about that," offered Diedra. "She's getting the help she needs over there."

"Thank you," replied Suzi. "Have a good day. We'll talk again soon, I'm sure. Enjoy your Redbirds. Love you."

Forty-eight

Mari only had to ponder for a second before she transported herself to a place that reminded her of Winery Hill. It was a beautiful hillside meadow overlooking the river valley of her home on Earth, surrounded by glorious mountains with rocky crags and snow-capped peaks. For her purposes, no buildings or roads marred the purest of nature, soft grasses moving with the slightest of a mountain breeze, refreshing her spirit. A smattering of wildflowers added touches of color to the beauty of her surroundings. The only thing out of place was her sophisticated party attire, but that was simple to change. In a wink, her body felt free in a gauzy white toga that was gathered at her shoulders with golden clips, and it blew softly around her in the gentle breeze. She added some pretty, wild poppies to her hair to complete the freedom of a flower child's appearance, because that was what she was feeling.

Now she was ready to sit lightly on the velvet grass and enjoy this special playtime that was just for her. She gently lifted the marvelous instrument, which felt like a close, sympathetic friend, and the energy that it emanated was in sync with her own. She caressed it lovingly as she played unbroken streams of melody with a precision that rose from deep inside her soul.

Tears rose as the healing vibrations flowed around and through her and blended with her own vibration. With every tear she felt the lightening of each agony that she had been holding on to.

With each note came the release of so much of what she carried over from her physical life. Each movement alluded to themes from that life as she allowed herself to feel it all in the vibration of the music and in the healing pastel colors that were beginning to whirl in melodious eddies around her. She felt alone with God in this moment of emotional resonance and let the unconditional love flow around and through her by way of the sweetly lyrical tunes that were only of this magical spirit world and from her heart. Through her creativity, she was relating to God as God was relating to creation within her. Her image of the Divine grew from her traditional ideas into an energy that was an all-inclusive essence beyond physical form. For her in this moment, God didn't need a face.

She played on into tunes that were not of memory but took their rise from the love that was within her heart, now aflutter with pure joy. Finally, the music faded, ending with a lullaby that put her soul to rest.

Mari discovered that there were many different types of peace to be found in her new existence. So much was possible. For now, it was just sitting quietly in the meadow as many colored birds began to fly and flit overhead. A cheerful Redbird landed in the wildflowers at her feet, as if her flute had beckoned it to join her. The Redbirds were becoming very important to her. She wasn't quite sure why.

With the musical colors settling around her, one area of violet grew vibrantly with a familiar energy. Mario took form within the light. He appeared as he had the first time. His garment was a glowing, white, other-worldly coat with gold and silver trim. His aura showed a loving pink intertwined with his natural lavender energy. But Mari's first reaction was one of shock and surprise. In all its glory, a huge bright red clown nose stood out on his otherwise handsome face. She started to giggle, and as

Mario joined in, it became the kind of infectious belly laughs that make speech impossible.

Even though she was enjoying their mutual levity, Mari caught a glimpse of a small aura out of the corner of her eye. As soon as she did, it faded out again. She thought nothing of it and her attention was back to Mario.

"Oh, you goof," she said between gales of laughter. She looked at him and the laughing started all over again. He dropped down beside her on the grass and smiled giving her a moment to enjoy her mirth. The red ball gave a loud pop as he pulled it off his nose and she snickered more at that.

"It's good to hear you laugh again," he said with a beautiful, bright smile.

"Well, you should have seen how silly you looked," she replied still grinning. "And I was totally surprised."

"You should talk, Flower Child. The only thing missing is a peace sign painted on your cheek."

Mari stood up and posed with a hand on her hip and the other behind her head.

"You don't like this look?" she asked sarcastically, with an air of drama and a pretty good Mae West imitation. "I think I look divine!"

"No doubt, you're beautiful, and I enjoy whatever look you want to come up with," he responded sweetly.

"Good," was her curt retort. And what, may I ask are you doing here?"

Mario took a deep breath and looked at her seriously as he formulated an answer. He remembered how direct she could be. "I heard your lullaby, and it sounded a little melancholy, so I thought I'd check in with you. But really, I only used that as an excuse. I can see now that you were only lowering your vibration from a higher experience."

"What do you mean you heard me playing?" she asked, looking at him through furrowed eyebrows. "I thought I was alone here. Maybe you'd better explain."

"It's not so much that I heard you as it is that you and I are very close and very much in tune to each other. Surely, you've sensed that by now."

"I know that there's something going on," said Mari. "And that you feel significant to my life here. And honestly, I think it's more than working and playing together as kindred spirits." She paused as she weighed her next words. Feeling bold in her insinuations but reserved in voicing them, she continued somewhat shyly, "There is a depth of connection that I feel with you more than anyone else. I can't help but feel that these meetings are leading up to something but I'm not sure what. Don't you think it's time to cut to the chase and fill me in? Who are you and why do I sense that you are a part of me?"

He was a little taken aback, but was pleased at the level of her evolution back to her direct, old self. He decided that since she was asking, it was time for her to know. Taking the flute from her and placing it on the grass, he took both her hands in his and breathed a sigh of relief that released a love that he had been holding in check long enough. The energy transferred from his hands to hers and made her feel more alive than she thought possible. There was to be no mincing of words with the look of determination in her eyes.

"I am your twin soul," Mario whispered tenderly with sweet breath that washed over her, quickening her heart and curing a secret loneliness with his ambrosial words. She was stunned to see that as she gazed into his beautiful and intense blue-violet eyes, she was seeing into a part of her own soul. And it was pure and good and worthy of all the love that she was experiencing in this world of spirit.

Reverently she bowed her head. "Oh, thank you," she said to Mario. As she absorbed this information, she quietly told Mario, "Please tell me more."

He was elated to be again joined with this loving, courageous part of himself, and felt her need to be told more. "Well," he began slowly, "what we have is not uncommon here, but it is somewhat different. Twin souls were created at the same time with complementary aspects. We are individuals but with a special bond. Soul mates are common here, but we are also all connected as kindred spirits. No relationship is more important than any other, it's just that ours has an especially strong attachment that keeps us connected wherever we are. We don't encroach into each other's minds without permission, but, as you release more of your physical life, you'll find that we have an empathetic relationship. When one of us is in another dimension or incarnation, the separation is felt as an unexplained loneliness, but a sweet knowing that there is more to who we really are."

He paused to let this sink in for Mari. "That answers a lot for me," she reflected. "The whole time I was on the other side, I felt like something was missing. I enjoyed some casual attractions to others there, but it just wasn't enough. I could never carry through with any kind of relationship. There was never a need. In fact, as I grew up, it was like I fought the whole maturity thing and oh my gosh," she gasped, and her hands flew to her face in realization. The anorexia. In a warped way, that's what kept me from growing up."

"Whoa, Kiddo," Mario interrupted. "You're getting ahead of yourself. Some twin souls do enjoy special relationships with their kindred souls over there if they write that into their plan. I respect that you didn't feel the need for other attachments, but I felt your loneliness. If we get deep here, and I don't want to, you're getting into issues of choices that you'll be dealing with..."

His voice trailed off for Mari as she remembered a short time before she left Earth.

The nurse had finished changing her bed with crisp fresh linens as Mari and Suzi strolled into the room from a visit to the roof garden. They had been sharing a story about Ann, Mari's nurse friend, who had confided that she was seeing a very cute intern, and the relationship seemed to be getting serious. Mari thought they were a darling couple.

When she tried to explain which intern he was, she had said, "Remember Mom. He's Doogie. The one who came in one day and we both giggled when he left and said at the same time, "Doogie!" He looked like the actor who played Doogie Howser on the TV series. When he first walked in, I thought he was just a visiting kid who went to the wrong room. He turned out to be one of my favorite doctors."

Suzi did, indeed, remember the giggle fit that they had shared at the young doctor's expense. And he was one of her favorites, also.

They were still smiling as they entered the room. The nurse was smoothing the covers and fluffing the pillow.

"There you go Dear," she said to Mari before she rushed off to her duties for other patients.

Suzi settled into the visitor's chair as Mari sat on the newly made bed. Suzi could see that her daughter was slipping deep into serious thought. She waited to see where it was going.

Finally, with a rather faraway look and still thinking about her friend's romance, Mari said slowly and thoughtfully, "You know Mom, I'm this family's only twenty-five-year-old virgin."

This serious statement threw Suzi for a loop at first, but she furrowed her brow and tilted her head in thought, reflecting on the history of family members. At last, she laughed. "You could very well be right. I don't know for certain, of course, but I can't think of anyone else who can make that statement."

Mari saw the humor in her revelation and added emphatically with a smile, "Well at least I've accomplished something in this life!'

Mother and daughter enjoyed a good laugh at the irony in Mari's voice.

Forty-nine

With a shake of her head, Mari came back to the meadow. Mario was staring at her. Slightly embarrassed, she shyly apologized. "Sorry about that. I slipped away for a moment there. What were you saying?"

"Never mind," he replied with a sly grin "From the pink in your cheeks, I'm getting the impression that you may have questions about intimacy in the spirit world."

He, indeed, had read as much of her curiosity as she would allow. She let him carry on with his speech as he lay back on the grass with his hands clasped behind his neck. "This should be interesting," she thought, as she gazed into the ethers above.

Very bluntly he stated, "We don't enjoy sex as it is known in the physical. It's too trivial for our ethereal bodies. Instead, when our souls agree, we unite in spirit. It's an experience that surpasses anything physical. We allow our auras to blend and join to become one soul."

As he spoke, Mari was feeling a warmth come over her that was nothing like the warmth of loins that she had read about in her Harlequin romance novel days. Instead, it was a glowing desire from her heart that was reaching upward in the purest love.

"Since it has nothing to do with procreation," he continued, "It's not a taboo subject like the physical thing. It's a beautiful experience. The best way I can describe it is that it's like climbing the colors of the rainbow until you merge with the pure white light that is God's love."

"Oh!" exclaimed Mari shyly as she pictured the glories of this colorful spectacle. She found that it wasn't the least bit uncomfortable discussing it. "I guess maybe I really didn't miss much over there after all," she teased.

Their discussion was interrupted by an obnoxious "pop" and they found Jane standing before them with her hands on her hips, bathed in her peachy pink aura.

"There you two are!" she stated curtly. "No fair blocking your friends out. But I'll forgive you this time. Having a nice talk?"

Jane's friends smiled at each other with a special smile that they shared between themselves, then they shrugged their shoulders as if to say, "Ok, you caught us."

"Well, I wouldn't bother you, but you two have had enough time alone," said Jane without much sympathy, "and I need to talk."

Part Three

THE GREAT REMEMBERING

Fifty

Jane stood in the grass in front of her two friends. Mario sat up and smiled at Jane with empathy and understanding. "How is Toby?" he asked without prompting.

"That's why I'm here," she said, her exasperation showing. "I'm blocked. He needs my help, but I'm stumped. I guess I'm too emotionally involved."

Mario turned to Mari and explained, "Toby is Jane's twin soul. He's been back here for some time now but is having difficulty transitioning."

"I was hoping," Jane looked at Mari pleading, "that since you are still in a similar mode, maybe the two of you, together, might have some input."

Mari could not only see but also feel the frustration that was showing up as some darkness in Jane's aura. "I don't know what help I could be but fill me in and we'll see." Just her friend's words of concern helped Jane to relax.

Jane took a deep breath, sat down on the grass, and ventured into the story that she needed to tell. "Toby arrived back here some time ago. He passed over at eleven years old from a tough life and seems to be stuck. His soul hasn't yet matured into its reality on this side. We're all trying to help him deal with that physical life so he can learn and move on, but we're blocked.

"Toby was raised by a nanny who took on the role of a real loving parent. She passed over before him, and that was a traumatic twist. His grief threw him into depression. She's with him here a lot now, trying to help. He holds onto her spirit very strongly. You'll know Toby when you see him, she said turning to Mari. "He has dark hair and freckles, and he's pigeon-toed and very nervous. He's carried all that back here with him, along with a bad stutter. Other kids made fun of him a lot on the other side. He was teased and bullied mercilessly. What a mess," she paused and shook her head in frustration.

"But he has a good soul. While he was in physical life, he even had a good ear and could listen on another level and hear things others couldn't. A lot of strength came from those conversations he's had with God. Toby is a sweetheart, and he helps me in the children's sector while he works on his own transition. Recently he made a wooden cradle for the babies there. He mostly just sits on the floor and rocks them in silence. It's good for the babies, but I'm not so sure about him. Occasionally he interacts with some of the older kids. He's a good storyteller as well as a good listener. I've even seen him visit the other side to help depressed kids who want to leave Earth too soon, and he's adept at calling in other energies to help where he can't. He's so good, but he's really stuck.

"He's here after a car accident with his father driving while intoxicated. But before that, even at his young age, he had thought about taking his own life. The thing that gets me is that he has every symptom of a soul after suicide. He's obsessed with babies that are coming back, and he's not transitioning."

Jane paused with her story and Mari processed the information she was getting. "I don't get the suicide connection. What does that have to do with babies?" she asked.

"That's right," volunteered Mario, "You wouldn't be up on that yet. When a person chooses suicide to end their life," he began with reverence and sympathy, "unless there is mental illness involved, they appear to have made a choice that is not in accord with their agreement before going into life. So they get another chance by going back by transference. The sad thing is that they don't get to transition here and enjoy the love and beauty of their true home before they go back into another life there. It's not a good choice. But with grace and perseverance, they will eventually make good choices and complete their learning on Earth, so they can be embraced with special care upon their return. I can understand Jane's concern about Toby being a little too focused on the infants. It's like he's thinking of going back there, to Earth, instead of adjusting to here. His transition seems to be complicated.

"What about his spirit guide and review?" he asked Jane.

She thought for a moment, then answered, "His spirit guide is great, but he's new and he came in after Toby had created his chart. They have been through the review and it didn't seem to be complete for him. He's still having trouble releasing that life. And you know what's weird? He keeps referring to a shiny silver knife. It's strange that nothing like that ever showed up in his review."

The three friends sat quietly pondering the dilemma, hoping for inspiration. Putting her thoughts into words, Mari said, "Symptoms of suicide with none apparently present makes me wonder, and I'm sure you've all thought of this, but does the review go back to any previous lives?"

Jane and Mario stared at her in amazement.

"Well," she added sheepishly, "just thought I'd ask."

"But of course!" Jane exclaimed as she slapped the side of her head in realization. "We've been so focused on his recent life that we weren't thinking beyond the box. Generally, the review only goes through the recent one, but we can go back further if need be. I knew that I was too involved to be thinking straight. Thank goodness we still get to work on perfection here. Wow! What a lesson. God bless you, my friend! I'm off to meet with a spirit guide."

With that, she popped out as quickly as she had popped in, leaving

Mari and Mario in the beautiful meadow.

"Good work, Lady," Mario complimented Mari. "That may be a tremendous help. The smallest detail can direct energy into the right direction. And we need each other's help here, too. It's a beautiful system to learn in even if the learning isn't as dramatic or as accelerated as on Earth."

"I guess being a newcomer," stated Mari, "I'm still carrying some of the drama of my physical life. I hope Toby gets straightened out. I'm still waiting to see if my own death will be deemed a suicide. I'm anxious about that."

"For now, we'll give it to the powers that be," said Mario as he stood and held out a hand for Mari. "And I promised you a concert. I'd say it's time, even though I don't believe anything can compare to the solo flute that I enjoyed earlier."

Mari welcomed the familiar love that passed between them as she took his hand and stood to receive an energy-filled embrace that hinted at the merging that he had told her about. She looked deeply into his big blue eyes and melted into a kiss that she had been waiting a lifetime to experience.

So, this was her twin soul, the one she was so lonesome for in physical life. She loved him because she was as much a part of him as he was a part of her. No wonder she had felt little connection to that life. It was difficult ending the embrace, but their smiles kept the feeling strong.

"I believe you mentioned a concert," said Mari, releasing the electric connection that held her gaze.

"That's right," answered Mario. "We should be on our way."

Ever the good granddaughter, she decided that she should check in with Lilly and Saria before she headed off in another direction.

"That's not really necessary," stated Mario. "They are with you in spirit, but if you would like to, we can do that."

Fifty-one

As they tapped into Lilly's energy, they found her in a classroom, intently listening to a lecture on writing poetry for the physical world. They didn't want to disturb her train of thought, so they left her a mental memo that they were off to a concert.

Saria was more available to them, getting ready for yet another party.

"Hey, Party Girl," said Mari. "Where's the merrymaking this time?"

Still being so closely connected to Mari, Saria wasn't the least bit surprised by the appearance of these two. She was always aware of her charge's whereabouts, and available when needed.

"I'm off to another welcome party celebration," she shared with them. "This time I get to welcome someone that I had been close to in my last life in the American West. I think I mentioned Pete to you. He was a rascal then, and we tangled several times. This is his second time here since I was with him physically. It's great to have him back. I've missed him. He is one of my teachers on this side."

As she spoke, she changed her appearance to that of the cowgirl that

Pete would be sure to recognize at his party. "So, you two are off to a concert. Which one is it?" she asked.

"I was thinking the philharmonic," said Mario, "if that suits my lady. It's a diverse program of some light guitar, working into some new stuff that has been recently composed here."

"Sounds great," said Mari. "I can't wait."

"I'm thrilled for you," said Saria. "It's a real experience. Thank you for checking in, but I'm always aware of you wherever you are. I do need to remind you that you and I have some important work coming up. Since you're having such a good time, maybe I'd better make an appointment with you to get down to brass tacks. Say, after the concert?"

Mari, play-acting the roll of one much put upon, replied, "Well if I must, then I guess I can fit you in."

Saria smiled to see Mari being lighthearted and turned to Mario. "Why don't you show Mari some of our public areas on your way there? Even show her the library that she and I will visit after the concert."

"Good idea," he replied. "Then we're off. Bye for now Saria."

The two spirits left Saria, preparing for her next rousing party.

Hand in hand, Mario and Mari found themselves fading from Saria's company and miraculously riding high above a marvelous cityscape. The basket of a voluminous, colorfully striped hot air balloon held them both, a white rose emblazoned on one side. Mari, a bit flummoxed, surprised herself at how comfortable she was at this altitude.

"Wonderful!" she exclaimed as she looked over the side. "I've always wanted to float away in a beautiful balloon. And the one I imagined was exactly these bright colors. The rose is a nice touch."

"I know what you like," Mario responded. "And I like it as much as you do."

Mari had lost track of the many times she wished that she could escape the drama that was her physical life. The heaviness would weigh her down to the point that she wished she would die and be done with it all. Now she was worried that suicidal thoughts would interfere with her transition here.

The view was far beyond the beauty and grandeur of the Seattle panorama that she had known so well on trips for medical treatments and appointments from her mountain home in the physical world. Every building in this spirit-world city had its own colorful inner light, glowing with the energy of activities taking place within.

The entire scene was a blend of many architectural styles. She could make out modern geometric structures, as well as gingerbread Victorian, domed Persian, provincial French, and touches of East Indian and Asian pagoda style infrastructure. The great variety somehow achieved harmony with beautiful gardens, lakes and streams interspersed throughout. Mari could feel at once the energy of this amazingly exciting place.

The harmony was especially evident radiating from an area of Romanesque buildings that caught her attention. The buildings appeared to be constructed of exotic varieties of marble, beautifully veined with gold and silver. Gleaming carved pillars supported arched and angled porticos.

"That's where we're headed," Mario interrupted Mari's study of the scene before her. "But, if you like, we'll take a little time to see some city sights along the way."

"Oh, I'd love that," Mari replied enthusiastically. "I always loved the energy of Seattle, but never got the chance to really spend much time there, except in hospitals."

The balloon eased gently downward until it landed in a park next to an intriguing open air market teeming with activity. Not only were the booths and shops a kaleidoscope of color, but the people were colorful as well. Everyone was attired for their own expression and comfort instead of adhering to any "popular" mode of dress. It was an international and even intergalactic gathering of souls from many lands and dimensions. Mari and Mario stepped from the balloon basket and joined the throngs of people. There seemed to be an absence of children, but Mari witnessed that many must be enjoying their inner child with playful antics, laughing and having a great time.

As they milled through vendors offering everything from works of art to practical tools masterfully crafted, Mario picked up on Mari's thought about money, wondering what sort of currency was being exchanged.

"That's another Earthly idea you'll learn to shake off. Here we exchange ideas and courtesies. We can create anything, so there is no need to buy anything. But there are many kinds of creativity, and we share those ideas with each other."

"For instance," he said as he walked toward a booth showcasing marvelous multicolored pottery that had caught her eye as well, "I've been thinking of changing the look of some of the things in my surroundings. The designs in this pottery would suit me well. If I decide to use this design, out of courtesy, I could possibly present the artisan with the idea of a new plant for his garden that I am working on in the greenhouse. It's the barter system in perfection. Just the exchange of ideas. And since there is no need for personal wealth, there is no need for those mixed energies that happen when money is involved, like competitiveness and greed. And really, we're not into owning things here anyway. We don't need things here. But we might occasionally enjoy them."

Just then, Mari remembered leaving her flute in the meadow.

"Don't sweat it, Kiddo," he encouraged her as she shared the thought with him. "It will always be yours, if you want it to be. All you have to do is wish it to be with you. Nothing ever gets lost here."

As they made their way through the colorful gathering place, they enjoyed the many street musicians. Infusing the scene with even more vigor, they were each vividly dressed to add to the richness of their melodies.

When Mari and Mario turned a corner at the end of the market, they walked through an ornate wrought iron gate, the figures of many animals woven into its grillwork. They followed a path that meandered through stands of trees, emerald areas of lush grass, and crystal ponds with sparkling iridescent fish.

Mari stopped in her tracks when they came upon a woman sitting peacefully petting a full grown, shaggy-maned lion. As she gazed around the scene, Mari began to see an amazing variety of animals interacting with just as many kinds of people. One man was gently brushing a lounging zebra, while another played what looked to be a hopscotch-like game with a friendly kangaroo. Animals and people were everywhere sharing the joy of each other's existence without the barriers of cages or barred fences. And as she watched, people and animals would appear or disappear at will. She finally turned to her partner, who was watching her with a big, silly grin.

"Our zoo," was all he said in answer to her questioning eyes, and they ventured on down the path. Continuing through a stand of fir trees, they were approached by a majestic elk that was almost twice Mari's height. He stopped and bowed his head so Mari could caress his velvety antlers and rub and scratch the warm brown fur on his neck. She even gave him a big loving hug, and he gave her a soft nudge in return before he continued on his way. This was so much better than any dream she could have conjured up in the limits of a physical mind.

The sights and sounds of this magical place began fading behind them as they approached another iron gate at the end of the trail.

Fifty-two

"Hey Mari!" called a glowing form that was trying to catch up to them. "This must be right up your alley, you little animal lover," smiled Jane, who was holding hands with a handsome auburn-haired man with a charming smattering of freckles across his nose. "We were just playing with a gaggle of geese across the way. May we join you?"

"You're always welcome," answered Mari. Mario nodded in agreement. "Introduce me to your friend, although I feel like I might already know him."

"You're so right," answered Jane. "Mari and Mario, please welcome Toby!"

"Hey guys," greeted Toby as he received warm hugs of welcome from his friends.

"Good work! Congratulations!" exclaimed Mario, giving his friend an affectionate shoulder nudge. He and Mari could see that Toby had finally succeeded in completing his transition. The mature soul before them was glowing with a radiant smile of elation.

"Thanks," was Toby's shy reaction. "And I do mean that with all my heart," he said looking at Mari. "Your observation made all the difference. The simplicity of it shook us out of our misunderstanding of the situation. It's good to be back."

"I couldn't be more pleased for you," Mari replied. "Your story really touched me. Sometime I'd like to know what happened."

"We were on our way to a coffee shop. Please join us," Jane invited.

Mari looked at Mario and he smiled in agreement. She was ecstatic to be enjoying such a warm friendship with kindred souls and peers in a friendly social situation. This camaraderie had been rare or, maybe more accurately, nonexistent in her last Earth experiences.

The four friends left the marvelous zoo through the iron gateway and entered a plaza surrounded by the many styled buildings that Mari had noticed before entering the city. Not as crowded as the market, it was still busy with the comings and goings of souls of every nationality and orientation. As they passed those who were conversing, Mari observed many languages being spoken that were unfamiliar to her ear, and she seemed to instinctively recognize the essence of what they were sharing. The conversations ranged from silly banter to serious, even heated, philosophical discussions, all in the wonderous spirit of joyful communication. Mostly, however, they were souls sharing the events of their everyday lives here in paradise. They were all having a great time.

The four friends walked through an outdoor area set with small intimate tables and entered a Tuscan-looking shop that emanated a heady aroma of brewing coffee. Roughly textured walls were draped with tapestries that depicted country panoramas of grazing sheep and lush vineyards. The shop was like walking into a scene from a travel poster. Mari had Italy on her list of places to visit someday, but she felt that she, indeed, was there now.

People sat at cozy marble tables sharing thoughts and ideas in the divinely glowing atmosphere. The focal point of the interior was a huge ornate brass machine that graced the back wall of the shop. Mari recognized it right away as an antique espresso machine like the one she had seen with her mother on a trip to Portland, Oregon. It was beautiful and had been from Italy. The one in her memory was almost as much a piece of art as this one, which had to be triple the size.

The baristas, creating the wonderful sounds and scents of brewing coffee and steamed milk, cheerfully presented their artful concoctions to those waiting patiently. Mari wondered about the necessity of all the trouble they were going to, but she appreciated that the creative process was being enjoyed as much as the beauty of the art that was produced.

Toby, coming out of his ordeal, desired the richness of a straight shot of espresso, while Mari ordered one of the luscious cappuccinos, complete with a swirl of foamy milk. She wasn't at all in need of refreshment, but she was up for the experience. Jane and Mario were simply enjoying their friends, delighted at the wonders of this world.

They decided to adjourn to a table outside and sat comfortably on the nicely cushioned chairs. "So, fill us in," said Mario to Toby and Jane as they settled in.

"Well," Jane began, "when I left you two, I went straight to Toby's guide, Joseph, and suggested that they go a little further back into Toby's life review. And they found what they needed. Toby should tell you the rest. He is a wonderful storyteller. The other kids where I work just love his silly fables." She affectionately turned to Toby as he was putting down his cup.

"Silly!" he exclaimed. "Why, why... Ok, I guess some of them are," he admitted. "But I have to say that it was easier to tell the kids tall tales than it was to relate to my own personal trials. I am still processing what I learned, and this isn't exactly a fairy tale. Anyway, Joseph and I went back to the library and took another look at my short life review. We started with what I was living through here and studied my lack of progress. Then we went into the car crash and backward through my ten years of physical life to the point of my soul transference into that incarnation. We were stumped, so we kept going. It was amazing. I had experienced a different kind of crash in the life before that one."

"I saw myself in a small airplane, high above a fleet of ships out in the ocean. My spirit guide and I were watching this all in reverse, but I will relate it to you in sequence.

"I was able to remember myself as a young Japanese pilot who had made the choice to join my other zealous comrades of a kamikaze crew. With our youthful passion, we believed that what we were doing was an honor and we would be blessed for it. I was intelligent, but let political fervor take precedence over my soul's contract for that life, to see that life to its agreed exit point. Instead, I consciously directed my plane into the ships below me and died in a fiery crash that took many other lives as well. It was a definite suicide that I was dealing with."

Toby paused with his narrative, giving Mari, who was mesmerized by his story, the chance to present a question that was on her mind. "I'm a little confused about the way you died," she commented with caution. "Jane said that you were obsessed with a silver knife. What was that about?"

"It had been an inheritance from my Japanese grandfather from that time. The knife was a beautiful antique that was intended for ceremonial purposes. I had taken it on that last flight and thought I was doing the honorable ancestral thing by using it on myself before the crash. I guess you could say that I experienced my own double suicide."

"Oh my gosh!" Mari exclaimed. "That is so dramatic. No wonder you were having such a tough time."

"It was a heavy lesson. I had consciously made that decision, and as a result, I immediately went into the next incarnation without getting to experience all of this. I had created what some refer to as karmic debt. I had misplaced my trust by putting it into inflated political egos, and did not look beyond that. I had carried over the misconception of my personal responsibility and felt that somehow the car crash had been my fault. Transition has been difficult because I had not released guilt because of the consequences of my actions. That was what I had gone there to learn, and it is what I have come to terms with here. Now I've learned to trust in higher purpose and in my own plan for personal evolution."

Toby paused and was clearly trying to organize his thoughts. He took a deep breath and exhaled slowly, continuing, "I'm too emotionally involved here to tell this story in a rational detached way. By trying to put it into words, I'm still processing what I've learned. While trying to understand my own situation, Ideas about understanding the whole picture of world conflict is hitting me hard. But I need to release it because that is getting beyond my purpose there. It wasn't to justify war. It was more about making a statement about attacks and suicide. You see, I was not rewarded for my actions. Instead, the people who lost their lives at my hand were blessed with the completion of their contracts and were instantaneously assimilated into this life and came here immediately with little or no transition. But I had to go back."

Mario rocked back in his chair and looked sympathetically but respectfully at his friend. "That's a real load to work on," he commented. "I for one, am grateful for the reminder of the negativity that we can get caught up in when we go to the Earth realm."

"So much there has to do with trust," interjected Jane. "Mostly trusting the messages that our soul receives about what our purpose is and what is true. Wow!" she smiled facetiously doing a dramatic hair flip. "I'm so wise today. Y'all remember that if you ever entertain any ideas about going back there."

"Not soon!" Toby and Mari yelled in unison, looked at each other in surprise, then laughed along with Jane.

But their attention shifted to Mario, who was not sharing their mirth.

Toby broke the momentary silence by asking, "So what's up with that look, my friend?"

"Since we're on the subject," Mario began, "I'm working on a plan to go there. It will be the first time for me. Claus and others are helping me to put it all together." He turned to Mari and continued, "I believe while you were touring his operations, he mentioned an associate who was planning to incarnate."

Mari did, indeed, remember the conversation, but she never imagined that the situation would involve someone so dear to her. Still feeling her own Earthly challenges, there was a tug on her heart, and she surprised herself with a momentary hint of separation anxiety.

She took a deep breath as she processed this new information. As much as she wanted Mario to do what was best for his soul, this news hit her hard. Was this to be part of her punishment? She had only just found her true love and twin soul. Was he going to be torn away from her and leave her heart yearning again? Could she bear to be alone that way? But mostly she was concerned about Mario and what he was going to have to endure. She would have to trust her higher self and his spirit guide.

Mario could see the love of his friends emanating from each of them. "I may as well ask now if you three will enlist to help from this side, since none of you seem to be going back soon yourselves."

"You bet," answered Toby, who turned to Jane.

"You couldn't leave me out if you tried," was her heartfelt response.

With the attention on Mari, she said shyly, putting her concerns aside, "I don't know right now what I have to offer in the mix, but I am pleased to be included. Absolutely count me in. Perhaps my work in the labs can contribute and, of course, my love is always with you."

Mario smiled as he gave Mari's hand an especially tender squeeze of gratitude.

Mari smiled and said, "Now I have even more reason to get on with my own review and assimilate into my life here. Toby, thank you for your story. It has a special meaning for me. It reminded me of a time when the thought of suicide occurred to me. Blindness because of diabetes was one complication that I imagined I wouldn't have the strength to come to terms with. I remember even writing about it in my diary, because I was having laser treatments on my eyes. Now I know that there are reasons why suicide's not a wise choice."

"Thank you, Mari," Toby replied. "It means a lot that someone else has been helped by my experiences. Believe me, it's no fun dealing with all the consequences of our decisions that can be carried over. The lessons just get harder each time we refuse to get them. Right now, I question your wisdom in going there," he said to Mario, "but you have my support just the same."

"I know going in that it's tough there, but the potential to learn and to give back is awesome," Mario said, justifying his decision. "Besides, I'll be back before you three will even miss me."

"That remains to be seen," Jane threw in sarcastically. "Don't think for one minute that you won't be missed. I will offer just one suggestion for you to remember about that place. If you don't remind yourself to look for the positive there, you can really get sucked into the negative. Toby can attest to that. But let's deal with the present. This conversation has gotten too serious. Where were you two headed when we caught up to you?"

Grateful for the change of subject, Mario answered, "After a quick walk by the library, we were headed to a concert. How about joining us?"

"Oh yes," agreed Mari. "That would be great."

"Thanks for the invitation," Jane answered glancing appreciatively toward Toby, "but we'll pass for now. Toby and I have catching up to do and he could use some healing meditation time. Let us know when you are going to another concert. It's an amazing experience. You will love it."

With that, Mari and Mario said their goodbyes and made their way across the tiled plaza to a magnificent building that towered over all the others.

Fifty-three

The library was the largest and most grand building on the square. It had six Roman columns of glossy white marble capped with gilded carvings of heavenly beings. The face of the portico had a carving of angels gazing wisely into open scrolls. Immense translucent marble steps led invitingly to massive doors adorned with more carvings of angels; each draped with a ribbon that revealed their designated phylum written across it. They were each holding many books and scrolls. Mari and Mario stopped and watched souls of every description coming and going up the steps and through the doors.

Obviously, everyone in the spirit world dressed for their comfort. Mari noticed silky sarongs, colorful serapes, business suits, brocade kimonos, and smoking jackets with ascots, but she was happy to see that Bermuda shorts and blue jeans with tee shirts were just as prevalent. Everyone was a definite component of the whole scene, and there was harmony to it. It held an atmosphere of souls in the quest for knowledge.

"This is probably the most important building in this area," Mario informed Mari. "It's the library where you will be visiting with Saria for your review. Some call it the Hall of Records. It houses not only literary works from the world's past, present, and future, but also scrolls with everyone's life plans and records of their experiences. It's awesome even for here."

"Wonderful," was all Mari could say as she took in the grandeur of the building and the lush gardens that surrounded it. Just the thought that all that literary work was available to her thrilled her beyond measure.

"For now," said Mario, "let's take a stroll through the garden to the amphitheater. You'll enjoy the inside later with Saria."

He took her hand and led her to a stairway leading into a sunken garden to the right of the library. They glided down the steps that were every bit as grand as those leading into the building. At the bottom they arrived at a multi-colored stone patio. Paths branched in different directions through flourishing gardens, verdant vegetation, and vast plantings of brilliant flowers that were a feast for all the senses.

The colors were amazing, with hues that Mari was sure would be considered unusual to the physical world. Artists would have to persevere to manifest them in their works in that reality. Of course, for her, musical tones that correspond with those colors were part of the totality of the experience. Fragrances swirled around her. She was sure that she was tasting the sweet atmosphere.

They walked on, hand in hand, in peaceful silence on a path that led to the theater. Around every turn there were luminous marble and gold statuary depicting many aspects of the creative arts in the spirit world as well as the physical world. There was one of a golden angel over the shoulder of a poet with a scroll in hand. Another was of Shakespearian actors, and there was one of a painter, with an ear missing, intently studying his canvas. It was appropriately titled Listening.

By now, Mari had learned when to open her thoughts to others, but also how to enjoy her private musing. As she took pleasure in the gardens, she thought how her experiences here so far were staggeringly wonderful and far beyond her expectations and imagination. The sensory feasts were amazing enough, but the love and peace that she was feeling had to be the best feature of all. She felt appreciated and at home.

However, she was aware that she was still surrounded by a bubble of Earthly concerns that she desperately wanted to pop. She wanted to finally realize her acceptance and her potential in the spirit world. She felt like a visitor in this atmosphere of spiritual delights. Perhaps it was Mario's mention of his plan to incarnate on Earth that was bringing all of this to her heart.

She had taken the news rather well, but it made the bubble feel thicker and more daunting. Then again, maybe it was that she didn't feel deserving of all the good that was coming her way. She was still weighed down by the gravity of the experiences she had in the physical world. Some of her choices seemingly made life not only tough for her but also unnecessarily tough for many others as well. What was it all going to amount to when her review was over? Would she find out that she didn't deserve to be here? What then? She had learned that some souls accomplish their transition in the flash of an eye, but apparently it was not to be so easy for her.

She returned to the present, finding Mario looking at her with concern. "You don't have to share your thoughts, but I can't ignore that your light is looking a little dim," he said. "What's up?"

"I didn't mean to worry you," she replied, avoiding an explanation. "I just drifted away in my thoughts for a moment there. I'm back now."

"That's good, because we've arrived."

They rounded a turn through a thick stand of trees that seemed to be dancing in harmony with some faint music. It came from a stage situated beneath a gently sloping hillside that had a backdrop shaped like a big iridescent crystal clam shell. Musicians were assembling there and beginning to tune their instruments. Even this supposedly unorganized music sounded wonderful with its varied tones.

Some souls were already lounging on the velvety emerald lawn, while others were still appearing from the many paths that emptied into the arena. The atmosphere was one of cheerful anticipation, an electric energy that grew as the area filled with joyful souls. The concert hadn't even started yet, and Mari was already feeling the enticing vigor of souls coming together. Every gathering she'd attended so far had held that special elevated vibration that seemed to reach out and upward, with God giving a nod of blessing to all those assembled.

Mari and Mario relaxed with the others on the green carpet of silky grass as a hush came over the crowd. Mari wasn't sure if the ambiance had dimmed around them, or if the light above the stage was growing in intensity. Either way, the focus was on the stage. There were no lighting fixtures, but a beautiful glow shone onto and from the stage, reflecting off the white coats of the musicians as they settled in for the performance. Despite their coordinated attire, the appearances of the souls of the orchestra comprised a diverse, colorful group of nationalities, each displaying a confident eagerness. A shimmering hum seemed to be originating from the instruments themselves, their anticipation of the virtuosic talents that were about to be presented bringing them alive before a single note had been struck.

Tingles of eagerness touched Mari's entire chakra system as the conductor took the stage. What a beautiful entity he was. His commanding height and rugged build emanated a presence of strength, but with a gentle creative nature.

His massive frame bowed graciously toward the musicians, then he turned to the audience. The entire orchestra stood and bowed with him in gratitude for their attendance, and with obvious pleasure for the opportunity to perform their craft. At that, the audience all stood around Mari and Mario. They joined and bowed to the stage in return. Mari was touched by this simple act of mutual respect. They were all an essential part of the collective experience.

Fifty-four

The conductor smiled, turned to face the orchestra and gave a light tap on the podium with his baton. Then he raised both arms, lowered his head in concentration and stood for a moment in suspended silence. Like a lightning bolt, he sharply threw his whole body into the demands of the opening notes of a powerful composition. The silence became filled with a dramatic cascade of chords. His arms moved with a rhythmic and powerful precision that was reflected in the music, which filled the air with a brilliant kaleidoscope of color.

The look of intense concentration on the conductor's face reminded Mari of the rapture she had seen in a film clip of Elvis singing his beloved gospel songs. For him, gospel wasn't just any music. It seemed to be an experience that he worked so hard to share with humankind.

Mari watched in fascination as she perceived different colors issuing forth from each instrumental section on the stage. Each one altered in hue from wispy yellow to shades of blue and mauve, shifting with the shifting melodic notes of music. It was like an aura borealis of sight as well as sound that undulated across the stage.

Mari's soul drank in the whole experience. Her eyes were wide with wonder as her heart expanded with joyful emotions simmering beneath the surface of her ethereal body. This is exactly what she had wished she could have described when she told her mom, "Music is color." It pulsated all around her as she sat wide-eyed in awe.

Music had always affected Mari with emotional resonance that helped her to access her feelings in profound ways. Now she completely immersed herself in the energy of the concert, which was a presentation of a variety of styles from hints of Jazz to Baroque chamber music. It went on and on, but time was foreign to all present. The clarity of the sound allowed Mari to distinguish the notes of each instrument within the acoustics of her surroundings. They flowed all around her, as they all blended in an awesome artistry with every chord.

As the music washed over her and filled her heart, Mari closed her eyes and imagined her soul rising into the sky above the scene. Her imagination soared and flew to places beyond even this world. The harmonics took her into a universe displaying samples of the wonders of even more worlds for her soul's exploration. She felt freedom beyond words until finally the performance brought her back to the love that was all around her in the music.

If only she could have known this universal love, maybe she could have dealt better with life on Earth. She had known love, but this was more. She was being given a hint that it is her very essence and that she was one with all that is. If only she could grip that knowing tightly and hold onto it through her review maybe she could realize a successful transition.

She opened her eyes and could see that all of nature was completely absorbed in the blending rhythms, The surrounding trees were swaying to the music, as multicolored birds engaged in an energetic aerial dance above the treetops.

The repertoire continued to migrate from lightness to powerful movements that vibrated the ground where they sat. It flowed freely from sweetly lyrical to eloquent and majestic works, with the occasional hint of the chants of angels, who would appear above the stage. Her soul was on a fantastic roller coaster of color, melody, and harmony, until the energy of the music slowly began dissipating and faded into a glorious stillness that was filled with the subtle energy of the heightened experience.

The audience was stunned into silence for only a moment, then erupted into enthusiastic applause as the conductor and orchestra bowed in acknowledgement and appreciation, creating a wave of love that washed over the crowd. Mari joined the others in standing with rousing applause, to send that love back to them from the carpeted hillside in the form of sincere gratitude for this experience that was far beyond her expectations. This world was so amazing, and she could only imagine what more there was to see, hear, and feel. At this juncture she couldn't conceive of ever having to leave.

The conductor turned back to his orchestra and bowed gracefully to them, in homage to their talents. Then he stood tall and turned again to the audience, taking a few steps forward as the applause decelerated and the atmosphere brightened with the light that welled up among the audience members.

When all was quiet again, he stated in a deeply sonorous voice that carried effortlessly over the hillside, "Our deepest thanks to you all for being a part of this presentation. Your enthusiasm as an audience has made this event as eloquent for us as you are demonstrating that it has been for you."

His words met with another stirring ovation from the audience. As Mari gazed at those involved, she was caught up in the flow of the pure elation of all these souls who had gathered to participate in this sensory experience. She turned and locked eyes with Mario, who was smiling at her, sharing in her elation.

"And it's not over," continued the conductor smiling with a warm and respectful tone to his voice. "We have a special treat. A new composition with a dance theme has come to us recently. I shared the idea of the work with a kindred spirit of mine who has recently returned here. Kamia is a choreographer and dancer with a particular appreciation for the freedom of her craft.

"She recently, and very bravely, I might add, gave up her dancing here to spend an entire manifestation on Earth confined to a wheelchair, and now she knows and appreciates her talents here with a refreshing new awareness. While in that incarnation, she was united with her partner, Jemel, who was a source of love and strength for her then, and was here to welcome her back home."

"Kamia and Jemel join us now to share their personally choreographed celebration of freedom set to this new work titled Victory."

Fifty-five

As the conductor turned back toward the orchestra, the atmosphere of the audience softened to a pinkish glow, drawing attention to the radiant white light of the stage. It appeared to be made of a smooth opaque glass that was back lit, emanating a warm incandescence.

A gently echoing melody began as the orchestra faded behind a gossamer veil, directing attention to the bare portion of the stage. The music reflected the hauntingly exotic tones of Middle Eastern music that Mari could imagine emanating from a Turkish café. Every lovely note was melded into the fluid movements of a gorgeous being who was magically appearing before them.

Kamia materialized on the left side of the stage, her long, silken black hair flowing in gentle waves around her shoulders and down the elegant curve of her back. Every graceful movement was synchronized perfectly with the music in the serpentine grace of her arms, which seemed to be speaking to the audience in a dialect all their own.

She was a vision of unusual beauty, with a warm bronze complexion and mystical, dark eyes. They revealed a triumphant soul totally in the moment and at one with her talent. Her delicately sinuous, white dress began in graceful folds over her left shoulder and stretched across the feminine curves of her torso to a softly flared knee-length skirt that revealed firm, finely muscular legs. Mari was mesmerized by the flow of the silky skirt. Her eyes followed the gleam of Kamia's glittering shoes with delicate straps, and heels that caressed her dainty feet. They moved with an exquisite loveliness to the exotic melody that filled the atmosphere around her. It was difficult to comprehend those same legs and feet misshapen and ineffective in a physical body.

Jemel eased into view on the right. He was a magnificent creature as well, with a strongly masculine countenance, and the purest love in his dark eyes, which were fixed on his beautiful partner. He wore a gleaming, white silk shirt that hugged his muscular midriff and tucked into form fitting white slacks, which flared ever so slightly over white flamenco-style boots. The talent in his energy was a wonder to behold as he moved in perfect unison with Kamia, and the music intensified and quickened as they were drawn closer together.

The dance and the music were indeed a "celebration of freedom." Every movement was a jubilant expression of joy and their unrestrained creativity. Every dip, sway, and turn in the light of the stage held Mari's gaze. She reveled in spirited blitheness and vitality.

As she watched the delightful display of artistic energy, Mari had to blink with surprise. She thought that she was imagining the two dancers becoming translucent, but they indeed were taking on a luminant transparency as they moved in front of each other, so the audience could see the form of one partner through the essence of the other. Their bodies were magically dipping and twirling together on the stage, a surface that was beginning to undulate with an enchanted vapor that fluttered at their feet. Their movements became more intimate, and they melded perfectly with the slowing rhythm of the music. A swirling rainbow of colors flowed around them.

Finally, well above the stage, their one glowing, celestially merged body floated within an amethyst essence that shifted into an opalescent cloud. The singular body of the dancers, which had now merged completely into one spirit, disappeared into the opaqueness. The cloud inhaled the energetic essence of the united spirit and expanded into the heavens, becoming a pure, dazzling white light that intensified with a penetrating brightness. It illuminated the atmosphere of the other-worldly theater and blessed every face present with a golden glow.

Mari had never experienced such a sublimely glorious demonstration of love. It grew warmly in her heart and vibrated throughout her essence. She was feeling God in God's own world. The dancers had taken them all into the experience of oneness with God's love. Their souls were now totally in tune with that love. It was the spirit, the very life, the quintessence of the combined strength of the music, the color and light that created the intense energy of this heavenly moment. Mari not only felt one with God, but also with all those around her. They were one pulsating blossom opening to the light of purest love.

Slowly, she began to focus on another light, within the white light, that was beginning to condense itself into a golden ball hovering over the stage. It began to shimmer and vibrate, breathing in the affection from the audience until they could hear a constant rhythm from the tympani drum in the orchestra, which was becoming visible once again on the stage. When the timpanist reached an intense pitch, the rest of the musicians joined in with an emphatic crash of cymbals as the golden ball exploded into glorious sparks. Each spark burst into sparkling crystals that fell with a light tinkling sound on the now marble stage, then melted into its light.

A peaceful silence filled the atmosphere. A blessing was bestowed on all who were present, and heads were instinctively bowed in reverence. Then suddenly they were aware of a rustling on the stage. They all looked up to see the dancers, each returning from opposite sides of the stage, radiant and glowing as they joined hands and bowed deeply.

Mari jumped up with Mario and the rest of the audience as they greeted the performers with hoots, hollers, and appreciative applause. Kamia and Jemel's faces were beaming with wide smiles as they bowed again and blew kisses, then receded behind a lowering curtain. The conductor stepped forward and simply said, "Thank you all."

As the enthusiastic applause began again, the stage and the performers all faded from view and disappeared. Mari and Mario found themselves, along with the rest of the audience, sitting once again on a beautiful hillside, stunned and feeling part of the bouquet of a world bound with a white satin ribbon of God's binding presence.

Mari was wonderstruck. She had been happy to be sitting beside her love, then the concert had started, transcending her to places that had only been in her dreams. What could she say? There were no words. It was all pure elated emotions at this point.

Mario's amused smile penetrated her blissful trance and pulled her back to their present as they sat quietly while the other audience members departed gleefully in couples and groups.

"What!" she blurted out, a little perturbed at his playful stare.

He let out a hearty laugh, then said sweetly, "You're beautiful and you are glowing."

She looked down shyly as he took her hands that were visibly displaying what she was feeling. They were indeed glowing with an aura that tingled as it danced from her fingertips like elegant, golden electricity.

Taking a deep breath, she found her voice, and asked cautiously in order not to lose the enchantment of the moment, "Is everything here this wonderful?"

"This and more," he answered lovingly. "This and more."

Mari became a little confused. She felt euphoric. Still, at the same time, there was the confusing dim hint of a shadow in the background of her thoughts that perhaps she was not yet deserving of all the marvels of this divine world that were being shown to her. Her Earthly self hadn't released her soul completely yet. She wanted so much to shake it off, but try as she might, it wouldn't leave. The heaviness of it was preventing her from accepting that all of this was hers, not just to behold, but also for her to claim as her present, her future, and her continuing story.

"There is so much more that I want to experience with you," said Mario. "Imagine skimming across an emerald sea in a crystal four-master with silken sails, or gliding atop Pegasus, unencumbered and fearless through a moonlit sky glistening with stars and planets that you can visit any time you wish. Or imagine yourself sitting in a grassy field with fascinating animals snuggling around you, all trying to be caressed at once. I can hear your delighted giggles that I know so well and long to hear again.

"But for now, try to be easy on yourself. We know that you must complete your orientation."

He paused, trying to think of what might help her as she faced the review that was coming up. She was a part of him, and he knew her better than she could even imagine. What she needed was something that her emotions could latch onto and give her strength. As he sought guidance, Mario instantly found an answer. "In the meantime, what would you think of visiting the place where you and Jane have worked together? Maybe it would help to know more about that part of your past here."

"I'd like that," Mari replied. "I guess it's another piece of the puzzle that I need to know about. I must admit that I'm more than a little curious."

"Well then, let's do it!" Mario exclaimed as he stood and offered Mari his hand.

Fifty-six

"Good afternoon," Deirdre said as Suzi answered her phone. "What's shakin' in your world today?"

"Not much," answered Suzi, "but now that you called, I have high hopes of it getting more interesting. What's new with you?"

"Not much here either," Dee replied, "but I just had to tell you, I had a colonoscopy this morning."

"That's not much fun," said Suzi. "Did it go well?"

"Oh yeah. I'm good," said Dee. "But it was so weird, while the meds were wearing off, I was feeling pretty good and I started getting information, so I laid there giving all the nurses and staff impromptu readings. It was pretty wild. I've never done anything like that before."

"That is hilarious," commented Suzi. "Goes to show you what you are capable of when you are relaxed."

"Yeah, I'll have to remember that," said Dee. "Not the drugs. Just letting myself relax. Speaking of relaxing into what we do, how about an update on your project?"

"Still slow," said Suzi. "I'm mostly making notes about memories with Mari. When I figure out what format flows for me, I'm sure I can refer back to those notes. I do get inspired impressions that I'm fairly certain are Mari trying to get my attention. I keep notes about that also. I've got notes everywhere."

"She is strongly around you, but you are still standing by that doorway blocking her," said Dee. "You need to get your ass out of the way, Sweetheart."

"I don't think it's that simple," offered Suzi. "I have a strong impression that she may still be processing her new existence and going through a transition experience over there. The veil is still feeling dense to me.

"I know she was with me after the dream I had about her, but it makes sense to me that visitations get more difficult as she grows into a higher vibration. I'm ok with that. I can be patient. And I'm getting more confident that it has to do with timing. I'm making efforts to raise my spiritual vibration to meet her when we are both ready."

"That will happen," said Deirdre. "I can feel it. You are meant to do this, and it sounds like you are getting a solid handle on it. Let me know if I can help."

"Yes, I will," said Suzi. "You have already helped by nagging me into it and I appreciate that. In a way, this is helping my own spiritual growth."

"I do what I can," said Dee.

"On another note, I have a story for you. I'm sure you remember me mentioning my sister-in-law, Mindy. Well, I was with her in her van the other day and there was a five-gallon bucket next to her seat. I'm curious, so I asked her what it was for."

"I would too," commented Suzi. "So, what did she say?"

"She answered, 'Oh, that's for my ashes when my body self-implodes.' If I wasn't as polite as I am, I would have bust a gut laughing, but she was deadpan serious. I just said, 'Well that's very tidy and considerate of you.' That girl is not normal, but she is loveable and amusing."

"Your world is just full of interesting people," said Suzi. "They must be out there seeking you out. Or you just attract them. But I can't say much. After all I am one of your weirdo entourages."

"You're one of the saner ones," said Dee. "Welcome to my world."

Fifty-seven

The atmosphere around Mari and Mario became a field dappled with multi-colored poppies and buttercups, as daisies occasionally lifted bright heads above the other flowers. Iridescent butterflies, with wings that looked like they were made of jewel-toned stained glass, fluttered from blossom to blossom, and colorful flocks of birds flew through rainbows and over billowing marshmallow clouds. Many of the birds landed in the emerald canopies of giant evergreen trees, as well as in trees that were heavy with pink and white blossoms. Mari felt that she was in an intensely vivid fairytale setting as she imagined that there surely was a castle somewhere off in the distance.

A glistening white gazebo with ivy and roses climbing its posts showed the landscape with just one other structure in view, a bridge over a crystal-clear brook. Over the bridge was a vibrant triple rainbow. Beyond that, the view was obscured in a vaporous mist that undulated with dull muted colors. Mari saw the striking contrast between the conflicting atmospheres and recognized the muted one. It was cloudy while she stood in a world of bright light and color

As Mari's eyes became accustomed to the scene around her, Jane slowly appeared, sitting on the steps of the gazebo with three children at her feet, staring up at her attentively. The two boys and a younger girl were engrossed in a lively conversation with Jane, who was glowing with a subtle white light tinted ever so softly with pinks and blues. Though her aura was pastel shades, she appeared bright compared to the dullness of the children's auras. Mari knew instinctively that they had just crossed over that marvelous bridge from the murky dimension where they lived on earth. Their faces shone with wonder and excitement, and their auras grew a bit brighter as they each spoke excitedly, telling individual stories of their crossing. Jane's demeanor was subdued, but her smile was warm and inviting as she listened intently.

The scene unfolded further, and Mari began to see many souls around the gazebo that she assumed were the loved ones who had met the children on their journey over the bridge. The tender devotion that permeated the atmosphere was intoxicating and she smiled at Mario, who was still beside her. He gave her hand a tender squeeze before he put his arm around her shoulder to pull her closer. They listened to the little dark-haired girl, who appeared to be about four years old. She was telling Jane she was happy to be free of her illness. As she spoke, a Redbird fluttered past her capturing the girl's attention. Then it flew by Mari and Mario, who were standing some distance to the side.

Her story halted mid-sentence, and she jumped up, her eyes as big and bright as a shiny blue Christmas ornament. She ran excitedly to Mari. "You're the lady with the flute!" she exclaimed. "You were in my dream before I died! You were in a field, and you had flowers in your hair. Then this guy showed up, she was beaming as she turned her gaze to Mario, and he had a big red nose. You were both laughing so hard. Then, I woke up and I felt like I really was there with you."

Mari bent down and smiled as she remembered a fleeting glimpse of a faint aura that she had noticed when she was amused by Mario's little joke.

"I think maybe you were indeed there," she answered with a twinkle in her eye. "I was sensing that there was someone with us. I'm glad you remember."

"It was neat," the girl responded. "I remember a lullaby in my dream first, then I went to that place, and I wanted to go there for real someday. It was so pretty and felt so good. Oh yeah. I'm Penny. Who are you?"

Touched by the enthusiasm of this precious soul, Mari said, "Well, welcome home, Penny. I'm Mari and my friend here is Mario. And you have arrived in that magical place." Penny took Mari's hand, and they chatted while Mari walked her back to her place with Jane and the others.

The two boys, who appeared to be about eight and eleven years old, were curious about what was going on. Penny wasted no time telling them about her wonderful dream.

When Penny finally slowed down, Jane greeted Mari and Mario and introduced the boys, Peter and Nicolas, and informed them that Mari was her coworker, but she was sort of on vacation right now.

"You mean we have to work here?" said the older and self-assuming, wiser boy, Peter.

"Sure thing," Jane informed him. "We work to help, but we play a lot and learn as we go along. It's something like where you came from but it's so much better. Our work here is more fun. And we have great parties. You just wait and see. You'll love it. Take like right now. You can't believe how much fun this is for me to be here with you. I'm having a great time, and this is part of my work."

"I agree whole heartedly," Mari concurred. "I just came from a concert that had the best music I've ever heard, but I'm just as excited to be here with you. It's all so amazing."

"Will you play your flute for us?" the quiet, eight-year-old Nicolas asked Mari.

She smiled a mischievous little smile and said, "Sure!" as she snapped her fingers for effect and her gleaming flute appeared in her hands. She added, "If that's ok with Jane."

"Oh cool!" exclaimed Nicolas as the instrument materialized.

Fifty-eight

The children sat open-mouthed and wide eyed at Mari's magic trick and Jane gave her a grateful nod. "That's a great idea," she said.

Mari started with the lullaby that Penny remembered from her dream, then segued into a lilting little ditty. Penny jumped up and began a sweet fairy-like dance through the wildflowers.

Nicolas hesitated to join in. His legs were new to him after being horribly crippled in his recent life. Mari gave Jane a questioning look. In return, she did a slight shoulder shrug and gave Mari a mental image that told her that Nicolas was an innocent victim in a recent war on the Earth plane.

She had a vision of him walking down a street with his mother. Then there was an awful red and orange flash as the air around them filled with black smoke and debris while people shouted and cried out in pain. Though shocked, Mari was certain that she was seeing a scene from the Middle East with domed buildings in the background. She found it interesting that, here in the spirit world, it didn't really matter which side of the conflict had caused his impairment or even what his nationality had been. Here he was a child's soul and a blameless victim.

A new emotion began to awaken in the core of her own soul. It flowed from pity to sadness, and finally settled in her heart as something that was a blend of love, empathy, and, more important, a profound gratitude for the souls who sign on with God to become innocent victims to inspire other souls struggling on the Earth plane.

She was becoming accustomed to this intense range of feelings. They were more powerful than any single emotion possible in the physical world. She heard Jane's soft whisper, "That's what we do as a spiritual family. We do what is needed there to try to get the attention of other souls who have become too absorbed in that reality and are working against the cause of higher good for the world."

Nicolas moved clumsily for a moment, but the appreciation of the new freedom of his agile spirit body spurred him on until he was out moving with the other children, laughing with an abandoned glee. He watched his feet as if they were dancing on their own.

Peter finally smiled and joined in with his own version of acrobatic hip hop moves.

Now the children, as well as Mari, were enjoying their merry dance as Jane, Mario, and the gathering of loved ones beamed with loving approval and swayed along to the tune. The atmosphere around the scene grew lighter and lighter and the dancers didn't even notice when their feet started lifting off the ground. They danced on and on and higher and higher until they approached the tops of the trees abandoning any vestiges of Earthly fears. They swayed with the trees and dipped with the twittering birds as they discovered their own higher vibratory selves.

Finally, Penny looked down and just giggled harder. The others caught on and showed no fear as they did flips, turns and wild aerodynamic acrobatics. They floated and soared through the forest and played hide and seek among the treetops. In their joy, the children's auras brightened and cleared until they became in sync with their bright new world and the glorious life that now awaited them. It was an event of healing for their precious bodies, minds, and spirits.

"She's still got it," Mario whispered to Jane.

"Oh yeah," she answered. "And I can't wait to have her back with us."

"Ditto," was all he could reply.

Jane cupped her hands around her mouth and yelled up to the children, "HEY YOU GUYS! YOU HAVE GOT A PARTY TO GO TO."

The children whooped and hollered in response, then lowered themselves back down to the gazebo. Each child's loved ones gathered around them, then slowly faded off to their welcome celebrations. Penny, Nicolas, and Peter waved enthusiastically to their tutors, who were throwing them kisses that took the form of little red hearts with wings fluttering off after them.

Mari was beaming with delight as she put her hand on her heart and gave a great sigh. "That was fabulous," she exclaimed, "and it did as much for me as it seemed to do for them. If this is work, bring it on is all I have to say. This is better than any amusement park."

"Yeah," Jane smiled. "Just another workday in Paradise. And we do have amusement parks here. Just imagine the rides. Why don't you get on with your exams so you can graduate from that worldly university that you need to leave behind.

"You're so right," Mari agreed. "I'm ready." Despite the awesome experience she had just enjoyed, she felt the weight of that old heaviness coming back and tempering her mood. She hadn't had any flashbacks for some time now, and was experiencing some anxiety about returning to those places in her mind. Some of the memories were good, of course, but others were darker and difficult to think about. She knew she had to face them so she could release them and move on. She wanted to have a real future in this new home, and was aching to get on with it.

Mari turned to Mario and said, "I'd like to touch base with my grandmother now and catch up with Saria."

"YEE HAW!" came a whopping cry from the treetops. Saria appeared, waving her cowgirl hat, still enjoying the romp in the verdant foliage. Mari laughed and realized that Saria had obviously been with her all this time, sharing her experiences. "You can really kick up your heels when you want to," she told Mari as she lowered herself to join the others. "Whew! That was fun. What's next?"

When she was lowered to their level, Saria could sense Mari's anxiety about her review.

"Okay," she said, "I get it. Where to then?"

"I'd like to see my grandmother," Mari answered. "I feel that I need to see her now."

"Your call, Kiddo," was her spirit guide's response. Then she addressed Jane and Mario. "How about you two? Coming along?"

"Back to work for me," replied Jane, as she turned her attention to some lights beginning to flicker on the bridge.

"Me, too," Mario answered as he touched Mari's hair with sweet affection. "It's back to the greenhouses. You're in good hands, and I have preparations to make. I'll catch up later."

He gave her a wink, and Mari and Saria proceeded to move through that familiar and comfortable void that transported them from place to place in this wonderful, multi-faceted world.

Fifty-nine

A shiny blue pick-up truck was sitting at the gate of Lilly's cottage. Mari was pleased that Claus must be there. They knocked at the familiar pink door out of respect. They could have just shown up in Lilly's living room, but that wouldn't be polite even here.

The door opened on its own, welcoming the visitors into the inviting warmth of the cozy cottage. Mari's eyes were met with the unexpectedly dazzling scene of four beings of brilliant heavenly light sitting comfortably and visiting. Their bodies radiated with a joyful light that was emanating from their hearts and illuminating every aspect of their bodies. Even their casual attire was aglow with the positive loving energy that filled the room with incredible brightness. As Mari's eyes adjusted to the dazzling light, she recognized three of the figures as Lilly, Claus and Lenora, Mari's great grandmother. She didn't recognize the energy of the fourth member, who was lovely with an equally glowing countenance.

The sight was beyond beautiful, and from Mari's perspective, it penetrated her own being as well as the walls of the room, which appeared translucent, revealing fabulous tromp l'oeil scenes of the abundant vegetation in the outside environment.

Lilly rose and approached her arriving guests. As she did so, the light of her essence dimmed and condensed within her body, making her appearance gentler for Mari to behold.

"There," she said when she reached Mari and gave her a big hug. "This should be more comfortable for you." Releasing the embrace, she informed Mari, "You've just seen us for the light beings that we really are. We've been toning it down for you in your travels here so far, but it was time for you to experience us in our true essences."

"Oh, thank you so much! You're all so beautiful!" Mari exclaimed, her eyes reflecting the gleaming light like tiny pieces of azure mirror.

Lilly gave Saria a welcoming smile, then took Mari's hand, leading her and Saria to a pair of armchairs that had appeared for them, forming a cozy conversational arrangement with the others. Greetings were exchanged all around and Lilly introduced the newcomer as her friend, Marabeth.

"She is part of my spiritual family here," she told Mari. "You wouldn't know her from your last life. She and I only made contact when we were children in that lifetime. I think I was about five and you," she addressed Marabeth, "were older, about seven years old."

"That's right," Marabeth chimed in with a delightful voice that had hints of a bell-like quality to it. "And little Lilly Mae was a real stinker, too," she added with a warm smile in Lilly's direction. "She teased me mercilessly about my big feet until I finally had to put her in her place. I gave her little feet a smirk and informed her that outhouses were built on small foundations."

Lilly blushed, "Ok, you got me with that, but we did become friends for just a short while over there. We're close friends here, but we only needed to make a brief contact, and that connection did our souls a lot of good."

Mari saw the genuine relationship between the two friends, but she was radiating question marks again. "I've been hearing references about spiritual family," she addressed the entire group. "Is that something unique to here?"

"Good question," Claus commented.

"Yeah, I've got a million of them," teased Mari with a facetious wink. "So can we just address this one?"

"Family is pretty much a universal concept," said Claus, with an air of the scientist. "On Earth it's an actual physical, genetic relationship. But, in reality, we are all joined on the soul level. The universe becomes a small place when it comes to connected souls."

"Now that's a pretty big idea for this little girl to get her mind around," Lenora threw into the conversation. "Let's look at a situation she can identify with. Your mom and her cousin, Deirdre, are connected genetically but it goes beyond that. Because they are also in our spiritual family here in this world, they can relate to each other because they know each other on a higher plane."

"The thing to know," Marabeth interjected, "is that before they went to Earth, the girls decided that they would connect on that level. They wrote it into their plans so they could be a support for each other. It's tough to be there without camaraderie."

"That's so true," Lilly added. "Then there are situations like Marabeth and me. We are in a spiritual family here, but we agreed to only meet briefly on Earth and when we did, we recognized each other on the soul level. Marabeth was only visiting my neighbors for a few days, but when we met there, I felt I had known her forever. That, indeed, was the case."

"To take it a bit further," Lilly went on to explain, "in that incarnation, Marabeth went on to have a daughter whom your mother, Suzi, is scheduled to meet in the new home on Hood Canal. She, along with a few others, make up a spiritual family. They will find a strong mutual bond that will help complete your mother's healing and be a blessing to them all. The term spiritual family can take in many souls who can be connected on many levels."

"That's reassuring," said Mari. "Thank you, Gramma."

"Lilly, do you remember the Redbirds?" Marabeth asked her sister-in-spirit.

Lilly gave her a big smile. "Oh, they were wonderful," she answered beaming, then turned to Mari. "We were in my back yard, in St. Louis, Missouri, when a whole flock of cardinals flew into the pine tree just whistling and singing their hearts out. They were so beautiful against the dark green of the tree. The Redbird has become sort of a totem for our spiritual family."

"I know they were important to you," Mari remembered. "You told me all about them when I was a kid, and you had ceramic Redbirds all over your house. Even Great-Gramma Lenora told me about them when she visited from Missouri." She gave Lenora a gentle smile, then continued to address Lilly. "We knew you loved them, so we always looked for them on gifts that we bought for you. We grew to love them, too. And I've enjoyed seeing them here for real. And I also remember that as a small child, I only knew them as Redbirds. In school I was surprised to find out that they were called cardinals."

"Oh, Doll Baby, where we come from that's what we all called them," offered Great-Grandma Lenora. "Cardinal was a less personal word for us. We just loved our Redbirds. Besides, we didn't have to know their fussy name to appreciate their song."

"They were one thing that I really missed living in the Northwest," Lilly volunteered. "Their song was so sweet. They reminded me of home. At the time, I thought that meant Missouri, but now I know it was more to do with my spiritual home. And here I can have them sing for me any time I fancy."

"Well, you ladies can reminisce all you like," said Claus as he stood to leave. "It's back to work for me. Thank you for the good company." He bowed to them all and faded away.

"Me, too," said Marabeth. "It's been a pleasure, but the library awaits my return. We have some new manuscripts going out to the other side. There's some exciting stuff. I'll probably see you there soon, Mari." She gave a wave and faded from Grandma Lilly's living room.

"So," said Lilly, addressing her granddaughter, "you're on your way to your review."

"Oh, Gramma," sighed Mari, "I'm so ready. With all that I've learned since I've been here, I know that I need to try to move on.

"You've all been so wonderful, but I'm getting weary of being an observer. It's time to be a participant in this life, if that is what is meant for me. I want to work and contribute to this amazing place, but I'm feeling my past like a weight around my ankles in a bottomless lake. From visions I've had of my memories, I think I can handle whatever it is that I have to deal with. At least I know it's time to try."

"You're wise to want to move on," Lilly added with concern, "and I'm glad that you're aware of the more intense impact of a total review. Saria will be there for you in any capacity that you need."

Up until now, Saria had been hovering in the background enjoying the conversation. She was well aware of what had to be done. Even though she could guide with confidence, she understood that she could not attempt to control the situation. Free will and no direct interference was the bane to spirit guides in so many situations. Fortunately for their clients, the love was there for them first and foremost.

Sixty

Suddenly a great rush of wind and the audible swish of powerful wings interrupted the conversation. Saria and Lilly looked at each other with grave concern.

"Oh my!" exclaimed a stunned Mari. "What was that?"

"It's an alarm. A call to action," Saria answered quickly. "Something serious is up on Earth and we need to be with our loved ones in the physical world. You know how to be with your mom. Do it now," she directed Mari. "Lilly and I can be present in many places at once, so you don't need to be concerned for anyone else. In fact, Lilly, why don't you send a part of yourself with Mari?"

"Consider it done," she replied as she took the startled Mari's hand. Together, they immediately went to Suzi's side in the physical world. Neither knew what to expect, but they were dedicated to help however they could.

They found Suzi in the stillness of an early Northwest autumn morning. She was just starting her day, pouring a cup of coffee and sitting down before the television to catch up on the morning news. Pressing the power button of the remote, she went directly into the Today Show, which had been interrupted by announcers who were in a state of panic. The newscasters were stunned as they reported that one of the twin towers of the World Trade Center in New York City had just been directly hit by an airplane.

Lilly and Mari were just as shocked as Suzi as they sat invisibly by her side, watching the horrific scene unfold. It was awful beyond words. Even through the television, Lilly and Mari were able to see the many angels and guides who were lifting a multitude of souls from the destruction.

Then, as if that weren't enough, a live shot showed a second plane heading for the other tower.

"Oh my god!" Suzi shrieked as the airplane hit the tower. In that moment she also heard the voice of her departed daughter Mari cry out, "OH NO! BUT THEY'RE INNOCENT!"

Even though she was in a state of shock, Suzi knew that voice instantly. She was overcome with a flood of her own emotions, as well as all the concern and love from the Other Side.

Tears and shock clouded the atmosphere as Lilly and Mari, along with all the other loving spirits who had arrived on that horrific scene to help, sent their love to Suzi and to all the other souls of the world who were now, and would be for a very long time, feeling the pain that was thrust upon the world of Earthly humanity in those few moments.

As Suzi spoke to Mitch on the phone sometime later, Lilly and Mari could see that she was in good hands. They had done their job to be with her, just as Mitch's "light team" and departed loved ones were with him. It was time to get back and assess the situation with other souls from the Other Side who had participated in the event. Many were needed to be there for those dead and dying victims crossing over whose transformations needed to be swift.

Mari was given a vision of the life-altering future effects of that historic event as she and Lilly left the scene. By instinct, she sent an emanation of her love and concern to flow through her beloved family, combined with the outpouring of love from the entire heavens to a troubled and confused world.

Sixty-one

"Well, Kiddo," Saria smiled tenderly at her determined charge as they returned their concentration to the business at hand and settled back into the warmth of Lilly's lovely home. "I can't tell you much about the review process because every soul is different. As you already know, we each go into physical life with our own self-assigned lessons and tasks to accomplish. This is your show, but I do get the feeling that the review system for you may have more to do with forgiveness than judgment.

"Good insight" Lilly agreed, "and all our love goes with you."

"Thank you," said Mari. She gave her grandmother and her great grandmother each a big hug and turned to Saria.

With a simple nod of her head, she and her spirit guide found themselves at the foot of the stairs leading up into the library. She remembered it from her time with Mario after they toured the marketplace, but that had been a much more relaxing time. Now the massive steps to the entrance were a little less inviting, and the atmosphere was free of the colorful souls she had seen on that previous visit. She and Saria were alone, looking up at the carved angels gazing down at them from the portico.

As Mari stood transfixed, her eyes took in the grand marble stairway before her. She felt a blend of emotions swirling somewhere between anticipation and dread, but she was driven forward knowing full well that something felt unfinished. Hopefully it was the review itself that would finalize so much for her or possibly send her back through the veil to another dreaded physical incarnation.

She tried to imagine what it would be like to go back. Was it true that if we don't complete our contract and accomplish our planned goals, it becomes even more difficult with each try? She saw herself in her last life crying alone in her apartment and feeling a total failure.

She and Saria began ascending the stairs, which resembled the stone stairways climbing toward the heavens on an Inca temple. With each step, questions started overcoming her in a tidal wave of uncertainty. Could she face her past? Did she do all that she had signed up for, and contribute to that life in a positive way? And, most of all, who was she, after all? Was she that sweet little girl, joyfully playing on the floor with her kitten. Or was she the desperate, troubled anorexic fighting back the pervasive hunger that haunted her whenever the food trays were delivered in the hospital? Or, would she find that, in fact, she truly was that flute-playing, working horticultural scientist who also served as counselor to precious innocent child souls who were returning to their heavenly home.

Despite feeling at one with every loving, self-assured soul she had met since crossing over, there was still a part of her that was holding on to Earthly insecurities. She was already judging herself before she knew what waited for her at the top of the stairway.

But she continued step by step, grateful to have Saria by her side. She tried so hard to gain control of her thoughts, but a vision of Toby suddenly appeared in her mind. A gripping fear began to slow her ascent as she recalled his story. She wondered about the idea that some souls don't transition here but instead return to Earth to finish their contract with God. Would her anorexia be mistaken for a suicidal desire? But, no, she hadn't wanted to die. She had felt out of control, and her eating was the only thing that she felt she could control. Her brain was in a constant fog due to the uncontrolled diabetes.

A weakness was beginning to seize her and she almost stumbled, but Saria was there to catch her. She held fast to Mari's shoulders as she gave her a serious, reproving glare and said softly, "This isn't the time to let your mind run amuck. Let's take a breather and get some perspective on this whole thing."

They sat down midway on the stairway and Saria encouraged Mari to take a few deep breaths to relax. "I guess I should have remembered how you have a tendency to create trouble in your mind before it happens," Saria began. "So, let's talk about the review."

"Oh, yes. Please do," Mari sighed. "I'd appreciate that."

"Well, you already know that you will see your entire life, but I can add that, like almost everything here, that too can be customized to accommodate our unique souls. Some choose to see it all on a huge Imax-like screen, and have it play out as if it were an academy-award-winning movie. Others prefer to sit at a computer-type screen to see it all. Or we have tables where souls can relax and view their lives as three-dimensional holographic images. Why, I have even heard of a circus performer who had his life displayed before him like a circus parade!"

That image helped Mari to smile and gain a little more composure.

"I can say," Saria continued on a serious note, "it's quite the experience however you choose to do it. I'll be available and a lot of love goes with you. So, shall we continue?"

Sixty-two

Mari nodded and rose with Saria. The steps seemed easier to manage now that she was a tad more at ease. They quickly reached the veranda with the enormous doors, carved so beautifully with angels of every phylum. From cherubim and seraphim to the archangels and principalities, all were depicted in the wondrous work of art. The eyes of the images sparkled and smiled at the two visitors as the door opened ever so slowly to allow their entry.

Mari gasped. She was struck by the immensity of the space, as well as the contents of this wonderful place. It was like another whole world that was vast and soaring, compared to heights that she had imagined from outside.

They entered a huge foyer and stepped onto the gold, and silver-veined marble floor, which was set in a classic diamond pattern. Softly muted paintings in ornate gilt frames did not hang on the walls but hovered at their eye level in the space above the floor. Each work of art subtly depicted scenes of angels giving comfort to souls of every nationality and creed. It was a beautiful demonstration and expression of the close relationship of faith and art.

As they walked slowly and reverently through the room, Mari's eyes were drawn from one painting which showed angels with Eskimos on the frozen tundra, to another that showed those heavenly protectors aboard what looked like a spacecraft. Then she saw one with multiple angels hovering over a group of frightened children. In the background was a city with a domed Mosque. Smoke was coming from the building that the children were staring at in shock.

As her eyes jumped from one picture to another, Mari noticed that the golden-framed pictures would magically mist over, then change to new scenes revealing other protected souls. Angels were everywhere and in every situation. The rendering to which she could identify most was a simple one of an angel sitting on a bed with her arm around a young blonde girl, who had her nose in a book and a gray kitten curled up on her lap. Tears clouded her eyes as she recognized her bedroom when she was a child. This frame didn't mist over as long as she gazed at it.

Mari stood transfixed until Saria took her by the elbow, leading her from the foyer and the hovering artwork. They approached a beautiful, crystal stairway, that led upward toward the lofts that soared above them. Those upper floors had rows upon rows of shelves filled with beautifully bound books, while others had shelves replete with rolled parchment scrolls. Comfortable furnishings invited a quiet read or serious study. Gilt and marble sculptures of serene figures in graceful poses rested at the end of each aisle. It even smelled like new books with rich leather bindings. Mari yearned to spend some time exploring those grand upper floors.

What she did not see, amidst all this grandeur and history, were any actual beings.

Her eyebrows furrowed, she turned to Saria. Saria, hearing and seeing Mari's unspoken questions, said, "This place appears empty of people to you because we are here in what might be referred to as a frozen moment in time. Your focus needs to be on you. This building is normally a hot bed of activity, with all of us coming and going constantly. We spirit guides spend a lot of time here to help you, by coming to check your chart to try to keep you on track. That's mostly what the scrolls are. They're soul charts."

"So, the charts are real tangible things. Where do we possibly find mine in all of this?" Mari asked as she gazed into the heights of this brightly lit building.

"That would be on the second floor," replied Saria. "It's a lot like when you go to a doctor's clinic and the receptionist already has your medical chart. In fact, this is where they got that idea on Earth. We're very organized here. Yours will be waiting for us."

She led Mari up the translucent stairs, which were clear with veined opaque inclusions on each step. Instead of posts to support the railings, there were huge gleaming crystal clusters on either side. She was feeling lighter and very blessed with every step as they glided to the second floor.

"I want to remind you," whispered Saria in the sacred atmosphere, "of what I said before. So much of your plan has to do with forgiveness."

"I'll keep that in mind," Mari whispered in reply. She was a little confused, because she thought that she had taken full responsibility for her life without blaming anyone else.

When they reached the top, they approached an arched doorway. It opened to a small sitting room that was waiting for them. To the left of the door sat a lovely, ivory, upholstered winged-back chair. Mari smiled to see that, here, a winged-back chair had actual wings. The curved wings on the back appeared to be made of the same soft feathers as the angel's wings in the portraits on the first floor. It was an inviting chair in which Mari was sure one could feel wrapped within an angel's wings. Across the room was an arched door leading to another room.

Saria turned Mari to face her, gently holding onto her shoulders as she looked deeply into her eyes with sincere compassion and said, "Well, Kid, I can go in there with you or just be available for you here. It's your call."

Mari turned and looked through the doorway. The room was inviting.

Cream-colored walls painted with a pearly, embossed paisley design shimmered subtly in a radiant glow of candlelight. She could see that in the center of the space was a small, ornately carved ivory desk with an ivory damask upholstered chair. On the desk stood a pedestal covered with a sheer white scarf, on which lay a scroll rolled out and ready for viewing. It shone brightly in the light of a large white candle, which glowed warmly on a carved alabaster pedestal. The entire room was serene and inviting, the elements perfectly customized for Mari's comfort.

She turned her attention to Saria. "I can do this," she stated confidently, "but I'd be pleased to have you waiting here for me."

Saria's face lifted with a gentle smile as she gave Mari's shoulders a supportive squeeze. She pulled Mari into a warm hug, then released her before she turned and lowered herself onto the winged chair and folded her hands on her lap. Mari smiled back as Saria settled in, sending her gratitude and love in the etheric form of a golden butterfly that fluttered between them. It landed on Saria's hand, then disappeared in a puff of mist.

Mari took a deep breath, turned, and entered the warm and welcoming room, passing into an atmosphere of pure love as she disappeared from Saria's view.

Sixty-three

She stopped just inside the doorway and, though feeling separated from her life-long spirit guide, Mari could sense that she was in the presence of something even closer to her. She took a moment to inhale the sublime elegance of the room. She'd been anxious about this moment, but she was surrounded by an enveloping grace and found herself surprisingly at ease.

The space was not as small as it first appeared, and a high, domed ceiling gave a feeling of openness. Everything was monochromatic ivory with gentle touches of soft beige. Each item gleamed with opaque white light, through a mist that mingled in the atmosphere of the parlor with a soft essence of jasmine. Mari felt as if this room was not even part of the grand and massive library that she had just left behind. It was as if she had stepped into a fragrant chamber that was floating in space.

Tall French doors stood on her right, opening to an enticing floral garden. The source of the jasmine fragrance was on either side of the door, with a profusion of delicate white flowers cascading over golden urns.

She could see a path leading to a charming white trellis laden with vines of velvety white roses. It was next to a pond, that was fed by a bubbling waterfall, that trickled through the crevices of a multicolored rock wall. Sheer curtains over the French doors swayed with a languid movement in response to the warm breeze that eased in from the garden.

Mari's attention returned to the center of the room where the scroll rested, upon the desk beside the candle, awaiting her examination.

The candle wasn't the only firelight in the room. An intricately carved white marble fireplace was on her left. A gentle flame radiated light.

Mari was at peace in this lovely, inviting parlor that was created just for her. As she took it all in, she began to hear a faint, light note coming from a harp that materialized to the right on the hearth. It played beautifully on its own, as if an invisible angel were caressing its strings. The music became clearer, and she felt a shift in the atmosphere. Her gaze was caught by a gold-framed painting that was revealing itself over the mantle, adjusting the energy in the room to one of a higher, even more beautiful intensity that she hadn't experienced since her spirit had been released from her physical body.

Sixty-four

Within the gilt frame, the art first appeared as undulant swirls of energy, glimmering with dancing, colorful shafts of light that began to merge into a hint of male and female faces. As the double portrait came into view, Mari began to recognize the features of her mother, Suzi, and her father, Mitch. The clarity and purity of their souls was set into the current of the etheric energy that surrounded them in the frame and pulsated around their luminous auras. They smiled down at her, and she could feel the warm glow of their love radiating from the light that shone from their eyes. It reached out and swirled around and through her. It was a familiar affection that she recognized immediately. She knew at once that they were with her in spirit, though they were still living in the physical world.

She tried to hold their adoring presence in her view, but new faces began to meld with theirs. She now saw in the two shining faces those of Claus and Lilly, her maternal grandparents, with the same loving countenance. Then those faded and became Bruce and Bertha, her paternal grandparents, sending their love.

Mari stood mesmerized as those two faces also faded into the wavy energy of the frame. More figures came into view that became her siblings, then extended family and friends that she was spiritually connected to appeared giving their love and support. She felt that she had never been, nor would she ever be, alone when she had so much pure love in the atmosphere around her.

Just as she was realizing the message of the miraculous artwork before her, with the harp music still magically filling the air, the faces completely misted over. She stood frozen and stunned until more features began to form in the energy of the frame. This time, however, they had both a magnificence beyond any she had witnessed so far, and, at the same time, the combined qualities and tender adoration of all the others.

Mari could make out male features that were amazingly strong and had no reference to any physical description. The eyes were intense with universal knowledge beyond Mari's imagination and the mouth was full and firm but lovingly gentle. Next to him, a being with female features offered a wonderful softness, with rounded cheeks that Mari's soul yearned to touch ever so gently. The smile was warm and engaging while the eyes glowed with an intensity of pure emotion and the incomprehensible love of a mother for her child.

An unimagined, pure joy swept over her as the two faces slowly merged into each other, creating a totality of one, supernatural-androgynous being with a smile that was warm and engaging. Unspoken words of love and appreciation were coming forth and filling her mind. The one set of eyes was divinely intense with heavenly knowledge, pure emotion, and unfathomable love that irresistibly drew Mari even closer.

Mari stretched her arms and reached just a bit further with her own loving heart and hands and, finally, touched the face that was the persona of all loving God.

She could feel the face in the palms of her hands, and a power the Earth had never known rushed through her as the single face disappeared, becoming a pure, almighty white light that encompassed her, melding it with her own pure light. At that divine moment, nothing else existed and she knew herself to be one with God. Her light, the pure energy of it, was one with the light of the universe.

Mari was finally introduced to and reminded of her true self, that part of her that never was, nor ever would be truly lost or separated from God. Her actions and decisions had only kept this knowledge at bay until she learned from her experiences. Perhaps the ultimate test of a good parent, was to know when to step back and do nothing but Love.

She was and would always be that very highest part of herself that was the creator of her own existence and every experience that she has had and will have, now and forever. And she remembered that, not only she, but also all other souls, were one and part of the whole of existence, all equally important and loved by God. They were all one with God, and along with all the others, she now knew in her heart that each soul plays an essential and important role in the creation of their world, the universe, and beyond.

With this personal truth and awareness, the face appeared to her again, bent to touch to her forehead, and graced her presence with a loving unconditional kiss of God, the kiss of peace.

He whispered to her, "You know, you could stay here with me."

The words resonated in her heart, and she answered simply, "I know."

"Thank you," was the whispered reply.

From the heavens came a simple, elegant melody that resonated from the harp bringing Mari back to the jasmine-infused ivory room, facing the little desk with her scroll rolled out, inviting her to partake of its knowledge. But Mari looked past the desk to the door. She walked, or perhaps she was gliding, over the plush carpet, so soft that she couldn't tell.

She was keenly aware that she was a new being, after her encounter with the Ultimate.

Sixty-five

Suzi went to the room where her computer was. Just inside the door, she stopped. She was overcome by the image that Deirdre had shared with her. She could feel Mari standing in the doorway, surrounded by bright light and became aware that she was blocking her daughter.

She stepped aside and sat down at the computer, put her hands on the keyboard and began to type.

She could feel a hand on her shoulder.

"Where are you now," she asked, "and what are you doing?"

The flow had begun.

Sixty-six

Saria sat down and got comfortable in the chair, then began to hear the melody of a harp and Mari was back. She wasn't sure what to expect, but it seemed like a flash of a second to Saria. Mari had transformed. She was a heavenly, translucent vision, suspended in her own vibrating white and golden aura of light that was filling the entire doorway. She was displaying the light entity that was the core of her being.

Mari smiled at Saria and her aura began to recede inside her as her essence began to mellow. The vibration that was filling the room was lowering in intensity to bring her back from the highest of high, back to her attentive and loving guide.

As Saria stared, spellbound by the vision before her, Mari spoke, helping to lower the vibrations further. Her voice started very high and fast as she attempted to explain her experience, but it only became clear to Saria as it began to resonate on their common level.

Saria finally heard Mari say emphatically and passionately clear, "... AND NOW I KNOW, I DON'T HAVE TO DO THIS!"

The spirit guide was stunned and sent Mari a questioning look. Mari closed her eyes and lowered her body's vibration more.

"Don't you see," she answered in the voice that her guide recognized, "that I know what I did? I know the big picture now and that there was a higher purpose to it all. I lived that life. It is a part of me. I don't have to relive it. It's done. I can just go on now."

Totally puzzled, Saria stared at her for what seemed like a very long minute, then rubbed her hand across her face. "Okkaay," was all she could reply. "So, what do we do now? Where would you like to go from here?"

"You're not getting it are you?" Mari smiled tenderly, answering the question with her own question. "I said that I don't have to do anything, but I now choose to do it. Oh yes, I choose to do this thing," she added passionately.

She paused until she saw the light of realization on Saria's sweet face.

"It's not necessary for me to go through the whole review thing. I thought it was a requirement and, as far as I know, it may not be required of anyone. But I want to. I really want to. I want to see the details. It is my desire to do so, and I know in my heart that there is much for me to learn in those details. And you said it had a lot to do with forgiveness. I want to experience how that plays out with others who touched my life and the ways I may have touched theirs. You told me to be open to that. And that is what life boils down to. It's experience. Even in the perfection of things, there is a corner of my heart that is telling me that there is more to learn, and I want the knowledge that is in those details."

Mari took a step forward to Saria and held out her hand.

"And furthermore, I want you to come with me! Will you please join me? It's a lovely room."

Saria stood and took Mari's hand and felt a surge of Mari's energy flowing through her whole body. "Thank you," she stated simply. "I will."

The two beautiful souls entered the room hand in hand and strode straight to the ivory desk. Mari sat in the chair and Saria stood behind her with her hand resting on Mari's shoulder in loving support.

The room was alive with dancing energy, and as Mari looked down at the parchment scroll with its golden rods and finials, a large, beautifully bound book materialized and replaced the scroll. This was perfect. Mari's love of books had followed her to this world, and now she could read her own story. She reached up and touched Saria's hand in an unspoken, affectionate, "Thank you."

Sixty-seven

The book was the size of a large coffee table book, and even thicker than those Mari had relished in her youth. Its cover was soft to the touch, like mottled pink and burgundy suede with a perfect, single white rose, her personal symbol, embossed into the fabric. Mari stroked the cover. She lifted it open with great reverence and care, wanting to relish each moment and word. But the book had a mind of its own and though Mari and Saria were able to savor every word and circumstance, the story-telling pages flipped very quickly. Their spirit minds were able to absorb every word with lightning speed.

Her story began with her decision to incarnate, and the formulation of the plan for the events of that life. A goal for her was to understand the power of forgiveness. She had remembered that factor with every circumstance that she experienced. When she had perceived that someone had slighted her, she now knew that it was all a part of her experience, and she realized that forgiving them wasn't necessary. Instead, she felt gratitude for the lesson and for those beautiful souls who played their part in presenting her with learning situations.

From being teased on the playground as a child, to doctors who only caused her confusion, and family members who rejected her because of her choices to exercise anorexic behavior instead of taking proper care of her diabetes, it had all happened to make her aware of her choices. In her mind she put out the thought, "God bless those souls who seemed to be making life difficult. They served me well." Compassion, the true ability to feel with others and enter their point of view, swept over her and filled her heart with unconditional love.

She and Saria rode the tide of her life and found blessings beyond measure in all the highs and the lows. Mari rode again on the speediest sled down the mountain side and snorkeled again in the South Pacific. She also sat alone in her apartment, crying in confusion after her mother had vented her frustration and told Mari that she couldn't do it anymore. On the next page Suzi was there for her with mother love. The beautiful tender times and the confusing heart-breaking times flashed vividly through Mari's awareness.

The succession of events continued to unfold before her in the turning pages. Mari saw all the memory flashbacks she'd been having but, with the gaps filled in, it all served a higher purpose, and she was reassured that God had never really abandoned her.

She relived those fears of abandonment as well as those of disappointment, failure, and the fear of life and death. She reveled in the fact that now she knew that there was no actual death. She merely passed through that thin veil that is all that exists between a physical life of toil and a spirit life of work, play, learning, and beauty beyond measure.

As the pages continued to turn, Mari and Saria both imagined a world where people still in physical life could experience something like this, standing back and seeing the flow of their lives and understanding the higher reasoning. If they could do this, couldn't some of the complications of the Earth realm be easier to deal with? If humanity could be aware of their own higher selves, how could they possibly do harm to another human soul? To be aware of the higher lessons and purpose and that we are the result of our own choices, and take responsibility for those choices. Wouldn't it be simpler? Wouldn't that help them to remember their own higher selves?

Sixty-eight

More pages turned, and Mari began to not only see, but also feel in her soul, the affects her actions had on those other souls who were traveling through life with her. It was painful. For all the physical pain she had felt back then, this empathetic spiritual pain was worse.

She remembered a lesson that she had learned in those moments with God. God did indeed give us the gift of freedom of choice of how to live our lives, but just as important, that choice encompasses the choice of our own emotions, and that we have the freedom to choose our reactions to any given situation. We even have the capacity to access the knowledge of higher good to help make those choices. She realized that, though she empathized with them, she could not be responsible for others' choices of their reactions. She was only responsible for her own.

Suddenly she felt the elation of the good that was in her essence, which balanced everything in divine perfection. She had been a person who abhorred aggression and resisted giving into unrighteous anger. She also resisted being unkind to others, and transcended her ego, moving into compassion to feel empathy with others. Through everything she had remained a gentle and compassionate soul.

Finally, she could see that her soul did learn, and her spirit did grow. This came to her as the pages became fewer, but continued with the story after she died, crossed over, and moved into the world of spirit.

Just as she saw how she was born into the physical world, she saw, again, her passing into this side of reality, and all that she had experienced since then. She witnessed being reunited with loved ones and reintroduced to kindred spirits like Mario, Jane and Toby, and to the beauty of this world.

Sixty-nine

With just a few pages remaining, the turning stopped abruptly as the story intersected perfectly with the present moment. Saria and Mari were in the ivory room, looking down at the suddenly still page. They both felt the perfect synchronicity of the moment, and the harp's melody once again filled the room.

Mari turned to Saria and saw a huge tear drop slowly working its way down her spirit guide's cheek. She rose and held Saria in a warm and loving embrace as Saria whispered, "Thank you so very much. That was the hardest thing I've ever done, being your guide, but by far the most valuable."

She stepped back and looked deeply into Mari's eyes. "You have come so very far. You've learned more than I even tried to show you, and your spirit is more beautiful than ever. I never imagined that being a guide could be so rewarding. Thank you, thank you, thank you!"

It was Mari's turn to feel a tear drop on her cheek. "And I thank you for your patience and persistence. I see now that you really had your hands full."

Saria smiled and touched Mari's cheek ever so gently to catch a tear as she said, "Well then, I thank you for thanking me." They both laughed, seeing that this thanking thing could go on and on.

"But Saria," Mari became serious, "I'm so very sorry."

Saria was taken aback. "Oh darlin'," she exclaimed incredulous, "after all that, what could you possibly be sorry for?"

"It's not in the story. I didn't see it," Mari answered sadly. She laid her hand on her heart and explained, "I am so full of gratitude for the opportunity God gave me to have those experiences for my soul's growth and learning, but there is a corner in my heart that hasn't yet filled and it's beginning to hurt." She paused and took a deep breath. "I don't yet understand what you said about forgiveness. I found that I didn't need to forgive anyone, so I'm perplexed. I feel something is missing. Can you explain what you meant?"

Now it was Saria's turn to be sad. "Oh honey, I was just passing on what I was hearing at the time and I'm not getting anything more now. It was meant for you to know when the time was right. I'm so sorry. This time I can't help you."

Mari felt a horrible tightness that told her that a torrent of tears was about to let loose. She couldn't believe that she wasn't feeling the total elation that should be overcoming her. She barely got out the words, "Excuse me," as she turned and hurried out the French doors down a set of steps, then ran quickly onto the garden path, barely able to see her way with the welling of her tears. She made it through the trellis and dropped onto a boulder that sat at the edge of the pond.

Seventy

Not only her tears, but great sobs were released from her soul as a flood of disappointment in herself overcame her. She couldn't believe that she could possibly feel so incomplete after all she had just experienced. There was supposed to be complete relief, and she was to go joyfully back into her life here in the spirit world. Her mind began to wander in her grief, and she began to feel a pull of separation from this world that was beginning to look dim and distant through her tears. Was she going to be denied all that beauty and love for what seemed to be such a small void in her story? Surely, she wouldn't have to go back into another incarnation to complete this last bit of learning. She started to feel herself being pulled away and closed her eyes, sobbing from the excruciating pain as she imagined herself being denied her true Home.

Through the lament she could hear a faint whistle-like bird song becoming clearer and closer. She raised her head to the skies, and through crystalline images created by her tears, she began to see flashes of red. She wiped her eyes to see, more clearly, a Redbird, the symbol of her spiritual family and her existence in this world, that was gliding toward her, singing its beautiful song. She finally felt a hint of hope and sat up on the boulder, reached out, and let the beautiful bird approach her and land gently on her hand.

The bird was a clear, brilliant red with distinct black markings, much like the ceramic replicas in her grandmother's china cabinet so long ago. This Redbird had a delicate golden aura that sparkled with bits of flashing light. It sat lightly on her finger, and Mari stared at this little messenger intently as the bird seemed to be looking into her soul and touching her heart.

Finally, Mari found her voice and whispered softly and sadly through her tears, "Little friend, can you tell me, what do I need to learn about forgiveness?"

The sweet creature only cocked its head to one side and gave her a puzzled look as if it were pondering her question. It gave a light whistle and turned its bright head and looked down into the ripples of the pond. Mari followed the bird's gaze and watched the ripples, seeing the contorted image of her own face. The pond surface began to smooth, and her face became clearer as she heard her own voice coming from the image.

"There is still a small part of you," the voice imparted, "that you are searching for. Your heart thinks you need to forgive yourself for the complications that you threw into your soul's path. You are holding onto that idea far too harshly. Won't you allow yourself to just let it go?"

With those words, Mari felt her heart fill to capacity with relief. Now she knew, as she looked at the Redbird through tears of pure joy and relief. She lifted her hand, allowing the gorgeous creature to lift off and soar above her, singing its glorious song.

Seventy-one

Saria was waiting at the French doors, watching Mari glide slowly and confidently down the garden path back toward her. Her strides were sure and steady in her new awareness of self-forgiveness, as she rose with each step toward Saria, who waited with a warm embrace.

"Just one more thing before we go," she said with newfound confidence. "I'd like to see those last few pages."

Saria smiled and they returned to the desk. They lifted the page that they had left off with, turned it and, slowly this time, finished the story.

After closing the book, they rose and walked out the door into the library that was, indeed, now teeming with activity. Souls were floating up, around, and between the stacks of books and scrolls. Others were enjoying a quiet read while some, who certainly must be spirit guides, were frantically looking through scrolls.

Mari and her guide paused when they joined the activity and watched innocent souls, still carrying burdens from their recent physical lives, marching up the stairway, their guides lovingly holding their hands.

Mari knew, firsthand, that they couldn't see her or Saria, but she sent them her love in the form of a golden butterfly. The two continued down the grand stairway and out through the library doors.

On the veranda, Mari paused and opened her arms wide, breathing in all the beauty of the world that she now claimed as her own. She turned to Saria and said, "You were a great spirit guide. Now will you just be my friend?"

"Try and stop me," answered Saria with a wink and a smile.

Mari smiled and offered a simple, "Thank you," knowing that nothing else needed to be said.

In a serious tone, she continued, "I need to be with my mom. She and I have work to do."

"I know," Saria replied, and Mari disappeared from her side.

Epilogue

Suzi carried her cup of coffee carefully down the stairs to her office space in her daylight basement and turned on some restful orchestral music. She lit a tea light candle under her infuser, which held a fragrant oil called "Essence of Vision." It subtly filled the air with the Earthy scents of her precious Northwest forests as she sat down at her computer.

Not knowing how to begin, Suzi held her face in her hands. She had work to do but she needed inspiration. She looked up and saw the picture of her deceased darling Mari. Through the beginning of welling tears, she asked, "Where are you now and what are you doing?"

She paused to listen.

"Oh my!" she exclaimed. "So that's the story you want to be told. Well, let's do this."

She took a sip of her coffee and placed her hands on the keyboard. As she took a deep breath and relaxed, she felt a warm hand touch her shoulder. She reached up and placed her own hand lovingly on the invisible hand of her daughter, then returned it to the keyboard and began typing.

These words appeared on the screen:

"I'm tired of dying, Gramma," whispered Mari. "I don't want to do it again."

Mari and Suzi both smiled. Their joint work had begun as they fulfilled the Redbird's sacred promise: To tell the story that generations had entrusted them to tell, and to share a world of unfathomable Beauty, everlasting Peace, and eternal, unconditional Love.

"To know that even one life has breathed easier because you have lived, that is to have succeeded."

Ralph Waldo Emerson

About the Author

Born and raised in the Pacific Northwest, USA, S.S. Wright is a wife, mom, grandmother, and great grandmother with roots in the Midwest and a story to tell. Fulfilling a promise she made to her daughter over thirty-five years ago, Wright has tenaciously tuned in to the story that wants to be told, encouraging her mind and heart and dreamspace to be available to hear and see and feel and share the extraordinary story of a daughter's journey. A talented crafter in needle work, dressmaking, quilting, jewelry design, stained glass, and doll and stuffed animal making, she is feeling extraordinarily pleased to bring forth *Singing the Redbird's Song*, her first published work of fiction and a project that has been a lifetime in the making.

www.singingtheredbirdssong.com

www.ingramcontent.com/pod-product-compliance
Lightning Source LLC
Chambersburg PA
CBHW071533110726
47908CB00007B/1869